Edward Frederic Benson was born in
1867 at Wellington College, where his
father, Edward White Benson (later
Archbishop of Canterbury), was
Headmaster. Educated at Marlborough
and King's College, Cambridge,
E. F. Benson's main interests were
classics and archaeology; from 1892–5
he studied and worked at the British
School of Archaeology in Athens.

In 1893 his first novel, *Dodo*, had
considerable success, and there
followed a stream of novels and
biographies, including his famous
social comedies, the *Lucia* series, cult
books since they were first published
in the 1920s.

Mayor of Rye from 1934–7, E. F. Benson
was awarded the O.B.E. and made an
Honorary Fellow of Magdalene
College, Cambridge. He died in 1940,
having published about eighty books.

Author photograph copyright Martello Bookshop

Also by E. F. Benson

and published by Black Swan

The Tale of an Empty House
and other ghost stories

E. F. Benson
Edited by Cynthia Reavell
with an Introduction by Susan Hill

BLACK SWAN

THE TALE OF AN EMPTY HOUSE AND OTHER GHOST STORIES

A BLACK SWAN BOOK 0 552 99222 4

First publication in Great Britain

PRINTING HISTORY
Black Swan edition published 1986

This book is set in 11/12 pt Mallard

Black Swan Books are published by
Transworld Publishers Ltd., 61–63
Uxbridge Road, Ealing, London W5 5SA, in
Australia by Transworld Publishers (Aust.)
Pty. Ltd., 15–23 Helles Avenue, Moorebank,
NSW 2170, and in New Zealand by
Transworld Publishers (N.Z.) Ltd., Cnr.
Moselle and Waipareira Avenues,
Henderson, Auckland.

Made and printed in Great Britain by
The Guernsey Press Co. Ltd.,
Guernsey, Channel Islands.

Dedicated to Tony with love, and to
Tilling Society members with affection.

Acknowledgements

Grateful thanks to Austin Seckerson and Rosemary Pardoe.

Contents

Foreword

E.F. Benson was born in 1867, just five years after M.R.
James – perhaps the master of the ghost story – and
their paths crossed at Cambridge in the late 1880s
when they were both at King's College, and Benson
became an admiring member of the group of which
'Monty' James was the leader.

Ghosts and the supernatural, and such associated
paraphernalia as mediums and table-tapping, always
held a strong fascination for E.F. Benson, even if his
feelings about them were somewhat ambivalent. He
arranged for a number of séances to be held at various
times (certainly more than were strictly necessary for
background material) and he had a definite belief in the
possibility of the power of the medium, while at the same
time recognising that many were frauds. As a schoolboy
he collaborated with his brothers and sisters in writing
a family play called The Spiritualist, which was 'a
slashing exposure of mediums'. But when his mother
left him a mysterious package when she died, he took
it to several different mediums, including one Eva
Kanderson, and asked them to find out what it contained
by spiritual means: all the answers were different.

His first psychic experience was probably in 1897 in
Egypt, apparently a case of second sight, when he had a
clairvoyant visit from a doctor, seeing and hearing his
exact words and gestures; it all happened identically in
reality two days later. His sister, Maggie, was seriously
ill at the time, and the doctor's words were reassuring
and marked a turning-point in the illness. One summer's

afternoon years later, Benson and his great friend, Canon Fowler, the local vicar, were sitting together in the secret garden at Lamb House in Rye when they both clearly saw the ghost of a man in black, wearing a cape and hose. And when Benson once held a séance in the Lamb House garden room, the medium said she saw a figure slumped in the very chair in which a man called Grebell had died after a murderous attack in the churchyard. Benson set several ghost stories in Lamb House – *Naboth's Vineyard*; *Machaon*; and *Roderick's Story* – and *James Lamp* is set in Hartshorn House in Mermaid Street in Rye, which is also the probable original for the Wyses' house in his Mapp & Lucia novels. Unfortunately these are not among the best of his stories and don't warrant inclusion in a short selection.

Of the 80 or so books of fiction Benson wrote (out of a total of 100 books) he is remembered for less than a dozen, and is best-loved for his series of six comic Mapp & Lucia novels, in the first of which he gently mocks those who are gullibly taken in by ouija boards and fraudulent mediums. The majority of his other novels seem sentimental and hopelessly dated now, with their tear-jerking moral endings. But, happily, Benson's ghost stories don't suffer from this weakness, and he is at his best working on the small canvas of the short story.

This selection includes *How Fear Departed from the Long Gallery*, chosen by Benson as his own favourite in a 1933 Faber anthology, *My Best Story*. The title story, *A Tale of an Empty House*, is chosen perhaps more for the evocative descriptions of the Norfolk marsh-scape than for its horror story, and *The Séance* for its humour. The long black magic story, *The Sanctuary*, has a great deal in common with part of Benson's novel *Colin II*. And, incidentally, the boy Dickie 'a delicate boy, rather queer and elfin', who becomes involved in strange rites, is obviously based on E.F. Benson's younger brother, Hugh (R.H.) Benson.

My own favourite is *Pirates*, Benson's most moving ghost story. This is quite unlike any of the others, and its

x

poignancy lies in its background setting which is so closely and feelingly based on Benson's own childhood and the family's happy years at *Lis Escop* – now Copeland Court – near Truro in Cornwall.

Cynthia Reavell

Introduction

Ghost stories are all atmosphere. The plot itself, detailed events leading to a climax, and the subsequent explanation, if any, is really of secondary interest and importance. If the atmosphere has been skilfully evoked, the scene well set, places clearly imagined and described, then the reader's attention will be gripped so firmly, his disbelief suspended so completely, that the author can get away with the creakiest of plots and still produce a brilliant story. For what we remember best about any good ghost story, and often remember for half a lifetime after reading it, is never exactly what happened, and to whom and how, but rather, in what kind of place, and weather, and how it aroused certain emotions, of fear, awe, gloom, menace, evil, or merely a sense of things being somehow 'out of joint.' And if the atmosphere of the ghost story is not exactly right, nothing else about it will follow successfully.

E.F. Benson's atmospheres are perfect, beautifully evoked from the opening sentences, carefully built up. He was a traditionalist in the form, knowing well what had always worked best for the classic writers, and preferring to make use of well-tried formulae, though never becoming merely a hollow imitator.

He takes us to remote parts of England, often by the sea, on the more deserted and bleak stretches of coastline. In *The Face*, Hester Ward is sent off to recuperate in an out-of-season hotel on the East coast, and in *Home, Sweet Home*, the exhausted nerve specialist Walter Mostyn, has prescribed a similar rest-cure for himself in a one-eyed village by the sea, at the end of a branch-line. Two bachelors take an August break in one of the remoter bits of Cornwall, one sultry summer, in *The Expiation*, and one of the finest pieces of scene-setting tells *A Tale of an Empty House*, set on wild, flat marshes.

The weather in such isolated spots is either misty, stormy, oppressively hot or bitingly cold – in other words, always extreme, always memorable, and always adding to the atmosphere.

The haunted house is, of course, the most popular of devices, but Benson might have invented it for himself, so vividly does he reconstruct these ugly, eerie, lonely buildings; we feel the draught down every long passageway, smell the musty, dead smell in empty rooms. Scarcely a story in this selection does not feature or centre around one of these terribly haunted places, yet every one is different, each has its own period and style, its own past history, and its own, particular ghost.

But certain themes recur, and these, too, are traditional. Generally, there has been a violent incident in the recent past, a dreadful murder, as in *A Tale of an Empty House*, and *Home, Sweet Home*, or a suicide – *The Other Bed*, *The Room in the Tower* – and either murderer or victim returns again and again to the scene, as a warning, or as a desperate attempt to escape from the past, or simply on some kind of dreadful treadmill, forced to go through the event endlessly. Sometimes, these ghosts are laid in a great climax that often involves dramatic, turbulent weather – a thunderstorm, or torrential rain and gales. In *How Fear Departed from the Long Gallery* the dénouement is unusual, in that it is by meeting and receiving love, instead of fear and horror, that the curse of the ghost – in this case, of twin babies – is lifted and the hauntings become peaceful and happy. Usually, however, after a particular, terrifying climax, perhaps involving a second act of violence, as in *Home, Sweet Home*, the ghost is vanquished, and the haunting simply ceases, without there being anything more than exhausted relief among the participants in the drama.

Another old device which Benson makes frighteningly successful use of is the dream of precognition. Again and again, there is a recurring dream – or, more accurately, nightmare – of a house visited, a room slept in, a face seen, and at some future date it all comes horribly true. The stories in which the face of evil, seen in the dream, is later recognised in a portrait – *The Face*, *The Room in the Tower*, are especially unpleasant, making us aware of our own dreams – and more than a little wary of picture galleries!

The one, essential ingredient of the true, classic ghost story is a ghost – that is, a spectre, either seen, heard or in some way sensed, and recognisably human, the ghost having come back from the dead to haunt a particular place or person. Most of Benson's stories fulfil this requirement, but one or two of those collected here do not fall into that category. They are really not ghost stories but stories of the macabre, of horror, of the supernatural in general. *Caterpillars* is a tale of creepy crawlies, *Mrs. Amworth* is about vampires, *And no Bird Sings* is a very odd, nasty little tale about evil made manifest in the form of a slug-like beast that gives off a terrible corrupt stench, and causes everything in its vicinity to die.

These, though they certainly cause a shudder to run up the spine, I find the least convincing of the stories, whose shadow falls for no longer than the brief time it takes to read them. Indeed, they even hover on that borderline of the horrible and the ridiculous, so that in certain moods we laugh rather than tremble at them. That is never true of the pure ghost story.

But laughter, or, at least, the emotions of happiness and warmth, and an air of light rather than of darkness, surround, and are evoked by, my two favourite stories here reprinted; *How Fear Departed from the Long Gallery* begins with horror and violent deeds, ends in resolution and joy, as the little ghostly children – and how successful childish ghosts in fiction always seem to be – receive a benediction of love. And *Pirates*, the most charming, gentle and evocative of all, whose resolution, though involving death, is still of a wholly different order from that of Benson's other ghost stories. It is a story of longing for a lost childhood, of a return to the past, of a house happily haunted, and of the wheel of life coming full circle. These ghosts have returned for a purpose, to beckon, to lead the way, to accompany, to fulfil a mission. It is a beautifully told, simple, yet many-layered tale, haunting in the best sense of the word, and taking its place at the end of the collection to lay all the ghosts of evil, terror and violence which have gone before, and restore peace, tranquillity, order and harmony, in an almost Shakespearian way.

Susan Hill

The Face

Hester Ward, sitting by the open window on this hot afternoon in June, began seriously to argue with herself about the cloud of foreboding and depression which had encompassed her all day, and, very sensibly, she enumerated to herself the manifold causes for happiness in the fortunate circumstances of her life. She was young, she was extremely good-looking, she was well-off, she enjoyed excellent health, and above all, she had an adorable husband and two small, adorable children. There was no break, indeed, anywhere in the circle of prosperity which surrounded her, and had the wishing-cap been handed to her that moment by some beneficent fairy, she would have hesitated to put it on her head, for there was positively nothing that she could think of which would have been worthy of such solemnity. Moreover, she could not accuse herself of a want of appreciation of her blessings; she appreciated enormously, she enjoyed enormously, and she thoroughly wanted all those who so munificently contributed to her happiness to share in it.

She made a very deliberate review of these things, for she was really anxious, more anxious, indeed, than she admitted to herself, to find anything tangible which could possibly warrant this ominous feeling of approaching disaster. Then there was the weather to consider; for the last week London had been stiflingly hot, but, if that was the cause, why had she not felt it before? Perhaps the effect of these broiling, airless days had been cumulative. That was an idea, but, frankly, it did not seem a very good one, for, as a matter of fact, she loved the heat; Dick, who hated it, said that it was odd he should have fallen in love with a salamander.

She shifted her position, sitting up straight in this low window-seat, for she was intending to make a call on her courage. She had known from the moment she awoke this morning what it was that lay so heavy on her, and now, having done her best to shift the reason of her depression on to anything else, and having completely failed, she meant to look the thing in the face. She was ashamed of doing so, for the cause of this leaden mood of fear which held her in its grip was so trivial, so fantastic, so excessively silly.

'Yes, there never was anything so silly,' she said to herself. 'I must look at it straight, and convince myself how silly it is.' She paused a moment, clenching her hands.

'Now for it,' she said.

She had had a dream the previous night, which, years ago, used to be familiar to her, for again and again when she was a child she had dreamed it. In itself the dream was nothing, but in those childish days whenever she had this dream which had visited her last night, it was followed on the next night by another, which contained the source and the core of the horror, and she would awake screaming and struggling in the grip of over-whelming nightmare. For some ten years now she had not experienced it, and would have said that, though she remembered it, it had become dim and distant to her. But last night she had had that warning dream, which used to herald the visitation of the nightmare, and now that whole store-house of memory, crammed as it was with bright things and beautiful, contained nothing so vivid.

The warning dream, the curtain that was drawn up on the succeeding night, and disclosed the vision she dreaded, was simple and harmless enough in itself. She seemed to be walking on a high sandy cliff covered with short down-grass; twenty yards to the left came the edge

12

of this cliff, which sloped steeply down to the sea that lay at its foot. The path she followed led through fields bounded by low hedges, and mounted gradually upwards. She went through some half-dozen of these, climbing over the wooden stiles that gave communication; sheep grazed there, but she never saw another human being, and always it was dusk, as if evening was falling, and she had to hurry on, because someone (she knew not whom) was waiting for her, and had been waiting not a few minutes only, but for many years. Presently, as she mounted this slope, she saw in front of her a copse of stunted trees, growing crookedly under the continual pressure of the wind that blew from the sea, and when she saw those she knew her journey was nearly done, and that the nameless one, who had been waiting for her so long, was somewhere close at hand. The path she followed was cut through this wood, and the slanting boughs of the trees on the sea-ward side almost roofed it in; it was like walking through a tunnel. Soon the trees in front began to grow thin, and she saw through them the grey tower of a lonely church. It stood in a graveyard, apparently long disused, and the body of the church, which lay between the tower and the edge of the cliff, was in ruins, roofless, and with gaping windows round which ivy grew thickly.

At that point this prefatory dream always stopped. It was a troubled, uneasy dream, for there was over it the sense of dusk and of the man who had been waiting for her so long, but it was not of the order of nightmare. Many times in childhood had she experienced it, and perhaps it was the subconscious knowledge of the night that so surely followed it which gave it its disquiet. And now last night it had come again, identical in every particular but one. For last night it seemed to her that in the course of these ten years which had intervened since last it had visited her the glimpse of the church and churchyard was changed. The edge of the cliff had come nearer to the tower, so that it now was within a yard or two of it, and the ruined body of the church, but for one broken arch that remained, had vanished. The sea had encroached, and for ten years had been busily eating at the cliff.

Hester knew well that it was this dream and this alone which had darkened the day for her, by reason of the nightmares that used to follow it, and, like a sensible woman, having looked it once in the face, she refused to admit into her mind any conscious calling-up of the sequel. If she let herself contemplate that, as likely or not the very thinking about it would be sufficient to ensure its return, and of one thing she was very certain, namely, that she didn't at all want it to do so. It was not like the confused jumble and jangle of ordinary nightmare, it was very simple, and she felt it concerned the nameless one who waited for her. . . But she must not think of it; her whole will and intention was set on not thinking of it, and to aid her resolution there was the rattle of Dick's latchkey in the front door and his voice calling her.

She went out into the little square front hall; there he was, strong and large, and wonderfully undream-like.

'This heat's a scandal, it's an outrage, it is an abomination of desolation,' he cried, vigorously mopping. 'What have we done that Providence should place us in this frying-pan? Let us thwart him, Hester! Let us drive out of this inferno and have our dinner at – I'll whisper it so that he shan't overhear – at Hampton Court!'

She laughed: this plan suited her excellently. They would return late, after the distraction of a fresh scene; and dining out at night was both delicious and stupefying.

'The very thing,' she said, 'and I'm sure Providence didn't hear. Let's start now!'

'Rather. Any letters for me?'

He walked to the table where there were a few rather uninteresting-looking envelopes with half-penny stamps.

'Ah, receipted bill,' he said. 'Just a reminder of one's

14

folly in paying it. Circular . . . unasked advice to invest
in German marks . . . Circular begging letter, beginning,
"Dear Sir or Madam." Such impertinence to ask one to
subscribe to something without ascertaining one's sex.
. . . Private view, portraits at the Walton Gallery. . .
Can't go; business meetings all day. You might like to
have a look in, Hester. Someone told me there were some
fine VanDycks. That's all: let's be off.'

Hester spent a thoroughly reassuring evening, and
though she thought of telling Dick about the dream that
had so deeply imprinted itself on her consciousness all
day, in order to hear the great laugh he would have given
her for being such a goose, she refrained from doing so,
since nothing that he could say would be so tonic to these
fantastic fears as his general robustness. Besides, she
would have to account for its disturbing effect, tell him
that it was once familiar to her, and recount the sequel
of the nightmares that followed. She would neither think
of them nor mention them: it was wiser by far just to
soak herself in his extraordinary sanity, and wrap herself in his affection. . . They dined out-of-doors at a
riverside restaurant and strolled about afterwards, and
it was very nearly midnight when, soothed with coolness
and fresh air, and the vigour of his strong companionship, she let herself into the house, while he took the
car back to the garage. And now she marvelled at the
mood which had beset her all day, so distant and unreal
had it become. She felt as if she had dreamed of ship-
wreck, and had awoke to find herself in some secure and
sheltered garden where no tempest raged nor waves
beat. But was there, ever so remotely, ever so dimly, the
noise of far-off breakers somewhere?

He slept in the dressing-room which communicated
with her bedroom, the door of which was left open for
the sake of air and coolness, and she fell asleep almost
as soon as her light was out, and while his was still
burning. And immediately she began to dream.

She was standing on the seashore; the tide was out,
for level sands strewn with stranded jetsam glimmered

in a dusk that was deepening into night. Though she had never seen the place it was awfully familiar to her. At the head of the beach there was a steep cliff of sand, and perched on the edge of it was a grey church tower. The sea must have encroached and undermined the body of the church, for tumbled blocks of masonry lay close to her at the bottom of the cliff, and there were grave-stones there, while others still in place were silhouetted whitely against the sky. To the right of the church tower there was a wood of stunted trees, combed sideways by the prevalent sea wind, and she knew that along the top of the cliff a few yards inland there lay a path through fields, with wooden stiles to climb, which led through a tunnel of trees and so out into the churchyard. All this she saw in a glance, and waited, looking at the sand-cliff crowned by the church tower, for the terror that was going to reveal itself. Already she knew what it was, and as so many times before, she tried to run away. But the catalepsy of nightmare was already on her; frantically she strove to move, but her utmost endeavour could not raise a foot from the sand. Frantically she tried to look away from the sand-cliffs close in front of her, where in a moment now the horror would be manifested. . .

It came. There formed a pale oval light, the size of a man's face, dimly luminous in front of her and a few inches above the level of her eyes. It outlined itself: short reddish hair grew low on the forehead; below were two grey eyes, set very close together, which steadily and fixedly regarded her. On each side the ears stood notice-ably away from the head, and the lines of the jaw met in a short, pointed chin. The nose was straight and rather long, below it came a hairless lip, and last of all the mouth took shape and colour, and there lay the crowning terror. One side of it, soft-curved and beauti-ful, trembled into a smile, the other side, thick and gath-ered together as by some physical deformity, sneered and lusted.

The whole face, dim at first, gradually focused itself into clear outline: it was pale and rather lean, the face of

16

a young man. And then the lower lip dropped a little, showing the glint of teeth, and there was the sound of speech. 'I shall soon come for you now,' it said, and on the words it drew a little nearer to her, and the smile broadened. At that the full, hot blast of nightmare poured in upon her. Again she tried to run, again she tried to scream, and now she could feel the breath of that terrible mouth upon her. Then with a crash and a rending like the tearing asunder of soul and body she broke the spell, and heard her own voice yelling and felt with her fingers for the switch of her light. And then she saw that the room was not dark, for Dick's door was open, and the next moment, not yet undressed, he was with her.

'My darling, what is it?' he said. 'What's the matter?'

She clung desperately to him, still distraught with terror.

'Ah, he has been here again,' she cried. 'He says he will soon come to me. Keep him away, Dick.'

For one moment her fear infected him, and he found himself glancing round the room.

'But what do you mean?' he said. 'No one has been here.'

She raised her head from his shoulder.

'No, it was just a dream,' she said. 'But it was the old dream, and I was terrified. Why, you've not undressed yet. What time is it?'

'You haven't been in bed ten minutes, dear,' he said. 'You had hardly put out your light when I heard you screaming.'

She shuddered.

'Ah, it's awful,' she said. 'And he will come again. . .'

He sat down by her.

'Now tell me all about it,' he said.

She shook her head.

'No, it will never do to talk about it,' she said, 'it will only make it more real. I suppose the children are all right, are they?'

'Of course they are. I looked in on my way upstairs.'

'That's good. But I'm better now, Dick. A dream hasn't anything real about it, has it? It doesn't mean anything?'

He was quite reassuring on this point, and soon she quieted down. Before he went to bed he looked in again on her, and she was asleep.

Hester had a stern interview with herself when Dick had gone down to his office next morning. She told herself that what she was afraid of was nothing more than her own fear. How many times had that ill-omened face come to her in dreams, and what significance had it ever proved to possess? Absolutely none at all, except to make her afraid. She was afraid where no fear was: she was guarded, sheltered, prosperous, and what if a nightmare of childhood returned? It had no more meaning now than it had then, and all those visitations of her childhood had passed away without trace. . . And then, despite herself, she began thinking over that vision again. It was grimly identical with all its previous occurrences, except . . . And then, with a sudden shrinking of her heart, she remembered that in earlier years those terrible lips had said: 'I shall come for you when you are older,' and last night they had said: 'I shall soon come for you now.' She remembered, too, that in the warning dream the sea had encroached, and it had now demolished the body of the church. There was an awful consistency about these two changes in the otherwise identical visions. The years had brought their change to them, for in the one the encroaching sea had brought down the body of the church, in the other the time was now near. . .

It was no use to scold or reprimand herself, for to bring her mind to the contemplation of the vision meant merely that the grip of terror closed on her again, it was far wiser to occupy herself, and starve her fear out by refusing to bring it the sustenance of thought. So she went about her household duties, she took the children out for their airing in the park, and then, determined to leave no moment unoccupied, set off with the card of invitation to see the pictures in the private view at the

Walton Gallery. After that her day was full enough; she was lunching out, and going on to a matinée, and by the time she got home Dick would have returned, and they would drive down to his little house at Rye for the week-end. All Saturday and Sunday she would be playing golf, and she felt that fresh air and physical fatigue would exorcise the dread of these dreaming fantasies.

The gallery was crowded when she got there; there were friends among the sightseers, and the inspection of the pictures was diversified by cheerful conversation. There were two or three fine Raeburns, a couple of Sir Joshuas, but the gems, so she gathered, were three Vandycks that hung in a small room by themselves. Presently she strolled in there, looking at her catalogue. The first of them, she saw, was a portrait of Sir Roger Wyburn. Still chatting to her friend she raised her eye and saw it. . .

Her heart hammered in her throat, and then seemed to stand still altogether. A qualm as of some mental sickness of the soul overcame her, for there in front of her was he who would soon come for her. There was the reddish hair, the projecting ears, the greedy eyes set close together, and the mouth smiling on one side, and on the other gathered up into the sneering menace that she knew so well. It might have been her own nightmare rather than a living model which had sat to the painter for that face.

'Ah, what a portrait, and what a brute!' said her companion. 'Look, Hester, isn't that marvellous?'

She recovered herself with an effort. To give way to this ever-mastering dread would have been to allow nightmare to invade her waking life, and there, for sure, madness lay. She forced herself to look at it again, but there were the steady and eager eyes regarding her; she could almost fancy the mouth began to move. All round her the crowd bustled and chattered, but to her own sense she was alone there with Roger Wyburn.

And yet, so she reasoned with herself, this picture of him – for it was he and no other – should have reassured her. Roger Wyburn, to have been painted by Vandyck, must have been dead near on two hundred years; how could he be a menace to her? Had she seen that portrait by some chance as a child; had it made some dreadful impression on her, since over-scored by other memories, but still alive in the mysterious subconsciousness, which flows eternally, like some dark underground river, beneath the surface of human life? Psychologists taught that these early impressions fester or poison the mind like some hidden abscess. That might account for this dread of one, nameless no longer, who waited for her.

That night down at Rye there came again to her the prefatory dream, followed by the nightmare, and clinging to her husband as the terror began to subside, she told him what she had resolved to keep to herself. Just to tell it brought a measure of comfort, for it was so outrageously fantastic, and his robust common sense upheld her. But when on their return to London there was a recurrence of these visions, he made short work of her demur and took her straight to her doctor.

'Tell him all, darling,' he said. 'Unless you promise to do that, I will. I can't have you worried like this. It's all nonsense, you know, and doctors are wonderful people for curing nonsense.'

She turned to him.

'Dick, you're frightened,' she said quietly.

He laughed.

'I'm nothing of the kind,' he said, 'but I don't like being awakened by your screaming. Not my idea of a peaceful night. Here we are.'

The medical report was decisive and peremptory. There was nothing whatever to be alarmed about; in brain and body she was perfectly healthy, but she was run down. These disturbing dreams were, as likely as not, an effect, a symptom of her condition, rather than the cause of it, and Dr. Baring unhesitatingly recommended a complete change to some bracing place. The wise thing would be to send her out of this stuffy furnace to some quiet place to where she had never been.

Complete change; quite so. For the same reason her husband had better not go with her; he must pack her off to, let us say, the East coast. Sea-air and coolness and complete idleness. No long walks; no long bathings; a dip, and a deck chair on the sands. A lazy, soporific life. How about Rushton? He had no doubt that Rushton would set her up again. After a week or so, perhaps, her husband might go down and see her. Plenty of sleep – never mind the nightmares – plenty of fresh air.

Hester, rather to her husband's surprise, fell in with this suggestion at once, and the following evening saw her installed in solitude and tranquillity. The little hotel was still almost empty, for the rush of summer tourists had not yet begun, and all day she sat out on the beach with the sense of a struggle over. She need not fight the terror any more; dimly it seemed to her that its malignancy had been relaxed. Had she in some way yielded to it and done its secret bidding? At any rate no return of its nightly visitations had occurred, and she slept long and dreamlessly, and woke to another day of quiet. Every morning there was a line for her from Dick, with good news of himself and the children, but he and they alike seemed somehow remote, like memories of a very distant time. Something had driven in between her and them, and she saw them as if through glass. But equally did the memory of the face of Roger Wyburn, as seen on the master's canvas or hanging close in front of her against the crumbling sand-cliff, become blurred and indistinct, and no return of her nightly terrors visited her. This truce from all emotion reacted not on her mind alone, lulling her with a sense of soothed security, but on her body also, and she began to weary of this day-long inactivity.

The village lay on the lip of a stretch of land reclaimed from the sea. To the north the level marsh, now beginning to glow with the pale bloom of the sea-lavender, stretched away featureless till it lost itself in distance, but to the south a spur of hill came down to the shore ending in a wooded promontory. Gradually, as her

21

physical health increased, she began to wonder what lay beyond this ridge which cut short the view, and one afternoon she walked across the intervening level and strolled up its wooded slopes. The day was close and windless, the invigorating sea breeze which till now had spiced the heat with freshness had died, and she looked forward to finding a current of air stirring when she had topped the hill. To the south a mass of dark cloud lay along the horizon, but there was no imminent threat of storm. The slope was easily surmounted, and presently she stood at the top and found herself on the edge of a tableland of wooded pasture, and following the path, which ran not far from the edge of the cliff, she came out into more open country. Empty fields, where a few sheep were grazing, mounted gradually upwards. Wooden stiles made a communication in the hedges that bounded them. And there, not a mile in front of her, she saw a wood, with trees growing slantingly away from the push of the prevalent sea winds, crowning the upward slope, and over the top of it peered a grey church tower.

For the moment, as the awful and familiar scene identified itself, Hester's heart stood still: the next a wave of courage and resolution poured in upon her. Here, at last, was the scene of that prefatory dream, and here was she presented with the opportunity of fathoming and dispelling it. Instantly her mind was made up, and under the strange twilight of the shrouded sky she walked swiftly on through the fields she had so often traversed in sleep, and up to the wood, beyond which he was waiting for her. She closed her ears against the clanging bell of terror, which now she could silence for ever, and unfalteringly entered that dark tunnel of wood. Soon in front of her the trees began to thin, and through them, now close at hand, she saw the church tower. In a few yards farther she came out of the belt of trees, and round her were the monuments of a graveyard long disused. The cliff was broken off close to the church tower: between it and the edge there was no more of the body of the church than a broken arch, thick-hung with ivy.

Round this she passed and saw below the ruin of fallen masonry, and the level sands strewn with headstones and disjected rubble, and at the edge of the cliff were graves already cracked and toppling. But there was no one here, none waited for her, and the churchyard where she had so often pictured him was as empty as the fields she had just traversed.

A huge elation filled her; her courage had been rewarded, and all the terrors of the past became to her meaningless phantoms. But there was no time to linger, for now the storm threatened, and on the horizon a blink of lightning was followed by a crackling peal. Just as she turned to go her eye fell on a tombstone that was balanced on the very edge of the cliff, and she read on it that here lay the body of Roger Wyburn.

Fear, the catalepsy of nightmare, rooted her for the moment to the spot; she stared in stricken amazement at the moss-grown letters; almost she expected to see that fell terror of a face rise and hover over his resting-place. Then the fear which had frozen her lent her wings, and with hurrying feet she sped through the arched pathway in the wood and out into the fields. Not one backward glance did she give till she had come to the edge of the ridge above the village, and, turning, saw the pastures she had traversed empty of any living presence. None had followed; but the sheep apprehensive of the coming storm, had ceased to feed, and were huddling under shelter of the stunted hedges.

Her first idea, in the panic of her mind, was to leave the place at once, but the last train for London had left an hour before, and besides, where was the use of flight if it was the spirit of a man long dead from which she fled? The distance from the place where his bones lay did not afford her safety; that must be sought for within. But she longed for Dick's sheltering and confident presence; he was arriving in any case tomorrow, but there were long dark hours before tomorrow, and who could say what the perils and dangers of the coming night might be? If he started this evening instead of to-morrow morning, he could motor down here in four hours, and would be with her by ten o'clock or eleven. She wrote an urgent telegram:

Come at once, (she said). *Don't delay.*

The storm which had flickered in the south now came quickly up, and soon after it burst in appalling violence. For preface there were but a few large drops that splashed and dried on the roadway as she came back from the post-office, and just as she reached the hotel again the roar of the approaching rain sounded, and the sluices of heaven were opened.

Through the deluge flared the fire of the lightning, the thunder crashed and echoed overhead, and presently the street of the village was a torrent of sandy, turbulent water, and sitting there in the dark, one picture leapt floating before her eyes – that of the tombstone of Roger Wyburn, already tottering to its fall at the edge of the cliff of the church tower. In such rains as these, acres of the cliffs were loosened; she seemed to hear the whisper of the sliding sand that would precipitate those perished sepulchres and what lay within to the beach below.

By eight o'clock the storm was subsiding, and as she dined she was handed a telegram from Dick, saying that he had already started and sent this off *en route*. By half past ten, therefore, if all was well, he would be here, and somehow he would stand between her and her fear. Strange how a few days ago both it and the thought of him had become distant and dim to her; now the one was as vivid as the other, and she counted the minutes to his arrival. Soon the rain ceased altogether, and looking out of the curtained window of her sitting-room where she was watching the slow circle of the hands of the clock, she saw a tawny moon rising over the sea. Before it had climbed to the zenith, before her clock had twice told the hour again, Dick would be with her.

It had just struck ten when there came a knock at her door, and the pageboy entered with the message that a

24

gentleman had come for her. Her heart leaped at the news; she had not expected Dick for half an hour yet, and now the lonely vigil was over. She ran downstairs, and there was the figure standing on the step outside. His face was turned away from her; no doubt he was giving some order to his chauffeur. He was outlined against the white moonlight, and in contrast with that, the gas-jet in the entrance just above his head gave his hair a warm, reddish tinge.

She ran across the hall to him.

'Ah, my darling, you've come,' she said. 'It was good of you. How quick you've been!' Just as she laid her hand on his shoulder he turned. His arm was thrown out round her, and she looked into a face with eyes close-set, and a mouth smiling on one side, the other, thick and gathered together as by some physical deformity, sneered and lusted.

The nightmare was on her; she could neither run nor scream, and supporting her dragging steps, he went forth with her into the night.

Half an hour later Dick arrived. To his amazement he heard that a man had called for his wife not long before, and that she had gone out with him. He seemed to be a stranger here, for the boy who had taken his message to her had never seen him before, and presently surprise began to deepen into alarm; inquiries were made outside the hotel, and it appeared that a witness or two had seen the lady whom they knew to be staying there walking, hatless, along the top of the beach with a man whose arm was linked in hers. Neither of them knew him, but one had seen his face and could describe it.

The direction of the search thus became narrowed down, and though with a lantern to supplement the moonlight they came upon footprints which might have been hers, there were no marks of any who walked beside her. But they followed these until they came to an end, a mile away, a great landslide of sand, which had fallen from the old churchyard on the cliff, and had brought down with it half the tower and a gravestone, with the body that had lain below.

The gravestone was that of Roger Wyburn, and his body lay by it, untouched by corruption or decay, though two hundred years had elapsed since it was interred there. For a week afterwards the work of searching the landslide went on, assisted by the high tides that gradually washed it away. But no further discovery was made.

Caterpillars

I saw a month or two ago in an Italian paper that the Villa Cascana, in which I once stayed, had been pulled down, and that a manufactory of some sort was in process of erection on its site. There is therefore no longer any reason for refraining from writing of those things which I myself saw (or imagined I saw) in a certain room and on a certain landing of the villa in question, nor from mentioning the circumstances which followed, which may or may not (according to the opinion of the reader) throw some light on, or be somehow connected with this experience.

This Villa Cascana was in all ways but one a perfectly delightful house, yet, if it were standing now, nothing in the world – I use the phrase in its literal sense – would induce me to set foot in it again, for I believe it to have been haunted in a very terrible and practical manner. Most ghosts, when all is said and done, do not do much harm; they may perhaps terrify, but the person whom they visit usually gets over their visitation. They may on the other hand be entirely friendly and beneficent. But the appearances in the Villa Cascana were not beneficent, and had they made their 'visit' in a very slightly different manner, I do not suppose I should have got over it any more than Arthur Inglis did.

The house stood on an ilex-clad hill not far from Sestri di Levante on the Italian Riviera, looking out over the iridescent blues of that enchanted sea, while behind it rose the pale green chestnut woods that climb up the hillsides till they give place to the pines that, black in contrast with them, crown the slopes. All round it the garden in the luxuriance of midspring bloomed and was fragrant, and the scent of magnolia and rose, borne on the salt freshness of the winds from the sea, flowed like a stream through the cool, vaulted rooms.

On the ground floor a broad pillared *loggia* ran round three sides of the house, the top of which formed a balcony for certain rooms of the first floor. The main staircase, broad and of grey marble steps, led up from the hall to the landing outside these rooms, which were three in number, namely, two big sitting-rooms and a bedroom arranged *en suite*. The latter was unoccupied, the sitting-rooms were in use. From these the main staircase was continued to the second floor, where were situated certain bedrooms, one of which I occupied, while from the other side of the first-floor landing some half-dozen steps led to another suite of rooms, where, at the time I am speaking of, Arthur Inglis, the artist, had his bedroom and studio. Thus the landing outside my bedroom at the top of the house, commanded both the landing of the first floor, and also the steps that led to Inglis' rooms. Jim Stanley and his wife, finally (whose guest I was), occupied rooms in another wing of the house, where also were the servants' quarters.

I arrived just in time for lunch on a brilliant noon of mid-May. The garden was shouting with colour and fragrance, and not less delightful after my broiling walk up from the *marina*, should have been the coming from the reverberating heat and blaze of the day into the marble coolness of the villa. Only (the reader has my bare word for this, and nothing more), the moment I set foot in the house I felt that something was wrong. This feeling, I may say, was quite vague, though very strong, and I remember that when I saw letters waiting for me on the table in the hall I felt certain that the explanation was here: I was convinced that there was bad news of some sort for me. Yet when I opened them I found no such explanation of my premonition: my correspondents all reeked of prosperity. Yet this clear miscarriage of a

28

presentiment did not dissipate my uneasiness. In that cool fragrant house there was something wrong.

I am at pains to mention this because to the general view it may explain that though I am as a rule so excellent a sleeper that the extinction of a light on getting into bed is apparently contemporaneous with being called on the following morning, I slept very badly on my first night in the Villa Cascana. It may also explain that fact that when I did sleep (if it was indeed in sleep that I saw what I thought I saw) I dreamed in a very vivid and original manner, original, that is to say, in the sense that something that, as far as I knew, had never previously entered into my consciousness, usurped it then. But since, in addition to this evil premonition, certain words and events occurring during the rest of the day, might have suggested something of what I thought happened that night, it will be well to relate them.

After lunch, then, I went round the house with Mrs. Stanley, and during our tour she referred, it is true, to the unoccupied bedroom on the first floor, which opened out of the room where we had lunched.

'We left that unoccupied,' she said, 'because Jim and I have a charming bedroom and dressing-room, as you saw, in the wing, and if we used it ourselves we should have to turn the dining-room into a dressing-room and have our meals downstairs. As it is, however, we have our little flat there, Arthur Inglis has his little flat in the other passage; and I remembered (aren't I extraordinary?) that you once said that the higher up you were in a house the better you were pleased. So I put you at the top of the house, instead of giving you that room.'

It is true, that a doubt, vague as my uneasy premonition, crossed my mind at this. I did not see why Mrs. Stanley should have explained all this, if there had not been more to explain. I allow, therefore, that the thought that there was something to explain about the unoccupied bedroom was momentarily present to my mind.

The second thing that may have borne on my dream was this.

At dinner the conversation turned for a moment on ghosts. Inglis, with the certainty of conviction, expressed his belief that anybody who could possibly believe in the existence of supernatural phenomena was unworthy of the name of an ass. The subject instantly dropped. As far as I can recollect, nothing else occurred or was said that could bear on what follows.

We all went to bed rather early, and personally I yawned my way upstairs, feeling hideously sleepy. My room was rather hot, and I threw all the windows wide, and from without poured in the white light of the moon, and the love-song of many nightingales. I undressed quickly, and got into bed, but though I had felt so sleepy before, I now felt extremely wide-awake. But I was quite content to be awake: I did not toss or turn, I felt perfectly happy listening to the song and seeing the light. Then, it is possible, I may have gone to sleep, and what follows may have been a dream. I thought anyhow that after a time the nightingales ceased singing and the moon sank. I thought also that if, for some unexplained reason, I was going to lie awake all night, I might as well read, and I remembered that I had left a book in which I was interested in the dining-room on the first floor. So I got out of bed, lit a candle, and went downstairs. I went into the room, saw on a side-table the book I had come to look for, and then, simultaneously, saw that the door into the unoccupied bedroom was open. A curious grey light, not of dawn nor of moonshine, came out of it, and I looked in. The bed stood just opposite the door, a big four-poster, hung with tapestry at the head. Then I saw that the greyish light of the bedroom came from the bed, or rather from what was on the bed. For it was covered with great caterpillars, a foot or more in length, which crawled over it. They were faintly luminous, and it was the light from them that showed me the room. Instead of the sucker-feet of ordinary caterpillars they had rows of pincers like crabs, and they moved by grasping what they lay on with their pincers, and then sliding their bodies forward. In colour these dreadful insects were yellowish-grey, and they were covered with irregular lumps and swellings. There must have been hundreds of them, for they formed a sort of writhing, crawling pyramid on the bed. Occasionally one fell off on to the floor, with a soft fleshy thud, and though the floor was of hard concrete, it yielded to the pincer-feet as if it had been putty, and crawling back, the caterpillar would mount on to the bed again, to rejoin its fearful companions. They appeared to have no faces, so to speak, but at one end of them there was a mouth that opened side-ways in respiration.

Then, as I looked, it seemed to me as if they all suddenly became conscious of my presence. All the mouths at any rate were turned in my direction, and next moment they began dropping off the bed with those soft fleshy thuds on to the floor, and wriggling towards me. For one second a paralysis as of a dream was on me, but the next I was running upstairs again to my room, and I remember feeling the cold of the marble steps on my bare feet. I rushed into my bedroom, and slammed the door behind me, and then – I was certainly wide-awake now – I found myself standing by my bed with the sweat of terror pouring from me. The noise of the banged door still rang in my ears. But, as would have been more usual, if this had been mere nightmare, the terror that had been mine when I saw those foul beasts crawling about the bed or dropping softly on to the floor did not cease then. Awake now, if dreaming before, I did not at all recover from the horror of dream: it did not seem to me that I had dreamed. And until dawn, I sat or stood, not daring to lie down, thinking that every rustle or movement that I heard was the approach of the caterpillars. To them and the claws that bit into the cement the wood of the door was child's play: steel would not keep them out.

But with the sweet and noble return of day the horror vanished: the whisper of wind became benignant again: the nameless fear, whatever it was, was smoothed out and terrified me no longer. Dawn broke, hueless at first;

31

then it grew dove-coloured, then the flaming pageant of light spread over the sky.

The admirable rule of the house was that everybody had breakfast where and when he pleased, and in consequence it was not till lunch-time that I met any of the other members of our party, since I had breakfast on my balcony, and wrote letters and other things till lunch. In fact, I got down to that meal rather late, after the other three had begun. Between my knife and fork there was a small pill-box of card-board, and as I sat down Inglis spoke.

'Do look at that,' he said, 'since you are interested in natural history. I found it crawling on my counterpane last night, and I don't know what it is.'

I think that before I opened the pill-box I expected something of the sort which I found in it. Inside it, anyhow, was a small caterpillar, greyish-yellow in colour, with curious bumps and excrescences on its rings. It was extremely active, and hurried round the box, this way and that. Its feet were unlike the feet of any caterpillar I ever saw: they were like the pincers of a crab. I looked, and shut the lid down again.

'No, I don't know it,' I said, 'but it looks rather unwholesome. What are you going to do with it?'

'Oh, I shall keep it,' said Inglis. 'It has begun to spin: I want to see what sort of a moth it turns into.'

I opened the box again, and saw that these hurrying movements were indeed the beginning of the spinning of the web of its cocoon. Then Inglis spoke again.

'It has got funny feet, too,' he said. 'They are like crabs' pincers. What's the Latin for crab? Oh, yes, Cancer. So in case it is unique, let's christen it: "Cancer Inglisensis." '

Then something happened in my brain, some momentary piercing together of all that I had seen or dreamed. Something in his words seemed to me to throw light on it all, and my own intense horror at the experience of the night before linked itself on to what he had just said. In effect, I took the box and threw it, caterpillar and all, out of the window. There was a gravel path just outside, and beyond it, a fountain playing into a basin. The box fell on to the middle of this.

Inglis laughed.

'So the students of the occult don't like solid facts,' he said. 'My poor caterpillar!'

The talk went off again at once on to other subjects, and I have only given in detail, as they happened, these trivialities in order to be sure myself that I have recorded everything that could have borne on occult subjects or on the subject of caterpillars. But at the moment when I threw the pill-box into the fountain, I lost my head: my only excuse is that, as is probably plain, the tenant of it was, in miniature, exactly what I had seen crowded on to the bed in the unoccupied room. And though this translation of those phantoms into flesh and blood – or whatever it is that caterpillars are made of – ought perhaps to have relieved the horror of the night, as a matter of fact it did nothing of the kind. It only made the crawling pyramid that covered the bed in the unoccupied room more hideously real.

After lunch we spent a lazy hour or two strolling about the garden or sitting in the *loggia,* and it must have been about four o'clock when Stanley and I started off to bathe, down the path that led by the fountain into which I had thrown the pill-box. The water was shallow and clear, and at the bottom of it I saw its white remains. The water had disintegrated the cardboard, and it had become no more than a few strips and shreds of sodden paper. The centre of the fountain was a marble Italian Cupid which squirted the water out of a wine-skin held under its arm. And crawling up its leg was the cater-pillar. Strange and scarcely credible as it seemed, it must have survived the falling-to-bits of its prison, and made its way to shore, and there it was, out of arm's reach, weaving and waving this way and that as it evolved its cocoon.

33

Then, as I looked at it, it seemed to me again that, like the caterpillar I had seen last night, it saw me, and breaking out of the threads that surrounded it, it crawled down the marble leg of the Cupid and began swimming like a snake across the water of the fountain towards me. It came with extraordinary speed (the fact of a caterpillar being able to swim was new to me), and in another moment was crawling up the marble lip of the basin. Just then Inglis joined us.

'Why, if it isn't old "Cancer Inglisensis" again,' he said, catching sight of the beast. 'What a tearing hurry it is in.'

We were standing side by side on the path, and when the caterpillar had advanced to within about a yard of us, it stopped, and began waving again, as if in doubt as to the direction in which it should go. Then it appeared to make up its mind, and crawled on to Inglis' shoe.

'It likes me best,' he said, 'but I don't really know that I like it. And as it won't drown I think perhaps –'

He shook it off his shoe on to the gravel path and trod on it.

All afternoon the air got heavier and heavier with the Sirocco that was without doubt coming up from the south, and that night again I went up to bed feeling very sleepy; but below my drowsiness, so to speak, there was the consciousness, stronger than before, that there was something wrong in the house, that something dangerous was close at hand. But I fell asleep at once, and – how long after I do not know – either woke or dreamed I awoke, feeling that I must get up at once, *or I should be too late.* Then (dreaming or awake) I lay and fought this fear, telling myself that I was but the prey of my own nerves disordered by Sirocco or what not, and at the same time quite clearly knowing in another part of my mind, so to speak, that every moment's delay added to the danger. At last this second feeling became irresistible, and I put on coat and trousers and went out of my room on to the landing. And then I saw that I had already delayed too long, and that I was now too late.

34

The whole of the landing of the first floor below was invisible under the swarm of caterpillars that crawled there. The folding doors into the sitting-room from which opened the bedroom where I had seen them last night, were shut, but they were squeezing through the cracks of it, and dropping one by one through the keyhole, elongating themselves into mere string as they passed, and growing fat and lumpy again on emerging. Some, as if exploring, were nosing about the steps into the passage at the end of which were Inglis' rooms, others were crawling on the lowest steps of the staircase that led up to where I stood. The landing, however, was completely covered with them: I was cut off. And of the frozen horror that seized me when I saw that, I can give no idea in words.

Then at last a general movement began to take place, and they grew thicker on the steps that led to Inglis' room. Gradually, like some hideous tide of flesh, they advanced along the passage, and I saw the foremost, visible by the pale grey luminousness that came from them, reach his door. Again and again I tried to shout and warn him, in terror all the time that they should turn at the sound of my voice and mount my stair instead, but for all my efforts I felt that no sound came from my throat. They crawled along the hinge-crack of his door, passing through as they had done before, and still I stood there making impotent efforts to shout to him, to bid him escape while there was time.

At last the passage was completely empty: they had all gone, and at that moment I was conscious for the first time of the cold of the marble landing on which I stood barefooted. The dawn was just beginning to break in the Eastern sky.

Six months later I met Mrs. Stanley in a country house in England. We talked on many subjects and at last she said:

'I don't think I have seen you since I got that dreadful news about Arthur Inglis a month ago.'

'I haven't heard,' said I.

'No? He has got cancer. They don't even advise an operation, for there is no hope of a cure: he is riddled with it, the doctors say.'

Now during all these six months I do not think a day had passed on which I had not had in my mind the dreams (or whatever you like to call them) which I had seen in the Villa Cascana.

'It is awful, is it not?' she continued, 'and I feel, I can't help feeling, that he may have –'

'Caught it at the villa?' I asked.

She looked at me in blank surprise.

'Why did you say that?' she asked. 'How did you know?'

Then she told me. In the unoccupied bedroom a year before there had been a fatal case of cancer. She had, of course, taken the best advice and had been told that the utmost dictates of prudence would be obeyed so long as she did not put anybody to sleep in the room, which had also been thoroughly disinfected and newly white-washed and painted. But –

Expiation

Philip Stuart and I, unattached and middle-aged persons, had for the last four or five years been accustomed to spend a month or six weeks together in the summer, taking a furnished house in some part of the country, which, by an absence of attractive pursuits, was not likely to be overrun by gregarius holiday-makers. When, as the season for getting out of London draws near, and we scan the advertisement columns which set forth the charms and the cheapness of residences to be let for August, and see the mention of tennis-clubs and esplanades and admirable golf-links within a stone's throw of the proposed front door, our offended and disgusted eyes instantly wander to the next item.

For the point of a holiday, according to our private heresy, is not to be entertained and occupied and jostled by glad crowds, but to have nothing to do, and no temptation which might lead to any unseasonable activity. London has held employments and diversion enough; we want to be without both. But vicinity to the sea is desirable, because it is easier to do nothing by the sea than anywhere else, and because bathing and basking on the shore cannot be considered an employment, but only an apotheosis of loafing. A garden also is a requisite, for that tranquillizes any fidgety notion of going for a walk.

In pursuance of this sensible policy we had this year taken a house on the south coast of Cornwall, for a relaxing climate conduces to laziness. It was too far off for us to make any personal inspection of it, but a perusal of the modestly worded advertisement carried conviction. It was close to the sea; the village Polwithy, outside which it was situated, was remote, and, as far as we knew, unknown; it had a garden, and there was attached to it a cook-housekeeper who made for simplification. No mention of golf-links or attractive resorts in the neighbourhood defiled the bald and terse specification, and though there was a tennis-court in the garden, there was no clause that bound the tenants to use it. The owner was Mrs. Hearne, who had been living abroad, and our business was transacted with a house-agent in Falmouth.

To make our household complete, Philip sent down a parlourmaid, and I a housemaid, and after leaving them a day in which to settle in, we followed. There was a six-mile drive from the station across high uplands, and at the end a long, steady descent into a narrow valley, cloven between the hills, that grew ever more luxuriant in verdure as we descended. Great trees of fuchsia spread up to the eaves of the thatched cottages which stood by the wayside, and a stream, embowered in green thickets, ran babbling along. Presently we came to the village, no more than a dozen houses, built of the grey stone of the district, and on a shelf just above it a tiny church with parsonage adjoining. High above us now flamed the gorse-clad slopes of the hills on each side, and now the valley opened out at its lower end, and the still, warm air was spiced and renovated by the breeze that drew up it from the sea. Then round a sharp angle of the road we came alongside a stretch of brick wall, and stopped at an iron gate above which flowed a riot of rambler rose.

It seemed hardly credible that it was this of which that terse and laconic advertisement had spoken; I had pictured something of villa-ish kind – yellow-bricked perhaps, with a roof of purplish slate, a sitting-room one side of the entrance, a dining-room the other; with a tiled hall and a pitch-pine staircase – and instead, here was this little gem of an early Georgian manor house, mellow and gracious, with mullioned windows and a roof of stone slabs. In front of it was a paved terrace, below which blossomed a herbaceous border, tangled and tropical, with no inch of earth visible through its luxuriance. Inside, too, was fulfilment of this fair exterior: a broad-balustered staircase led up from the odiously entitled 'lounge hall', which I had pictured as a medley of Benares ware and saddle-bagged sofas, but which proved to be cool, broad and panelled with a door opposite that through which we entered, leading on to the further area of garden at the back. There was the advertised but innocuous tennis-court, bordered on the length of its far side by a steep grass bank, along which was planted a row of limes, once pollarded, but now allowed to develop at will. Thick boughs, some fourteen or fifteen feet from the ground, interlaced with each other, forming an arcaded row; above them, where Nature had been permitted to go her own way, the trees broke into feathered and honey-scented branches. Beyond lay a small orchard climbing upwards; above that the hillside rose more steeply, in broad spaces of short-cropped turf and ablaze with gorse, the Cornish gorse that flowers all the year round, and spreads its sunshine from January to December.

There was time for a stroll through this perfect little domain before dinner, and for a short interview with the housekeeper, a quiet, capable-looking woman, slightly aloof, as is the habit of her race, from strangers and foreigners, for so the Cornish account the English, but who proved herself at the repast that followed to be as capable as she appeared. The evening closed in hot and still, and after dinner we took chairs out on to the terrace in front of the house.

'Far the best place we've struck yet,' observed Philip. 'Why did no one say Polwithy before?'

'Because nobody had ever heard of it, luckily,' said I.

'Well, I'm a Polwithian. At least, I am in spirit. But how aware Mrs. – Mrs. Criddle made me feel that I wasn't really.'

Philip's profession, a doctor of obscure nervous

diseases, has made him preternaturally acute in the diagnosis of what other people feel, and for some reason quite undefined I wanted to know what exactly he meant by this. I was in sympathy with his feeling, but I could not analyse it.

'Describe your symptoms,' I said.

'I have. When she came up and talked to us, and hoped we should be comfortable, and told us that she would do her best, she was just gossiping. Probably it was perfectly true gossip. But it wasn't she. However, as that's all that matters, there's no reason why we should probe further.'

'Which means that you have,' I said.

'No; it means that I tried to and couldn't. She gave me an extraordinary sense of her being aware of something which we knew nothing of; of being on a plane which we couldn't imagine. I constantly meet such people; they aren't very rare. I don't mean that there's anything the least uncanny about them, or that they know things that are uncanny. They are simply aloof, as hard to understand as your dog or your cat. She would find us equally aloof if she succeeded in analysing her sensations about us, but like a sensible woman she probably feels not the smallest interest in us. She is there to bake and to boil, and we are there to eat her bakings and appreciate her boilings.'

The subject dropped, and we sat on in the dusk that was rapidly deepening into night. The door into the hall was open at our backs, and a panel of light from the lamps within was cast out on to the terrace. Wandering moths, invisible in the darkness, suddenly became manifest as they fluttered into this illumination, and vanished again as they passed out of it. One moment they were there, living things with life and motion of their own, the next they had quite disappeared. How inexplicable that would be, I thought, if one did not know from long familiarity that light of the appropriate sort and strength is needed to make material objects visible.

Philip must have been following precisely the same

train of thought, for his voice broke in, carrying it a little further.

'Look at that moth,' he said, 'and even while you look it has gone like a ghost, even as like a ghost it appeared. Light made it visible. And there are other sorts of light, interior psychical light which similarly makes visible the beings which people the darkness of our blindness.'

Just as he spoke I thought for the moment that I heard the tingle of a telephone bell. It sounded very faintly, and I could not have sworn that I had actually heard it. At the most it gave one staccato little summons and was silent again.

'Is there a telephone in the house?' I asked. 'I haven't noticed one.'

'Yes, by the door into the back garden,' said he. 'Do you want to telephone?'

'No, but I thought I heard it ring. Didn't you?'

He shook his head, then smiled.

'Ah, that was it,' he said.

Certainly now there was the clink of glass, rather bell-like, as the parlourmaid came out of the dining-room with a tray of syphon and decanter, and my reasonable mind was quite content to accept this very probable explanation. But behind that, quite unreasonably, some little obstinate denizen of my consciousness rejected it. It told me that what I had heard was like the moth that came out of darkness and went on into darkness again. . .

My room was at the back of the house, overlooking the lawn-tennis-court, and presently I went up to bed. The moon had risen, and the lawn lay in bright illumination bordered by a strip of dark shadow below the pollarded limes. Somewhere along the hillside an owl was foraging, softly hooting, and presently it swept whitely across the lawn. No sound is so intensely rural, yet none, to my mind, so suggests a signal. But it seemed to signal nothing, and, tired with the long, hot journey, and soothed by the deep tranquillity of the place, I was soon asleep. But often during the night I woke, though never to more than a dozing, dreamy consciousness of where I was, and each

41

time I had the notion that some slight noise had roused me, and each time I found myself listening to hear whether the tingle of a telephone bell was the cause of my disturbance. There came no repetition of it, and again I slept, and again I woke with drowsy attention for the sound which I felt I expected, but never heard.

Daylight banished these imaginations, but though I must have slept many hours all told, for these wakings had been only brief and partial, I was aware of a certain weariness, as if though my bodily senses had been rested, some part of me had been wakeful and watching all night. This was fanciful enough to disregard, and certainly during the day I forgot it altogether. Soon after breakfast we went down to the sea, and a short ramble along a shingly shore brought us to a sandy cove framed in promontories of rock that went down into deep water. The most fastidious connoisseur in bathing could have pictured no more ideal scene for his operations, for with hot sand to bask on and rocks to plunge from, and a limpid ocean and a cloudless sky, there was indeed no lacuna in perfection. All morning we loafed here, swimming and sunning ourselves, and for the afternoon there was the shade of the garden, and a stroll later on up through the orchard and to the gorse-clad hillside. We came back through the churchyard, looked into the church, and coming out, Philip pointed to a tombstone which from its newness among its dusky and moss-grown companions easily struck the eye. It recorded without pious or scriptural reflection the date of the birth and death of George Hearne; the latter event had taken place close on two years ago, and we were within a week of the exact anniversary. Other tombstones near were monuments to those of the same name, and dated back for a couple of centuries and more.

'Local family,' said I, and strolling on we came to our own gate in the long brick wall. It was opened from inside just as we arrived at it, and there came out a brisk, middle-aged man in clergyman's dress, obviously our vicar.

He very civilly introduced himself.

'I heard that Mrs. Hearne's house had been taken, and that the tenants had come,' he said, 'and I ventured to leave my card.'

We performed our part of the ceremony, and in answer to his inquiry professed our satisfaction with our quarters and our neighbourhood.

'That is good news,' said Mr. Stephens; 'I hope you will continue to enjoy your holiday. I am Cornish myself, and like all natives think there is no place like Cornwall!'

Philip pointed with his stick towards the churchyard. 'We noticed that the Hearnes are people of the place,' he said. Quite suddenly I found myself understanding what he had meant by the aloofness of the race. Something between reserve and suspicion came into Mr. Stephens' face.

'Yes, yes, an old family here,' he said, 'and large landowners. But now some remote cousin . . . The house, however, belongs to Mrs. Hearne for life.'

He stopped, and by that reticence confirmed the impression he had made. In consequence, for there is something in the breast of the most incurious which, when treated with reserve becomes inquisitive, Philip proceeded to ask a direct question.

'Then I take it that the George Hearne who, as I have just seen, died two years ago, was the husband of Mrs. Hearne, from whom we took the house?'

'Yes; he was buried in the churchyard,' said Mr. Stephens quickly. Then, for no reason at all, he added:

'Naturally he was buried in the churchyard here.'

Now my impression at that moment was that Mr. Stephens had said something he did not mean to say, and had corrected it by saying the same thing again.

He went on his way, back to the vicarage, with an amiably expressed desire to do anything that was in his power for us, in the way of local information, and we went in through the gate. The post had just arrived; there was the London morning paper and a letter for Philip which cost him two perusals before he folded it up

43

and put it into his pocket. But he made no comment, and presently, as dinner-time was near, I went up to my room. Here in this deep valley with the great westerly hill towering above us, it was already dark, and the lawn lay beneath a twilight as of deep, clear water. Quite idly as I brushed my hair in front of the glass on the table in the window, of which the blinds were not yet drawn, I looked out and saw that on the bank along which grew the pollarded limes there was lying a ladder. It was just a shade odd that it should be there, but the oddity of it was quite accounted for by the supposition that the gardener had had business among the trees in the orchard, and had left it there, for the completion of his labours tomorrow. It was just as odd as that, and no odder, just worth a twitch of the imagination to account for it, but now completely accounted for.

I went downstairs, and passing Philip's door heard the swish of ablutions which implied he was not quite ready, and in the most loaferlike manner I strolled round the corner of the house. The kitchen window which looked on to the tennis-court was open, and there was a good smell, I remember, coming from it. And still without thought of the ladder I had just seen, I mounted the slope of grass on to the tennis-court. Just across it was the bank where the pollarded limes grew; but there was no ladder lying there. Of course the gardener must have remembered he had left it, and had returned to remove it exactly as I came downstairs. There was nothing singular about that, and I could not imagine why the thing interested me at all. But for some inexplicable reason I found myself saying: 'But I did see the ladder just now.'

A bell – no telephone bell, but a welcome harbinger to a hungry man – sounded from inside the house, and I went back on to the terrace, just as Philip got downstairs. At dinner our speech rambled pleasantly over the accomplishments of today, and the prospects of tomorrow, and in due course we came to the consideration of Mr. Stephens. We settled that he was an aloof fellow, and then Philip said:

'I wonder why he hastened to tell us that George Hearne was buried in the churchyard, and then added that naturally he was!'

'It's the natural place to be buried in,' said I.

'Quite. That's just why it was hardly worth mentioning.'

I felt then, just momentarily, just vaguely, as if my mind was regarding stray pieces of a jigsaw puzzle. The fancied ringing of the telephone bell last night was one of them, this burial of George Hearne in the churchyard was another, and, even more inexplicably, the ladder I had seen under the trees was a third. Consciously I made nothing whatever out of them, and did not feel the least inclination to devote any ingenuity to so fortuitous a collection of pieces. Why shouldn't I add, for that matter, our morning's bathe, or the gorse on the hillside? But I had the sensation that, though my conscious brain was presently occupied with piquet, and was rapidly growing sleepy with the day of sun and sea, some sort of mole inside it was digging passages and connecting-corridors below the soil.

Five eventless days succeeded; there were no more ladders, no more phantom telephone bells, and emphatically no more Mr. Stephens. Once or twice we met him in the village street and got from him the curtest salutation possible short of a direct cut. And yet somehow he seemed charged with information, so we lazily concluded, and he made for us a field of imaginative speculation. I remember that I constructed a highly fanciful romance, which postulated that George Hearne was not dead at all, but that Mr. Stephens had murdered some inconvenient black-mailer, whom he had buried with the rites of the Church. Or – these romances always broke down under cross-examination from Philip – Mr. Stephens himself was George Hearne, who had fled from justice, and was supposed to have died. Or Mrs. Hearne was really George Hearne, and our admirable housekeeper was the real Mrs. Hearne. From such indications you may judge how the intoxication of the sun and the sea had overpowered us.

45

But there was one explanation of why Mr. Stephens had so hastily assured us that George Hearne was buried in the churchyard which never passed our lips. It was just because both Philip and I really believed it to be the true one that we did not mention it. But just as if it was some fever or plague, we both knew that we were sickening with it. And then these fanciful romances stopped because we knew that the Real Thing was approaching. There had been faint glimpses of it before, like distant sheet-lightning; now the noise of it, authentic and audible, began to rumble.

There came a day of hot, overclouded weather. We had bathed in the morning, and loafed in the afternoon, but Philip, after tea, had refused to come for our usual ramble, and I set out alone. That morning Mrs. Criddle had rather peremptorily told me that a room in the front of the house would prove much cooler for me, for it caught the sea breeze, and though I objected that it would also catch the southerly sun, she had clearly made up her mind that I was to move from the bedroom overlooking the tennis-court and the pollarded limes, and there was no resisting so polite and yet determined a woman.

When I set out for my ramble after tea, the change had already been effected, and my brain nosed slowly about as I strolled, sniffing for her reason, for no self-respecting brain could accept the one she gave. But in this hot, drowsy air, I entirely lacked nimbleness, and when I came back the question had become a mere silly, unanswerable riddle. I returned through the church-yard, and saw that in a couple of days we should arrive at the anniversary of George Hearne's death.

Philip was not on the terrace in front of the house, and I went in at the door of the hall, expecting to find him there or in the back garden. Exactly as I entered my eye told me that there he was, a black silhouette against the glass door, at the end of the hall, which was open, and led through into the back garden. He did not turn round at the sound of my entry, but took a step or two in the direction of

46

the far door, still framed in the oblong of it. I glanced at the table, where the post lay, found letters both for me and him, and looked up again. There was no one there.

He had hastened his steps, I supposed, but simultaneously I thought how odd it was that he had not taken his letters, if he was in the hall, and that he had not turned when I entered. However, I should find him just round the corner, and with his post and mine in my hand I went towards the far door. As I approached it I felt a sudden cold stir of air, rather unaccountable, for the day was notably sultry, and went out. He was sitting at the far end of the tennis-court.

I went up to him with his letters.

'I thought I saw you just now in the hall,' I said. But I knew already that I had not seen him in the hall.

He looked up quickly.

'And have you only just come in?' he said.

'Yes; this moment. Why?'

'Because half an hour ago I went in to see if the post had come, and thought I saw you in the hall.'

'And what did I do?' I asked.

'You went out on to the terrace. But I didn't find you there.'

There was a short pause as he opened his letters.

'Damned interesting,' he observed. 'Because there's someone here who isn't you or me.'

'Anything else?' I asked.

He laughed, pointing at the row of trees.

'Yes, something too silly for words,' he said. 'Just now I saw a piece of rope dangling from the big branch of that pollarded lime. I saw it quite distinctly. And then there wasn't any rope there at all, any more than there is now.'

Philosophers have argued about the strongest emotion known to man. Some say 'love', others 'hate', others 'fear'. I am disposed to put 'curiosity' on a level, at least, with these august sensations, just mere simple inquisitiveness. Certainly at the moment it rivalled fear in my mind, and there was a hint of that.

47

As he spoke the parlourmaid came out into the garden with a telegram in her hand. She gave it to Philip, who without a word scribbled a line on the reply-paid form inside it, and handed it back to her.

'Dreadful nuisance,' he said, 'but there's no help for it. A few days ago I got a letter which made me think I might have to go up to town, and this telegram makes it certain. There's an operation possible on a patient of mine, which I hoped might have been avoided, but my locum tenens won't take the responsibility of deciding whether it is necessary or not.'

He looked at his watch.

'I can catch the night train,' he said, 'and I ought to be able to catch the night train back from town tomorrow. I shall be back, that is to say, the day after tomorrow in the morning. There's no help for it. Ha, that telephone of yours will come in useful. I can get a taxi from Falmouth, and needn't start till after dinner.'

He went into the house, and I heard him rattling and tapping at the telephone. Soon he called for Mrs. Criddle, and presently came out again.

'We're not on the telephone service,' he said. 'It was cut off a year ago, only they haven't removed the apparatus. But I can get a trap in the village, Mrs. Criddle says, and she's sent for it. If I start at once I shall easily be in time. Spicer's packing a bag for me, and I'll take a sandwich.'

He looked sharply towards the pollarded trees.

'Yes, just there,' he said. 'I saw it plainly, and equally plainly I saw it not. And then there's that telephone of yours.'

I told him now about the ladder I had seen below the tree where he saw the dangling rope.

'Interesting,' he said, 'because it's so silly and unexpected. It is really tragic that I should be called away just now, for it looks as if the – well, the matter were coming out of the darkness into a shaft of light. But I'll be back, I hope, in thirty-six hours. Meantime do observe very carefully, and whatever you do, don't make a theory.

Darwin says somewhere that you can't observe without a theory, but to make a theory is a great danger to an observer. It can't help influencing your imagination; you tend to see or hear what falls in with your hypothesis. So just observe; be as mechanical as a phonograph and a photographic lens.'

Presently the dog-cart arrived, and I went down to the gate with him. 'Whatever it is that is coming through, is coming through in bits,' he said. 'You heard a telephone; I saw a rope. We both saw a figure, but not simultaneously nor in the same place. I wish I didn't have to go.'

I found myself sympathizing strongly with this wish, when after dinner I found myself with a solitary evening in front of me, and the pledge to 'observe' binding me. It was not mainly a scientific ardour that prompted this sympathy, and the desire for independent combination; but, quite emphatically, fear of what might be coming out of the huge darkness which lies on all sides of human experience. I could no longer fail to connect together the fancied telephone bell, the rope, and the ladder, for what made the chain between them was the figure that both Philip and I had seen. Already my mind was seething with conjectural theory, but I would not let the ferment of it ascend to my surface consciousness; my business was not to aid, but rather stifle, my imagination.

I occupied myself, therefore, with the ordinary devices of a solitary man, sitting on the terrace, and subsequently coming into the house, for a few spots of rain began to fall. But though nothing disturbed the outward tranquillity of the evening, the quietness administered no opiate to that seething mixture of fear and curiosity that obsessed me. I heard the servants creep bedwards up the back stairs and presently I followed them. Then, forgetting for the moment that my room had been changed, I tried the handle of the door of that which I had previously occupied. It was locked.

Now here, beyond doubt, was the sign of a human agency, and at once I was determined to get into the room. The key, I could see, was not in the door, which must therefore have been locked from outside. I therefore searched the usual cache for keys along the top of the door-frame, found it, and entered.

The room was quite empty, the blinds not drawn, and after looking round it I walked across to the window. The moon was up, and though obscured behind clouds, gave sufficient light to enable me to see objects outside with tolerable distinctness. There was the row of pollarded limes, and then with a sudden intake of my breath I saw that a foot or two below one of the boughs there was suspended something whitish and oval which oscillated as it hung there. In the dimness I could see nothing more than that, but now conjecture crashed into my conscious brain. But even as I looked it was gone again; there was nothing there but deep shadow, the trees steadfast in the windless air. Simultaneously I knew that I was not alone in the room.

I turned swiftly about, but my eyes gave no endorsement of that conviction, and yet their evidence that there was no one here except myself failed to shake it. The presence, somewhere close to me, needed no such evidence; it was self-evident though invisible, and I knew that my forehead was streaming with the abject sweat of terror. Somehow I knew that the presence was that of the figure both Philip and I had seen that evening in the hall, and, credit it or not as you will, the fact that it was invisible made it infinitely the more terrible. I knew, too, that though my eyes were blind to it, it had got into closer touch with me; I knew more of its nature now: it had had tragic and awful commerce with evil and despair. Some sort of catalepsy was on me, while it thus obsessed me; presently, minutes afterwards, or perhaps mere seconds, the grip and clutch of its power was relaxed, and with shaking knees I crossed the room and went out, and again locked the door. Even as I turned the key I smiled at the futility of that. With my emergence the terror completely passed; I went across the passage leading to my room, got into bed, and was soon asleep. But I had no more need to question myself as to why Mrs.

Criddle made the change. Another guest, she knew, would come to occupy it as the season arrived when George Hearne died and was buried in the churchyard.

The night passed quietly and then succeeded a day hot and still and sultry beyond belief. The very sea had lost its coolness and vitality, and I came in from my swim tired and enervated instead of refreshed. No breeze stirred; the trees stood motionless as if cast in iron, and from horizon to horizon the sky was overlaid by an ever-thickening pall of cloud. The cohorts of storm and thunder were gathering in the stillness, and all day I felt that power, other than that of these natural forces, was being stored for some imminent manifestation.

As I came near to the house the horror deepened, and after dinner I had a mind to drop into the vicarage, according to Mr. Stephens' general invitation, and get through an hour or two with other company than my own. But I delayed till it was past any reasonable time for such an informal visit, and ten o'clock still saw me on the terrace in front of the house. My nerves were all on edge, a stir or step in the house was sufficient to make me turn round in apprehension of seeing I knew not what, but presently it grew still. One lamp burned in the hall behind me; by it stood the candle which would light me to bed.

I went indoors soon after, meaning to go up to bed, then suddenly, ashamed of this craven imbecility of mind, took the fancy to walk round the house for the purpose of convincing myself that all was tranquil and normal, and that my fear, that nameless indefinable load on my spirit, was but a product of this close and thundery night. The tension of the weather could not last much longer; soon the storm must break and the relief come, but it would be something to know that there was nothing more than that. Accordingly I went out again on to the terrace, traversed it and turned the corner of the house where lay the tennis-lawn.

Tonight the moon had not yet risen, and the darkness was such that I could barely distinguish the outline of the house, and that of the pollarded limes, but through the glass door that led from this side of the house into the hall there shone the light of the lamp that stood there. All was absolutely quiet, and half reassured I traversed the lawn, and turned to go back. Just as I came opposite the lit door, I heard a sound very close at hand from under the deep shadow of the pollarded limes. It was as if some heavy object had fallen with a thump and rebound on the grass, and with it there came the noise of a creaking bough suddenly strained by some weight. Then interpretation came upon me with the unreasoning force of conviction, though in the blackness I could see nothing. But at the sound a horror such as I have never felt laid hold on me. It was scarcely physical at all: it came from some deep-seated region of the soul.

The heavens were rent, a stream of blinding light shot forth, and straight in front of my eyes, a few yards from where I stood, I saw. The noise had been of a ladder thrown down on the grass, and from the bough of the pollarded lime there was the figure of a man, white-faced against the blackness, oscillating and twisting on the rope that strangled him. Just that I saw before the stillness was torn to atoms by the roar of thunder, and as from a hose the rain descended. Once again, even before that first appalling riot had died, the clouds were shredded again by the lightning, and my eyes which had not moved from the place, saw only the framed shadows of the trees, and their upper branches bowed by the pelting rain. All night the storm raged and bellowed, making sleep impossible, and for an hour at least, between the peals of thunder, I heard the ringing of the telephone bell.

Next morning Philip returned, to whom I told exactly what is written here, but watch and observe as we might, neither of us, in the three further weeks which we spent at Polwithy, heard or saw anything that could interest the student of the occult. Pleasant lazy days succeeded each other; we bathed and rambled and played piquet of an evening, and incidentally we made friends with the vicar.

He was an interesting man, full of curious lore concerning local legends and superstitions, and one night, when in our ripened acquaintanceship he had dined with us, he asked Philip directly whether either of us had experienced anything unusual during our tenancy.

Philip nodded towards me.

'My friend saw most,' he said.

'May I hear it?' asked the vicar.

When I had finished, he was silent awhile.

'I think the – shall we call it explanation? – is yours by right,' he said. 'I will give it you if you care to hear it.'

Our silence, I supposed, answered him.

'I remember meeting you two on the day after your arrival here,' he said, 'and you inquired about the tombstone in the churchyard erected to the memory of George Hearne. I did not want to say more of him then, for a reason that you will presently know. I told you, I recollect, perhaps rather hurriedly, that it was Mrs. Hearne's husband who was buried there. Already, I imagine, you guess that I concealed something. You may even have guessed it at the time.'

He did not wait for any confirmation or repudiation of this. Sitting out on the terrace in the deep dusk, his communication was very impersonal. It was just a narrating voice, without identity, an anonymous chronicle.

'George Hearne succeeded to the property here, which is considerable, only two years before his death. He was married shortly after he succeeded. According to any decent standard, his life both before and after his marriage was vile. I think – God forgive me if I wrong him – he made evil his good; he liked evil for its own sake. But out of the middle of the mire of his own soul there sprang a flower: he was devoted to his wife. And he was capable of shame.

'A fortnight before his – his death, she got to know what his life was like, and what he was in himself. I need not tell you what was the particular disclosure that came to her knowledge; it is sufficient to say that it was revolting. She was here at the time; he was coming down

53

from London that night. When he arrived he found a note from her saying that she had left him and could never come back. She told him that he must give her opportunity for her to divorce him, and threatened him with exposure if he did not.

'He and I had been friends, and that night he came to me with her letter, acknowledged the justice of it, but asked me to intervene. He said that the only thing that could save him from utter damnation was she, and I believe that there he spoke sincerely. But, speaking as a clergyman, I should not have called him penitent. He did not hate his sin, but only the consequences of it. But it seemed to me that if she came back to him he might have a chance, and next day I went to her. Nothing that I could say moved her one atom, and after a fruitless day I came back, and told him of the uselessness of my mission.

'Now, according to my view, no man who deliberately prefers evil to good, just for the sake of wickedness, is sane, and this refusal of hers to have anything more to do with him I fully believe upset the unstable balance of his soul altogether. There was just his devotion to her which might conceivably have restored it, but she refused – and I can quite understand her refusal – to come near him. If you knew what I know you could not blame her. But the effect of it on him was portentous and disastrous, and three days afterwards I wrote to her again, saying quite simply that the damnation of his soul would be on her head unless, leaving her personal feelings altogether out of the question, she came back. She got that letter the next evening, and already it was too late.

'That afternoon, two years ago, on the fifteenth of August, there was washed up in the harbour here a dead body, and that night George Hearne took a ladder from the fruit-wall in the kitchen garden and hanged himself. He climbed into one of the pollarded limes, tied the rope to a bough, and made a slip-knot at the other end of it. Then he kicked the ladder away.

'Mrs. Hearne meantime had received my letter. For a couple of hours she wrestled with her own repugnance and then decided to come to him. She rang him up on the telephone, but the housekeeper here, Mrs. Criddle, could only tell her that he had gone out after dinner. She continued ringing him up for a couple of hours, but there was always the same reply.

'Eventually she decided to waste no more time, and motored over from her mother's house where she was staying at the north end of the county. By then the moon had risen, and looking out from his bedroom window, she saw him.'

He paused.

'There was an inquest,' he said, 'and I could truthfully testify that I believed him to be insane. The verdict of suicide during temporary insanity was brought in, and he was buried in the churchyard. The rope was burned, and the ladder was burned.'

The parlourmaid brought out drinks, and we sat in silence till she had gone again.

'And what about the telephone my friend heard?' asked Philip.

He thought a moment.

'Don't you think that great emotion like that of Mrs. Hearne's may make some sort of record,' he asked, 'so that if the needle of a sensitive temperament comes in contact with it a reproduction takes place? And it is the same perhaps about that poor fellow who hanged himself. One can hardly believe that his spirit is bound to visit and revisit the scene of his follies and his crimes year by year.'

'Year by year?' I asked.

'Apparently. I saw him myself last year; Mrs. Criddle did also.'

He got up.

'How can one tell?' he said. 'Expiation, perhaps. Who knows?'

The Tale of the Empty House

It had been a disastrous afternoon: rain had streamed incessantly from a low grey sky, and the road was of the vilest description. There were sections consisting of sharp flints, newly laid down and not yet rolled into amenity, and the stretches in between were worn into deep ruts and bouncing holes, so that it was impossible anywhere to travel at even a moderate speed. Twice we had punctured, and now, as the stormy dusk began to fall, something went wrong with the engine, and after crawling on for a hundred yards or so we stopped. My driver, after a short investigation, told me that there was a half-hour's tinkering to be done, and after that we might, with luck, trundle along in a leisurely manner, and hope eventually to arrive at Crowthorpe, which was the proposed destination.

We had come, when this stoppage occurred, to a crossroad. Through the driving rain I could see on the right a great church, and in front a huddle of houses. A consultation of the map seemed to indicate that this was the village of Riddington, the guide-book added the information that Riddington possessed an hotel, and the signpost at the corner endorsed them both. To the right along the main road, into which we had just struck, was Crowthorpe, fifteen miles away and straight in front of us, half a mile distant, was the hotel.

The decision was not difficult. There was no reason why I should get to Crowthorpe tonight instead of tomorrow, for the friend whom I was to meet there would not arrive until next afternoon and it was surely better to limp half a mile with a spasmodic engine than to attempt fifteen on this inclement evening.

'We'll spend the night here,' I said to my chauffeur. 'The road dips downhill, and it's only half a mile to the hotel. I dare say we shall get there without using the engine at all. Let's try, anyhow.'

We hooted and crossed the main road, and began to slide very slowly down a narrow street. It was impossible to see much, but on either side there were little houses with lights gleaming through blinds, or with blinds still undrawn, revealing cosy interiors. Then the incline grew steeper, and close in front of us I saw masts against a sheet of water that appeared to stretch unbroken into the rain-shrouded gloom of the gathering night.

Riddington, then, must be on the open sea, though how it came about that boats should be tied up to an open quay-wall was a puzzle, but perhaps there was some jetty, invisible in the darkness, which protected them. I heard the chauffeur switch on his engine as we made a sharp turn to the left, and we passed below a long row of lighted windows, shining out on to a rather narrow road, on the right edge of which the water lapped. Again he turned sharply to the left, described a half-circle on crunching gravel, and drew up at the door of the hotel. There was a room for me, there was a garage, there was a room for him, and dinner had not long begun.

Among the little excitements and surprises of travel there is none more delightful than that of waking in a new place at which one has arrived after nightfall on the previous evening. The mind has received a few hints and dusky impressions, and probably during sleep it has juggled with these, constructing them into some sort of coherent whole, and next morning its anticipations are put to the proof. Usually the eye has seen more than it has consciously registered, and the brain has fitted together as in the manner of a jigsaw puzzle a very fair presentment of its immediate surroundings. When I woke next morning a brilliantly sunny sky looked in at my windows; there was no sound of wind or of breaking waves, and before getting up and verifying my impressions of the night before I lay and washed in my imagined picture. In front of my windows there would be a narrow roadway bordered by a quay-wall: there would be a breakwater, forming a harbour for the boats that lay at anchor there, and away, away to the horizon would stretch an expanse of still and glittering sea. I ran over these points in my mind; they seemed an inevitable inference from the glimpses of the night before and then, assured of my correctness, I got out of bed and went to the window.

I have never experienced so complete a surprise. There was no harbour, there was no breakwater, and there was no sea. A very narrow channel, three-quarters choked with sand-banks on which now rested the boats whose masts I had seen the previous evening, ran parallel to the road, and then turned at right-angles and went off into the distance. Otherwise no water of any sort was visible; right and left and in front stretched a limitless expanse of shining grasses with tufts of shrubby growth, and great patches of purple sea-lavender. Beyond were tawny sand-banks, and further yet a line of shingle and scrub and sand-dunes. But the sea which I had expected to fill the whole circle of the visible world till it met the sky on the horizon had totally disappeared.

After the first surprise at this colossal conjuring trick was over, I dressed quickly, in order to ascertain from local authorities how it was done. Unless some hallucination had poisoned my perceptive faculties, there must be an explanation of this total disappearance, alternately, of sea and land, and the key, when supplied, was simple enough. That line of shingle and scrub and sand-dunes on the horizon was a peninsula running for four or five miles parallel with the land, forming the true beach, and it enclosed this vast basin of sand-banks and mud-banks and level lavender-covered marsh, which was submerged at high tide, and made an estuary. At low tide it was altogether empty but for the stream that struggled out through various channels to the mouth of it two miles away to the left, and there was easy passage across it for a man who carried his shoes and stockings, to the far sand-dunes and beaches which terminated at Riddington Point, while at high tide you could sail out from the quay just in front of the hotel and be landed there.

The tide would be out of the estuary for five or six hours yet; I could spend the morning on the beach, or, taking my lunch, walk out to the Point, and be back before the returning waters rendered the channel impassable. There was good bathing on the beach, and there was a colony of terns who nested there.

Already, as I ate my breakfast at a table in the window overlooking the marsh, the spell and attraction of it had begun to work. It was so immense and so empty; it had the allure of the desert about it, with none of the desert's intolerable monotony, for companies of chiding gulls hovered over it, and I could hear the pipe of redshank and the babble of curlews. I was due to meet Jack Granger in Crowthorpe that evening, but if I went I knew that I should persuade him to come back to Riddington, and from my knowledge of him I was aware that he would feel the spell of the place no less potent than I. So, having ascertained that there was a room for him here, I wrote him a note saying that I had found the most amazing place in the world, and told my chauffeur to take the car into Crowthorpe to meet the train that afternoon and bring him here. And with a perfectly clear conscience I set off with a towel and a packet of lunch in my pocket to explore vaguely and goallessly that beckoning immensity of lavender-covered, bird-haunted expanse.

My way, as pointed out to me, led first along a sea-bank which defended the drained pastureland on the right of it from the high tides, and at the corner of that I struck into the basin of the estuary. A contour-line of jetsam, withered grass, strands of seaweed, and the bleached shells of little crabs showed where the last tide had reached its height, and inside it the marsh-growth was still wet. Then came a stretch of mud and pebbles, and presently I was wading through the stream that flowed down to the sea. Beyond that were banks of ribbed sand swept by the incoming tides, and soon I regained the wide green marshes on the further side, beyond which was the bar of shingle that fringed the sea.

I paused as I reshod myself. There was not a sign of any living human being within sight, but never have I found myself in so exhilarating a solitude. Right and left were spread the lawns of sea-lavender, starred with pink tufts of thrift and thickets of suaeda bushes. Here and there were pools left in depressions of the ground by the retreated tide, and here were patches of smooth black mud, out of which grew, like little spikes of milky-green asparagus, a crop of glasswort, and all these happy vegetables flourished in sunshine, or rain, or the salt of the flooding tides with impartial amphibiousness. Overhead was the immense arc of the sky, across which flew now a flight of duck, hurrying with necks outstretched, and now a lonely black-backed gull, flapping his ponderous way seawards. Curlews were bubbling, and redshank and ringed plover fluting, and now as I trudged up the shingle-bank, at the bottom of which the marsh came to an end, the sea, blue and waveless, lay stretched and sleeping, bordered by a strip of sand, on which far off a mirage hovered. But from end to end of it, as far as eye could see, there was no sign of human presence.

I bathed and basked on the hot beach, walked along for half a mile, and then struck back across the shingle into the marsh. And then with a pang of disappointment I saw the first evidence of the intrusion of man into this paradise of solitude, for on a stony spit of ground that ran like some great rib into the amphibious meadows, there stood a small square house built of brick, with a tall flagstaff set up in front of it. It had not caught my eye before, and it seemed an unwarrantable invasion of the emptiness. But perhaps it was not so gross an infringement of it as it appeared, for it wore an indefinable look of desertion, as if man had attempted to domesticate himself here and had failed. As I approached it this impression increased, for the chimney was smokeless, and the closed windows were dim with the film of salt air and the threshold of the closed door was patched with lichen and strewn with debris of withered grasses. I walked twice round it, decided that it was certainly uninhabited, and finally, leaning against the sunbaked wall, ate my lunch.

The glitter and heat of the day were at their height. Warmed and exercised, and invigorated by my bathe, I felt strung to the supreme pitch of physical well-being, and my mind, quite vacant except for these felicitous impressions, followed the example of my body, and basked in an unclouded content. And, I suppose by a sense of the Lucretian luxury of contrast, it began to picture to itself, in order to accentuate these blissful conditions, what this sunlit solitude would be like when some November night began to close in underneath a low, grey sky and a driving storm of sleet. Its solitariness would be turned into an abominable desolation: if from some unconjecturable cause one was forced to spend the night here, how the mind would long for any companionship, how sinister would become the calling of the birds, how weird the whistle of the wind round the cavern of this abandoned habitation. Or would it be just the other way about, and would one only be longing to be assured that the seeming solitude was real, and that no invisible but encroaching presence, soon to be made manifest, was creeping nearer under cover of the dusk, and be shuddering to think that the wail of the wind was not only the wind, but the cry of some discarnate being, and that it was not the curlews who made that melancholy piping? By degrees the edge of thought grew blunt, and melted into inconsequent imaginings, and I fell asleep.

61

I woke with a start from the trouble of a dream that faded with waking, but felt sure that some noise close at hand had aroused me. And then it came again: it was the footfall of someone moving about inside the deserted house, against the wall of which my back was propped. Up and down it went, then paused and began again; it was like that of a man who waited with impatience for some expected arrival. I noticed also that the footfall had an irregular beat, as if the walker went with a limp. Then in a minute or two the sound ceased altogether.

An odd uneasiness came over me, for I had been so certain that the house was uninhabited. Then turning my head I noticed that in the wall just above me was a window, and the notion, wholly irrational and unfounded, entered my mind that the man inside who tramped was watching me from it. When once that idea got hold of me, it became impossible to sit there in peace any more, and I got up and shovelled into my knapsack my towel and the remains of my meal. I walked a little further down the spit of land which ran out into the marsh, and turning looked at the house again, and again to my eyes it seemed absolutely deserted. But, after all, it was no concern of mine and I proceeded on my walk, determining to inquire casually on my return to the hotel who it was that lived in so hermetical a place, and for the present dismissed the matter from my mind.

It was some three hours later that I found myself opposite the house again, after a long, wandering walk. I saw that, by making an only slightly longer detour, I could pass close to the house again, and I knew that the sound of those footsteps within it had raised in me a curiosity that I wanted to satisfy. And then, even as I paused, I saw that a man was standing by the door: how he came there I had no idea, for the moment before he had not been there, and he must have come out of the house. He was looking down the path that led through the marsh, shielding his eyes against the sun, and presently he took a step or two forward, and he dragged his left leg as he walked, limping heavily. It was his step, then, which I had heard within, and any mystery about the matter was of my own making. I therefore took the shorter path, and got back to the hotel to find that Jack Granger had just arrived.

We went out again in the gleam of the sunset, and watched the tide sweeping in and pouring up the dykes, until again the great conjuring trick was accomplished, and the stretch of marsh with its fields of sea-lavender was a sheet of shining water. Far away across it stood the house by which I had lunched, and just as we turned Jack pointed to it.

'That's a queer place for a house,' he said. 'I suppose no one lives there.'

'Yes, a lame man,' said I; 'I saw him today. I'm going to ask the hotel porter who he is.'

The result of this inquiry was unexpected.

'No; the house has been uninhabited several years,' he said. 'It used to be a watch-house from which the coastguards signalled if there was a ship in distress, and the lifeboat went out from here. But now the lifeboat and the coastguards are at the end of the Point.'

'Then who is the lame man I saw walking about there, and heard inside the house?' I asked.

He looked at me, I thought, queerly.

'I don't know who that could be,' he said. 'There's no lame man about here to my knowledge.'

The effect on Jack of the marshes and their gorgeous emptiness, of the sun and the sea, was precisely what I had anticipated. He vowed that any day spent anywhere than on these beaches and fields of sea-lavender was a day wasted, and proposed that the tour, of which the main object had originally been the golf links of Norfolk, should for the present be cancelled. In particular, it was the birds of this long solitary headland that enchanted him.

'After all, we can play golf anywhere,' he said. 'There's an oyster-catcher scolding, do you hear? – and how silly to whack a little white ball – ringed plover, but what's that calling as well? – when you can spend the

63

day like this! Oh, don't let us go and bathe yet: I want to wander along that edge of the marsh – ha, there's a company of turnstones; they make a noise like the drawing of a cork – there they are, those little chaps with chestnut-coloured patches! Let's go along the near edge of the marsh, and come out by the house where your lame man lives.'

We took, therefore, the path with the longer detour, which I had abandoned last night. I had said nothing to him of what the hotel porter had told me that the house was unlived in, and all he knew was that I had seen a lame man, apparently in occupation there. My reason for not doing so (to make the confession at once) was that I already half believed that the steps I had heard inside, and the lame man I had seen watching outside, did not imply in the porter's sense of the word that the house was occupied, and I wanted to see whether Jack as well as myself would be conscious of any such tokens of a presence there. And then the oddest thing happened.

All the way up to the house his attention was alert on the birds, and in especial on a piping note which was unfamiliar to him. In vain he tried to catch sight of the bird that uttered it, and in vain I tried to hear it. 'It doesn't sound like any bird I know,' he said; 'in fact, it doesn't sound like a bird at all, but like some human being whistling. There it is again! Is it possible you don't hear it?'

We were now quite close to the house.

'There must be someone there who is whistling,' he said; 'it must be your lame man . . . Lord, yes, it comes from inside the house. So that's explained, and I hoped it was some new bird. But why can't you hear it?'

'Some people can't hear a bat's squeak,' said I.

Jack, satisfied with the explanation, took no more interest in the matter, and we struck across the shingle, bathed and lunched, and tramped on to the tumble of sand-dunes in which the Point ended. For a couple of hours we strolled and lazed there in the liquid and sunny air, and reluctantly returned in order to cross the ford before the tide came in. As we retraced our way, I saw coming up from the west a huge continent of cloud; and just as we reached the spit of land on which the house stood, a jagged sword of lightning flickered down to the low-lying hills across the estuary, and a few big raindrops plopped on the shingle.

'We're in for a drenching,' he said. 'Ha! Let's ask for shelter at your lame man's house. Better run for it!' Already the big drops were falling thickly, and we scuttled across the hundred yards that lay between us and the house, and came to the door just as the sluices of heaven were pulled wide. He rapped on it, but there came no answer; he tried the handle of it, but the door did not yield, and then, by a sudden inspiration, he felt along the top of the lintel and found a key. It fitted into the wards and next moment we stood within.

We found ourselves in a slip of a passage, at the end of which went up the staircase to the floor above. On each side of it was a room, one a kitchen, the other a living-room, but in neither was there any stick of furniture. Discoloured paper was peeling off the walls, the windows were thick with spidery weavings, the air heavy with unventilated damp.

'Your lame man dispenses with the necessities as well as the luxuries of life,' said Jack. 'A spartan fellow.'

We were standing in the kitchen: outside the hiss of the rain had grown to a roar, and the bleared window was suddenly lit up with a flare of lightning. A crack of thunder answered it, and in the silence that followed there came from just outside, audible now to me, the sound of a piping whistle. Immediately afterwards I heard the door by which we had just entered violently banged, and I remembered that I had left it open.

His eyes met mine.

'But there's no breath of wind,' I said. 'What made it bang like that?'

'And that was no bird that whistled,' said he.

There was the shuffle in the passage outside of a limping step: I could hear the drag of a man's lame foot along the boards.

'He has come in,' said Jack.

Yes, he had come in, and who had come in? At that moment no fright, but fear, which is a very different matter, closed in on me. Fright, as I understand it, is an emotion, startling, but not unnerving; you may under the finger of fright spring aside, you may scream, you may shout, you have the command of your muscles. But as that limping step moved down the passage I felt fear, the hand of the nightmare that, as it clutches, paralyses and inhibits not action only, but thought. I waited frozen and speechless for what should happen next.

Exactly opposite the open door of the kitchen in which we stood the step stopped. And then, soundlessly and invisibly, the presence that had made itself manifest to the outward ear entered. Suddenly I heard Jack's breath rattle in his throat.

'Oh, my God!' he cried in a voice hoarse and strangled, and he threw his left arm across his face as if defending himself, and his right arm, shooting out seemed to hit at something which I could not see, and his fingers crooked themselves as if clutching at that which had evaded his blow. His body was bent back as if resisting some invisible pressure, then lunged forward again, and I heard the noise of a resisting joint, and saw on his throat the shadow (or so it seemed) of a clutching hand. At that some power of movement came back to me, and I remember hurling myself at the empty space between him and me, and felt under my grip the shape of a shoulder and heard on the boards of the floor the slip and scoop of a foot. Something invisible, now a shoulder, now an arm, struggled in my grasp, and I heard a panting respiration that was not Jack's, nor mine, and now and then in my face I felt a hot breath that stank of corruption and decay. And all the time this physical contention was symbolical only: what he and I wrestled with was not a thing of flesh and blood, but some awful spiritual presence. And then . . .

There was nothing. The ghostly invasion ceased as suddenly as it had begun, and there was Jack's face gleaming with sweat close to mine, as we stood with dropped arms opposite each other in an empty room, with the rain beating on the roof and the gutters chuckling. No word passed between us, but next moment we were out in the pelting rain, running for the ford. The deluge was sweet to my soul, it seemed to wash away that horror of great darkness and that odour of corruption in which we had been plunged.

Now, I have no certain explanation to give of the experience which has here been shortly recounted, and the reader may or may not connect with it a story that I heard a week or two later on my return to London.

A friend of mine and I had been dining at my house one evening, and we had discussed a murder trial then going on of which the papers were full.

'It isn't only the atrocity that attracts,' he said, 'I think it is the place where the murder occurs that is the cause of the interest in it. A murder at Brighton, or Margate, or Ramsgate, any place which the public associates with pleasure trips, attracts them because they know the place and can visualize the scene. But when there is a murder at some small, unknown spot, which they have never heard of, there is no appeal to their imagination. Last spring, for instance, there was the murder at that small village on the coast of Norfolk. I've forgotten the name of the place, though I was in Norwich at the time of the trial and was present in court. It was one of the most awful stories I ever heard, as ghastly and sensational as this last affair, but it didn't attract the smallest attention. Odd that I can't remember the name of the place when all the rest is so vivid to me!'

'Tell me about it,' I said; 'I never heard of it.'

'Well, there was this little village, and just outside it was a farm, owned by a man called John Beardsley. He lived there with his only daughter, an unmarried woman of about thirty, a good-looking, sensible creature apparently, the last in the world you would have thought to do anything unexpected. There worked at the farm as a day-labourer a young fellow called Alfred Maldon, who in the trial of which I am speaking was the prisoner. He had one of the most dreadful faces I ever saw, a catlike receding forehead, a broad, short nose, and a great red sensual mouth, always on the grin. He seemed positively to enjoy being the central figure around whom all the interest of those ghoulish women who thronged the court was concentrated, and when he shambled into the witness-box –'

'Shambled?' I asked.

'Yes; he was lame; his left foot dragged along the floor as he walked. As he shambled into the witness-box he nodded and smiled to the judge, and clapped his counsel on the shoulder, and leered at the gallery. . . He worked on the farm, as I was saying, doing jobs that were within his capacity, among which was certain house-work, carrying coals and what-not, for John Beardsley, though very well-off, kept no servant, and this daughter Alice – that was her name – ran the house. And what must she do but fall in love, it was no less than that, with this monstrous and misshapen fellow. One afternoon her father came home unexpectedly and caught them together in the parlour, kissing and cuddling. He turned the man out of the house, neck and crop, gave him his week's wages, and dismissed him, threatening him with a fine thrashing if he ever caught him hanging about the place. He forbade his daughter ever to speak to him again, and in order to keep watch over her, got in a woman from the village who would be there all day while he was out on the farm.

'Young Maldon, deprived of his job, tried to get work in the village, but none would employ him, for he was a black-tempered fellow ready to pick a quarrel with anyone, and an unpleasant opponent, for, with all his lameness, he was of immense muscular strength. For some weeks he idled about in the village, getting a chance job occasionally, and no doubt, as you will see, Alice Beardsley managed to meet him. The village – its name still escapes me – lay on the edge of a big tidal

68

estuary, full at high water, but on the ebb of a broad stretch of marsh and sand and mud-banks, beyond which ran a long belt of shingle that formed the seaward side of the estuary. On it stood a disused coastguard house, a couple of miles away from the village, and in as lonely a place as you would find anywhere in England. At low tide there was a shallow ford across to it, and in the sand-banks round about it some beds of cockle. Maldon, unable to get regular work, took to cockle-digging, and during the summer, when the tide was low, Alice (it was no new thing with her) used to go over the ford to the beach beyond and bathe. She would go across the sand-banks where the cockle-diggers, Maldon among them, were at work, and if he whistled as she passed that was the signal between them that he would slip away presently and join her at the disused coastguard house, and there throughout the summer they used to meet.

'As the weeks went on her father saw the change that was coming in her, and suspecting the cause, often left his work and, hidden behind some sea-bank, used to watch her. One day he saw her cross the ford, and soon after she had passed he saw Maldon, recognizable from a long way off by his dragging leg, follow her. He went up the path to the coastguard house, and entered. At that John Beardsley crossed the ford, and hiding in the bushes near the house, saw Alice coming back from her bathe. The house was off the direct path to the ford, but she went round that way, and the door was opened to her, and closed behind her. He found them together, and mad with rage attacked the man. They fought and Maldon got him down and then and there in front of his daughter strangled him.

'The girl went off her head, and is in the asylum at Norwich now. She sits all day by the window whistling. The man was hanged.'

'Was Riddington the name of the village?' I asked.

'Yes. Riddington, of course,' he said. 'I can't think how I forgot it.'

The Bus-Conductor

My friend, Hugh Grainger, and I had just returned from a two days' visit in the country, where we had been staying in a house of sinister repute which was supposed to be haunted by ghosts of a peculiarly fearsome and truculent sort. The house itself was all that such a house should be, Jacobean and oak-panelled, with long dark passages and high vaulted rooms. It stood, also, very remote, and was encompassed by a wood of sombre pines that muttered and whispered in the dark, and all the time that we were there a south-westerly gale with torrents of scolding rain had prevailed, so that by day and night weird voices moaned and fluted in the chimneys, a company of uneasy spirits held colloquy among the trees, and sudden tattoes and tappings beckoned from the window-panes. But in spite of these surroundings, which were sufficient in themselves, one would almost say, spontaneously to generate occult phenomena, nothing of any description had occurred. I am bound to add, also, that my own state of mind was peculiarly well adapted to receive or even to invent the sights and sounds we had gone to seek, for I was, I confess, during the whole time that we were there, in a state of abject apprehension, and lay awake both nights through hours of terrified unrest, afraid of the dark, yet more afraid of what a lighted candle might show me.

Hugh Grainger, on the evening after our return to town, had dined with me, and after dinner our conversation, as was natural, soon came back to these entrancing topics.

'But why you go ghost-seeking I cannot imagine,' he said, 'because your teeth were chattering and your eyes starting out of your head all the time you were there, from sheer fright. Or do you like being frightened?'

Hugh, though generally intelligent, is dense in certain ways; this is one of them.

'Why, of course, I like being frightened,' I said. 'I want to be made to creep and creep and creep. Fear is the most absorbing and luxurious of emotions. One forgets all else if one is afraid.'

'Well, the fact that neither of us says anything,' he said, 'confirms what I have always believed.'

'And what have you always believed?'

'That these phenomena are purely objective, not subjective, and that one's state of mind has nothing to do with the perception that perceives them, nor have circumstances or surroundings anything to do with them either. Look at Osburton. It has had the reputation of being a haunted house for years, and it certainly has all the accessories of one. Look at yourself, too, with all your nerves on edge, afraid to look round or light a candle for fear of seeing something! Surely there was the right man in the right place then, if ghosts are subjective.'

He got up and lit a cigarette, and looking at him – Hugh is about six feet high, and as broad as he is long – I felt a retort on my lips, for I could not help my mind going back to a certain period in his life, when, from some cause which, as far as I knew, he had never told anybody, he had become a mere quivering mass of disordered nerves. Oddly enough, at the same moment and for the first time, he began to speak of it himself.

'You may reply that it was not worth my while to go either,' he said, 'because I was so clearly the wrong man in the wrong place. But I wasn't. You for all your apprehensions and expectancy have never seen a ghost. But I have, though I am the last person in the world you would have thought likely to do so, and, though my nerves are steady enough again now, it knocked me all to bits.'

He sat down again in his chair.

'No doubt you remember my going to bits,' he said, 'and since I believe that I am sound again now, I should rather like to tell you about it. But before I couldn't; I couldn't speak of it at all to anybody. Yet there ought to have been nothing frightening about it; what I saw was certainly a most useful and friendly ghost. But it came from the shaded side of things; it looked suddenly out of the night and the mystery with which life is surrounded.

'I want first to tell you quite shortly my theory about ghost-seeing,' he continued, 'and I can explain it best by a simile, an image. Imagine then that you and I and everybody in the world are like people whose eye is directly opposite a little tiny hole in a sheet of cardboard which is continually shifting and revolving and moving about. Back to back with that sheet of cardboard is another, which also, by laws of its own, is in perpetual but independent motion. In it too there is another hole, and when, fortuitously it would seem, these two holes, the one through which we are always looking, and the other in the spiritual plane, come opposite one another, we see through, and then only do the sights and sounds of the spiritual world become visible or audible to us. With most people these holes never come opposite each other during their life. But at the hour of death they do, and then they remain stationary. That, I fancy, is how we "pass over".

'Now, in some natures, these holes are comparatively large, and are constantly coming into opposition. Clair-voyants, mediums are like that. But, as far as I knew, I had no clairvoyant or mediumistic powers at all. I there-fore am the sort of person who long ago made up his mind that he never would see a ghost. It was, so to speak, an incalculable chance that my minute spy-hole should come into opposition with the other. But it did: and it knocked me out of time.'

I had heard some such theory before, and though Hugh put it rather picturesquely, there was nothing in the least convincing or practical about it. It might be so, or again it might not.

'I hope your ghost was more original than your theory,' said I, in order to bring him to the point.

'Yes, I think it was. You shall judge.'

I put on more coal and poked up the fire. Hugh has got, so I have always considered, a great talent for telling stories, and that sense of drama which is so necessary for the narrator. Indeed before now, I have suggested to him that he should take this up as a profession, sit by the fountain in Piccadilly Circus, when times are, as usual, bad, and tell stories to the passers-by in the street. Arabian fashion, for reward. The most part of mankind, I am aware, do not like long stories, but to the few, among whom I number myself, who really like to listen to lengthy accounts of experiences, Hugh is an ideal narrator. I do not care for his theories, or for his similes, but when it comes to facts, to things that happened, I like him to be lengthy.

'Go on, please, and slowly,' I said. 'Brevity may be the soul of wit, but it is the ruin of story-telling. I want to hear when and where and how it all was, and what you had for lunch and where you had dined and what –'

Hugh began:

'It was the 24th of June, just eighteen months ago,' he said. 'I had let my flat, you may remember, and come up from the country to stay with you for a week. We had dined alone here –'

I could not help interrupting.

'Did you see the ghost here?' I asked. 'In this square little box of a house in a modern street?'

'I was in the house when I saw it.'

I hugged myself in silence.

'We had dined alone here in Graeme Steet,' he said, 'and after dinner I went out to some party, and you stopped at home. At dinner your man did not wait, and when I asked where he was, you told me he was ill, and, I thought, changed the subject rather abruptly. You gave me your latch-key when I went out, and on coming back, I found you had gone to bed. There were, however, several letters for me, which required answers. I wrote them

73

there and then, and posted them at the pillar-box opposite. So I suppose it was rather late when I went upstairs.

'You had put me in the front room, on the third floor, overlooking the street, a room which I thought you generally occupied yourself. It was a very hot night, and though there had been a moon when I started to my party, on my return the whole sky was cloud-covered, and it both looked and felt as if we might have a thunderstorm before morning. I was feeling very sleepy and heavy, and it was not till after I had got into bed that I noticed by the shadows of the window-frames on the blind that only one of the windows was open. But it did not seem worth while to get out of bed in order to open the other, though I felt rather airless and uncomfortable, and I went to sleep.

'What time it was when I awoke I do not know, but it was certainly not yet dawn, and I never remember being conscious of such an extraordinary stillness as prevailed. There was no sound either of foot-passengers or wheeled traffic; the music of life appeared to be absolutely mute. But now instead of being sleepy and heavy, I felt, though I must have slept an hour or two at most, since it was still quite dark, perfectly fresh and wide-awake, and the effort which had seemed not worth making before, that of getting out of bed and opening the other window, was quite easy now, and I pulled up the blind, threw it wide open, and leaned out, for somehow I parched and pined for air. Even outside the oppression was very noticeable, and though, as you know, I am not easily given to feel the mental effects of climate, I was aware of an awful creepiness coming over me. I tried to analyse it away, but without success; the past day had been pleasant, I looked forward to another pleasant day tomorrow, and yet I was full of some nameless apprehension. I felt, too, dreadfully lonely in this stillness before the dawn.

'Then I heard suddenly and not very far away the sound of some approaching vehicle, I could distinguish the tread of two horses walking at a slow foot's pace.

74

They were, though yet invisible, coming up the street, and yet this indication of life did not abate that dreadful sense of loneliness which I have spoken of. Also in some dim unformulated way that which was coming seemed to me to have something to do with the cause of my oppression.

'Then the vehicle came into sight. At first I could not distinguish what it was. Then I saw that the horses were black and had long tails, and that what they dragged was made of glass, but had a black frame. It was a hearse. Empty.

'It was moving up this side of the street. It stopped at your door.

'Then the obvious solution struck me. You had said at dinner that your man was ill, and you were, I thought, unwilling to speak more about his illness. No doubt, so I imagined now, he was dead, and for some reason, perhaps because you did not want me to know anything about it, you were having the body removed at night. This, I must tell you, passed through my mind quite instantaneously, and it did not occur to me how unlikely it really was, before the next thing happened.

'I was still leaning out of the window, and I remember also wondering, yet only momentarily, how odd it was that I saw things – or rather the one thing I was looking at – so very distinctly. Of course, there was a moon behind the clouds, but it was curious how every detail of the hearse and the horses was visible. There was only one man, the driver, with it, and the street was otherwise absolutely empty. It was at him I was looking now. I could see every detail of his clothes, but from where I was, so high above him, I could not see his face. He had on grey trousers, brown boots, a black coat buttoned all the way up, and straw hat. Over his shoulder there was a strap, which seemed to support some sort of little bag. He looked exactly like – well, from my description what did he look exactly like?'

'Why – a bus-conductor,' I said instantly.

'So I thought, and even while I was thinking this, he

75

looked up at me. He had a rather long thin face, and on his left cheek there was a mole with a growth of dark hair on it. All this was as distinct as if it had been noonday, and as if I was within a yard of him. But – so instantaneous was all that takes so long in telling – I had not time to think it strange that the driver of a hearse should be so unfunereally dressed.

'Then he touched his hat to me, and jerked his thumb over his shoulder.

' "Just room for one inside, sir," he said.

'There was something so odious, so coarse, so unfeeling about this that I instantly drew my head in, pulled the blind down again, and then, for what reason I do not know, turned on the electric light in order to see what time it was. The hands of my watch pointed to half-past eleven.

'It was then for the first time, I think, that a doubt crossed my mind as to the nature of what I had just seen. But I put out the light again, got into bed, and began to think. We had dined; I had gone to a party, had come back and written letters, had gone to bed and had slept. So how could it be half-past eleven? . . . Or – *what* half-past eleven was it?

'Then another easy solution struck me; my watch must have stopped. But it had not; I could hear it ticking.

'There was stillness and silence again. I expected every moment to hear muffled footsteps on the stairs, footsteps moving slowly and smally under the weight of a heavy burden, but from inside the house there was no sound whatever. Outside, too, there was the same dead silence, while the hearse waited at the door. And the minutes ticked on and ticked on, and at length I began to see a difference in the light in the room, and knew that the dawn was beginning to break outside. But how had it happened then that if the corpse was to be removed at night it had not gone, and that the hearse still waited, when morning was already coming?

'Presently I got out of bed again, and with the sense of strong physical shrinking I went to the window and pulled back the blind. The dawn was coming fast; the whole street was lit by that silver hueless light of morning. But there was no hearse there.

'Once again I looked at my watch. It was just a quarter-past four. But I would swear that not half an hour had passed since it had told me that it was half-past eleven.

'Then a curious double sense, as if I was living in the present and at the same moment had been living in some other time, came over me. It was dawn on June 25th, and the street, as natural, was empty. But a little while ago the driver of a hearse had spoken to me, and it was half-past eleven. What was that driver, to what plane did he belong? And again *what* half-past eleven was it that I had seen recorded on the dial of my watch?

'And then I told myself that the whole thing had been a dream. But if you ask me whether I believed what I told myself, I must confess that I did not.

'Your man did not appear at breakfast next morning, nor did I see him again before I left that afternoon. I think if I had, I should have told you about all this, but it was still possible you see, that what I had seen was a real hearse, driven by a real driver, for all the ghastly gaiety of the face that had looked up to mine, and the levity of his pointing hand. I might possibly have fallen asleep soon after seeing him, and slumbered through the removal of the body and the departure of the hearse. So I did not speak of it to you.'

There was something wonderfully straightforward and prosaic in all this; here were not Jacobean houses oak-panelled and surrounded by weeping pine-trees, and somehow the very absence of suitable surroundings made the story more impressive. But for a moment a doubt assailed me.

'Don't tell me it was all a dream,' I said.

'I don't know whether it was or not. I can only say that I believe myself to have been wide awake. In any case the rest of the story is – odd.

'I went out of town again that afternoon,' he continued, 'and I may say that I don't think that even for a moment did I get the haunting sense of what I had seen or dreamed that night out of my mind. It was present to me always as some vision unfulfilled. It was as if some clock had struck the four quarters, and I was still waiting to hear what the hour would be.

'Exactly a month afterwards I was in London again, but only for the day. I arrived at Victoria about eleven, and took the Underground to Sloane Square in order to see if you were in town and would give me lunch. It was a baking hot morning, and I intended to take a bus from the King's Road as far as Graeme Street. There was one standing at the corner just as I came out of the station, but I saw that the top was full, and the inside appeared to be full also. Just as I came up to it the conductor who, I suppose, had been inside, collecting fares or what not, came out on to the step within a few feet of me. He wore grey trousers, brown boots, a black coat buttoned, a straw hat, and over his shoulder was a strap on which hung his little machine for punching tickets. I saw his face, too; it was the face of the driver of the hearse, with a mole on the left cheek. Then he spoke to me, jerking his thumb over his shoulder.

' "Just room for one inside, sir," he said.

'At that a sort of panic-terror took possession of me, and I knew I gesticulated wildly with my arms, and cried, "No, no!" But at that moment I was living not in the hour that was then passing, but in that hour which had passed a month ago, when I leaned from the window of your bedroom here just before the dawn broke. At this moment, too, I knew that my spy-hole had been opposite the spy-hole into the spiritual world. What I had seen there had some significance, now being fulfilled, beyond the significance of the trivial happenings of today and tomorrow. The Powers of which we know so little were visibly working before me. And I stood there on the pavement shaking and trembling.

'I was opposite the post-office at the corner, and just

as the bus started my eye fell on the clock in the window there. I need not tell you what the time was.

'Perhaps I need not tell you the rest, for you probably conjecture it, since you will not have forgotten what happened at the corner of Sloane Square at the end of July, the summer before last. The bus pulled out from the pavement into the street in order to get round a van that was standing in front of it. At the moment there came down the King's Road a big motor going at a hideously dangerous pace. It crashed full into the bus, burrowing into it as a gimlet burrows into a board.'

He paused.

'And that's my story,' he said.

How Fear Departed from the Long Gallery

Church-Peveril is a house so beset and frequented by spectres, both visible and audible, that none of the family which it shelters under its acre and a half of green copper roofs takes physical phenomena with any seriousness. For to the Peverils the appearance of a ghost is a matter of hardly greater significance than is the appearance of the post to those who live in more ordinary houses. It arrives, that is to say, practically every day, it knocks (or makes other noises), it is observed coming up the drive (or in other places). I myself, when staying there have seen the present Mrs. Peveril, who is rather short-sighted, peer into the dusk, while we were taking our coffee on the terrace after dinner, and say to her daughter:

'My dear, was not that the Blue Lady who has just gone into the shrubbery? I hope she won't frighten Flo. Whistle for Flo, dear.'

(Flo, it may be remarked, is the youngest and most precious of many dachshunds).

Blanche Peveril gave a cursory whistle, and crunched the sugar left unmelted at the bottom of her coffee-cup between her very white teeth.

'Oh, darling, Flo isn't so silly as to mind,' she said. 'Poor blue Aunt Barbara is such a bore! Whenever I meet her she always looks as if she wanted to speak to me, but when I say "What is it, Aunt Barbara?" she never speaks, but only points somewhere towards the house, which is so vague. I believe there was something she wanted to confess about two hundred years ago, but she has forgotten what it is.'

Here Flo gave two or three short pleased barks, and came out of the shrubbery wagging her tail, and capering round what appeared to me to be a perfectly empty space on the lawn.

'There! Flo has made friends with her,' said Mrs. Peveril. 'I wonder why she dresses in that very stupid shade of blue.'

From this it may be gathered that even with regard to psychical phenomena there is some truth in the proverb that speaks of familiarity. But the Peverils do not exactly treat their ghosts with contempt, since most of that delightful family never despised anybody except such people as avowedly did not care for hunting or shooting, or golf or skating. And as all of their ghosts are of their family, it seems reasonable to suppose that they all, even the poor Blue Lady, excelled at one time in field-sports. So far then they harbour no such unkindness or contempt, but only pity. Of one Peveril, indeed, who broke his neck in vainly attempting to ride up the main staircase on a thoroughbred mare after some monstrous and violent deed in the back-garden, they are very fond, and Blanche comes downstairs in the morning with an eye unusually bright when she can announce that Master Anthony was 'very loud' last night. He (apart from the fact of his having been so foul a ruffian) was a tremendous fellow across country, and they like these indications of the continuance of his superb vitality. In fact, it is supposed to be a compliment, when you go to stay at Church-Peveril, to be assigned a bedroom which is frequented by defunct members of the family. It means that you are worthy to look on the august and villainous dead, and you will find yourself shown into some vaulted or tapestried chamber, without benefit of electric light, and are told that great-great grandmamma Bridget occasionally has vague business by the fire-place, but it is better not to talk to her, and that you will hear Master Anthony 'awfully well' if he attempts the front staircase any time before morning. There you are left for your night's repose, and, having quakingly undressed, begin reluctantly to put out your candles. It is draughty in these great chambers, and the solemn tapestry swings and bellows and subsides, and the firelight dances on the forms of huntsmen and warriors and stern pursuits. Then you climb into your bed, a bed so huge that you feel as if the desert of Sahara was spread for you, and pray, like the mariners who sailed with St. Paul, for day. And, all the time, you are aware that Freddy and Harry and Blanche and possibly even Mrs. Peveril are quite capable of dressing up and making disquieting tappings outside your door, so that when you open it some inconjecturable horror fronts you. For myself, I stick steadily to the assertion that I have an obscure valvular disease of the heart, and so sleep undisturbed in the new wing of the house where Aunt Barbara, and great-great-grandmamma Bridget and Master Anthony never penetrate. I forget the details of great-great-grandmamma Bridget, but she certainly cut the throat of some distant relation before she disembowelled herself with the axe that had been used at Agincourt. Before that she had led a very sultry life, crammed with amazing incidents.

But there is one ghost at Church-Peveril at which the family never laugh, in which they feel no friendly and amused interest, and of which they only speak just as much as is necessary for the safety of their guests. More properly it should be described as two ghosts, for the 'haunt' in question is that of two very young children, who were twins. These, not without reason, the family take very seriously indeed. The story of them, as told me by Mrs. Peveril, is as follows:

In the year 1602, the same being the last of Queen Elizabeth's reign, a certain Dick Peveril was greatly in favour at Court. He was brother to Master Joseph Peveril, then owner of the family house and lands, who two years previously, at the respectable age of seventy-four, became father of twin boys, first-born of his progeny. It is known that the royal and ancient virgin had said to handsome Dick, who was nearly forty years his brother's junior, "Tis pity that you are not master of Church-Peveril,' and these words probably suggested to him a sinister design. Be that as it may, handsome Dick, who very adequately sustained the family reputation for wickedness, set off to ride down to Yorkshire, and found that, very conveniently, his brother Joseph had just been seized with an apoplexy, which appeared to be the result of a continued spell of hot weather combined with the necessity of quenching his thirst with an augmented amount of sack, and had actually died while handsome Dick, with God knows what thoughts in his mind, was journeying northwards. Thus it came about that he arrived at Church-Peveril just in time for his brother's funeral. It was with great propriety that he attended the obsequies, and returned to spend a sympathetic day or two of mourning with his widowed sister-in-law, who was but a faint-hearted dame, little fit to be mated with such hawks as these. On the second night of his stay, he did that which the Peverils regret to this day. He entered the room where the twins slept with their nurse, and quietly strangled the latter as she slept. Then he took the twins and put them into the fire which warms the long gallery. The weather, which up to the day of Joseph's death had been so hot, had changed suddenly to bitter cold, and the fire was heaped high with burning logs and was exultant with flame. In the core of this conflagration he struck out a cremation-chamber, and into that he threw the two children, stamping them down with his riding-boots. They could just walk, but they could not walk out of that ardent place. It is said that he laughed as he added more logs. Thus he became master of Church-Peveril.

The crime was never brought home to him, but he lived no longer than a year in the enjoyment of his blood-stained inheritance. When he lay a-dying he made his confession to the priest who attended him, but his spirit struggled forth from its fleshly coil before Absolution could be given him. On that very night there began in Church-Peveril the haunting which to this day is but seldom spoken of by the family, and then only in low tones and with serious mien. For, only an hour or two after handsome Dick's death, one of the servants passing the door of the long gallery heard from within peals of the loud laughter so jovial and yet so sinister, which he had thought would never be heard in the house again. In a moment of that cold courage, which is so nearly akin to mortal terror, he opened the door and entered, expecting to see he knew not what manifestation of him who lay dead in the room below. Instead he saw two little white-robed figures toddling towards him hand in hand across the moon-lit floor.

The watchers in the room below ran upstairs startled by the crash of his fallen body, and found him lying in the grip of some dread convulsion. Just before morning he regained consciousness and told his tale. Then pointing with trembling and ash-grey finger towards the door, he screamed aloud, and so fell back dead.

During the next fifty years this strange and terrible legend of the twin-babies became fixed and consolidated. Their appearance, luckily for those who inhabit the house, was exceedingly rare, and during these years they seem to have been seen four or five times only. On each occasion they appeared at night, between sunset and sunrise, always in the same long gallery, and always as two toddling children scarcely able to walk. And on each occasion the luckless individual who saw them died either speedily or terribly, or with both speed and terror, after the accursed vision had appeared to him. Sometimes he might live for a few months: he was lucky if he died, as did the servant who first saw them, in a few hours. Vastly more awful was the fate of a certain Mrs. Canning, who had the ill-luck to see them in the middle of the next century, or to be quite accurate, in the year 1760. By this time the hours and the place of their appearance were well-known, and, as up till a year ago, visitors were warned not to go between sunset and sunrise into the long gallery.

But Mrs. Canning, a brilliantly clever and beautiful woman, admirer also and friend of the notorious sceptic M. Voltaire, wilfully went and sat night after night, in spite of all protestations, in the haunted place. For four evenings she saw nothing, but on the fifth she had her will, for the door in the middle of the gallery opened, and there came toddling towards her the ill-omened, innocent little pair. It seemed that even then she was not frightened, but she thought good, poor wretch, to mock at them, telling them it was time for them to get back into the fire. They gave no word in answer, but turned away from her, crying and sobbing. Immediately after, they disappeared from her vision and she rustled downstairs to where the family and guests in the house were waiting for her, with the triumphant announcement that she had seen them both, and must needs write to M. Voltaire, saying that she had spoken to spirits made manifest. It would make him laugh. But when some months later the whole news reached him he did not laugh at all.

Mrs. Canning was one of the great beauties of her day, and in the year 1760 she was at the height and zenith of her blossoming. The chief beauty, if it is possible to single out one point where all was so exquisite, lay in the dazzling colour and incomparable brilliance of her complexion. She was now just thirty years of age, but, in spite of the excesses of her life, retained the snow and roses of girlhood, and she courted the bright light of day which other women shunned, for it but showed to greater advantage the splendour of her skin. In consequence she was very considerably dismayed one morning, about a fortnight after her strange experience in the long gallery, to observe on her left cheek an inch or two below her turquoise-coloured eyes, a little greyish patch of skin, about as big as a threepenny piece. It was in vain that she applied her accustomed washes and unguents: vain, too, were the arts of her *fardeuse* and of her medical adviser. For a week she kept herself secluded, martyring herself with solitude and unaccustomed physics, and for result at the end of the week she had no amelioration to comfort herself with: instead, this woeful grey patch had doubled itself in size. Thereafter the nameless disease, whatever it was, developed in new and terrible ways. From the centre of the discoloured place there sprouted forth little lichen-like tendrils of greenish-grey, and another patch appeared on her lower lip. This, too, soon vegetated, and one morning on opening her eyes to the horror of a new day, she found that her vision was strangely blurred. She sprang to her looking-glass, and what she saw caused her to shriek aloud with horror. From under her upper eyelid a fresh growth had spung up, mushroom-like, in the night, and its filaments extended downwards, screening the pupil of her eye. Soon after her tongue and throat were attacked: the air passages became obstructed, and death by suffocation was merciful after such suffering.

More terrible yet was the case of a certain Colonel Blantyre who fired at the children with his revolver. What he went through is not to be recorded here.

It is this haunting, then, that the Peverils take quite seriously, and every guest on his arrival in the house is told that the long gallery must not be entered after nightfall on any pretext whatever. By day, however, it is a delightful room and intrinsically merits description, apart from the fact that the due understanding of its geography is necessary for the account that here follows. It is full eighty feet in length, and is lit by a row of six tall windows looking over the gardens at the back of the house. A door communicates with the landing at the top of the main staircase, and about half-way down the gallery in the wall facing the windows is another door communicating with the back staircase and servants' quarters, and thus the gallery forms a constant place of passage for them in going to the rooms on the first landing. It was through this door that the baby-figures came when they appeared to Mrs. Canning, and on several other occasions they have been known to make their entry here, for the room out of which handsome Dick took them lies just beyond at the top of the back stairs. Further on again in the gallery is the fireplace into which he thrust them, and at the far end a large bow-window looks straight down the avenue. Above this fireplace, there hangs with grim significance a portrait of handsome Dick, in the insolent beauty of early manhood, attributed to Holbein, and a dozen other portraits of great merit face the windows. During the day this is the most frequented sitting-room in the house, for its other visitors never appear there then, nor does it then ever resound with the harsh jovial laugh of handsome Dick, which sometimes, after dark has fallen, is heard by passers-by on the landing outside. But Blanche does not grow bright-eyed when she hears it: she shuts her ears and hastens to put a greater distance between her and the sound of that atrocious mirth.

But during the day the long gallery is frequented by many occupants, and much laughter in no wise sinister or saturnine resounds there. When summer lies hot over the land, those occupants lounge in the deep window seats, and when winter spreads his icy fingers and blows shrilly between his frozen palms, congregate round the fireplace at the far end, and perch, in companies of cheerful chatterers, upon sofa and chair, and chair-back and floor. Often have I sat there on long August evenings up till dressing-time, but never have I been there when anyone has seemed disposed to linger over-late without hearing the warning: 'It is close on sunset: shall we go?' Later on in the shorter autumn days they often have tea laid there, and sometimes it has happened that, even while merriment was most uproarious, Mrs. Peveril has suddenly looked out of the window and said, 'My dears, it is getting so late: let us finish our nonsense downstairs in the hall.' And then for a moment a curious hush always falls on loquacious family and guests alike, and as if some bad news had just been known, we all make our silent way out of the place. But the spirits of the Peverils (of the living ones, that is to say) are the most mercurial imaginable, and the blight

which the thought of handsome Dick and his doings casts
over them passes away again with amazing rapidity.

A typical party, large, young, and peculiarly cheerful,
was staying at Church-Peveril shortly after Christmas
last year, and as usual on December 31, Mrs. Peveril
was giving her annual New Year's Eve ball. The house
was quite full, and she had commandeered as well the
greater part of the Peveril Arms to provide sleeping-
quarters for the overflow from the house. For some days
past a black and windless frost had stopped all hunting,
but it is an ill windlessness that blows no good (if so
mixed a metaphor may be forgiven), and the lake below
the house had for the last day or two been covered with
an adequate and admirable sheet of ice. Everyone in the
house had been occupied all the morning of that day in
performing swift and violent manoeuvres on the elusive
surface, and as soon as lunch was over we all, with one
exception, hurried out again. This one exception was
Madge Dalrymple who had had the misfortune to fall
rather badly earlier in the day, but hoped, by resting her
injured knee, instead of joining the skaters again, to be
able to dance that evening. The hope, it is true, was of
the most sanguine sort, for she could but hobble ignobly
back to the house, but with the breezy optimism which
characterizes the Peverils (she is Blanche's first cousin),
she remarked that it would be but tepid enjoyment that
she could, in her present state, derive from further
skating, and thus she sacrificed little, but might gain
much.

Accordingly after a rapid cup of coffee which was
served in the long gallery, we left Madge comfortably
reclined on the big sofa at right-angles to the fireplace,
with an attractive book to beguile the tedium till tea.
Being of the family, she knew all about handsome Dick
and the babies, and the fate of Mrs. Canning and Colonel
Blantyre, but as we went out I heard Blanche say to her,
'Don't run it too fine, dear,' and Madge had replied, 'No,

I'll go away well before sunset.' And so we left her alone in the long gallery.

Madge read her attractive book for some minutes, but failing to get absorbed in it, put it down and limped across to the window. Though it was still but little after two, it was but a dim and uncertain light that entered, for the crystalline brightness of the morning had given place to a veiled obscurity produced by flocks of thick clouds which were coming sluggishly up from the north-east. Already the whole sky was overcast with them, and occasionally a few snowflakes fluttered waveringly down past the long windows. From the darkness and bitter cold of the afternoon, it seemed to her that there was like to be a heavy snowfall before long, and these outward signs were echoed inwardly in her by that muffled drowsiness of the brain, which to those who are sensitive to the pressures and lightnesses of weather portends storm. Madge was peculiarly the prey of such external influences: to her a brisk morning gave an ineffable brightness and briskness of spirit, and correspondingly the approach of heavy weather produced a somnolence in sensation that both drowsed and depressed her.

It was in such mood as this that she limped back again to the sofa beside the log-fire. The whole house was comfortably heated by water-pipes, and though the fire of logs and peat, an adorable mixture, had been allowed to burn low, the room was very warm. Idly she watched the dwindling flames, not opening her book again, but lying on the sofa with face towards the fireplace, intending drowsily and not immediately to go to her own room and spend the hours, until the return of the skaters made gaiety in the house again, in writing one or two neglected letters. Still drowsily she began thinking over what she had to communicate: one letter several days overdue should go to her mother, who was immensely interested in the psychical affairs of the family. She would tell her how Master Anthony had been prodigiously active on the staircase a night or two ago, and how the Blue Lady, regardless of the severity of the weather, had been seen by Mrs. Peveril that morning, strolling about. It was rather interesting: the Blue Lady had gone down the laurel walk and had been seen by her to enter the stables, where, at the moment, Freddy Peveril was inspecting the frost-bound hunters. Identically then, a sudden panic had spread through the stables, and the horses had whinnied and kicked, and shied, and sweated. Of the fatal twins nothing had been seen for many years past, but, as her mother knew, the Peverils never used the long gallery after dark.

Then for a moment she sat up, remembering that she was in the long gallery now. But it was still but a little after half-past two, and if she went to her room in half an hour, she would have ample time to write this and another letter before tea. Till then she would read her book. But she found she had left it on the window-sill, and it seemed scarcely worth while to get it. She felt exceedingly drowsy.

The sofa where she lay had been lately re-covered, in a greyish green shade of velvet, somewhat the colour of lichen. It was of very thick, soft texture, and she luxuriously stretched her arms out, one on each side of her body, and pressed her fingers into the nap. How horrible that story of Mrs. Canning was: the growth on her face was of the colour of lichen. And then without further transition or blurring of thought Madge fell asleep.

She dreamed. She dreamed that she awoke and found herself exactly where she had gone to sleep, and in exactly the same attitude. The flames from the logs had burned up again, and leaped on the walls, fitfully illuminating the picture of handsome Dick above the fire-place. In her dream she knew exactly what she had done today, and for what reason she was lying here now instead of being out with the rest of the skaters. She remembered also (still dreaming), that she was going to write a letter or two before tea, and prepared to get up in order to go to her room. As she half-rose she caught sight of her own arms lying out on each side of her on the grey velvet sofa. But she could not see where her hands ended, and where the grey velvet began: her fingers seemed to have melted into the stuff. She could see her wrists quite clearly, and a blue vein on the backs of her hands, and here and there a knuckle. Then, in her dream she remembered, the last thought which had been in her mind before she fell asleep, namely the growth of the lichen-coloured vegetation on the face and the eyes and the throat of Mrs. Canning. At that thought the strangling terror of real nightmare began: she knew that she was being transformed into this grey stuff, and she was absolutely unable to move. Soon the grey would spread up her arms, and over her feet; when they came in from skating they would find here nothing but a huge misshapen cushion of lichen-coloured velvet, and that would be she. The horror grew more acute, and then by a violent effort she shook herself free of the clutches of this very evil dream, and she awoke.

For a minute or two she lay there, conscious only of the tremendous relief at finding herself awake. She felt again with her fingers the pleasant touch of the velvet, and drew them backwards and forwards, assuring herself that she was not, as her dream had suggested, melting into greyness and softness. But she was still, in spite of the violence of her awakening, very sleepy, and lay there till, looking down, she was aware that she could not see her hands at all. It was very nearly dark.

At that moment a sudden flicker of flame came from the dying fire, and a flare of burning gas from the peat flooded the room. The portrait of handsome Dick looked evilly down on her, and her hands were visible again. And then a panic worse than the panic of her dreams seized her. Daylight had altogether faded, and she knew that she was alone in the dark in the terrible gallery. This panic was of the nature of nightmare, for she felt unable to move for terror. But it was worse than nightmare because she knew she was awake. And then the full cause of this frozen fear dawned on her; she knew with the certainty of absolute conviction that she was about to see the twin-babies.

She felt a sudden moisture break out on her face, and within her mouth her tongue and throat went suddenly dry, and she felt her tongue grate along the inner surface of her teeth. All power of movement had slipped from her limbs, leaving them dead and inert, and she stared with wide eyes into the blackness. The spurt of flame from the peat had burned itself out again, and darkness encompassed her.

Then on the wall opposite her, facing the windows, there grew a faint light of dusky crimson. For a moment she thought it but heralded the approach of the awful vision, then hope revived in her heart, and she remembered that thick clouds had overcast the sky before she went to sleep, and guessed that this light came from the sun not yet quite sunk and set. This sudden revival of hope gave her the necessary stimulus, and she sprang off the sofa where she lay. She looked out of the window and saw the dull glow on the horizon. But before she could take a step forward it was obscured again. A tiny sparkle of light came from the hearth which did no more than illuminate the tiles of the fireplace, and snow falling heavily tapped at the window panes. There was neither light nor sound except these.

But the courage that had come to her, giving her the power of movement, had not quite deserted her, and she began feeling her way down the gallery. And then she found that she was lost. She stumbled against a chair, and, recovering herself, stumbled against another. Then a table barred her way, and, turning swiftly aside, she found herself up against the back of a sofa. Once more she turned and saw the dim gleam of the firelight on the side opposite to that on which she expected it. In her blind gropings she must have reversed her direction. But which way was she to go now? She seemed blocked in by furniture. And all the time insistent and imminent was the fact that the two innocent terrible ghosts were about to appear to her.

Then she began to pray, 'Lighten our darkness, O Lord,' she said to herself. But she could not remember how the prayer continued, and she had sore need of it. There was something about the perils of the night. All this time she felt about her with groping, fluttering hands. The fire-glimmer which should have been on her left was on her right again; therefore she must turn herself round again. 'Lighten our darkness,' she whispered, and then aloud she repeated, 'Lighten our darkness.'

She stumbled up against a screen, and could not remember the existence of any such screen. Hastily she felt beside it with blind hands, and touched something soft and velvety. Was it the sofa on which she had lain? If so, where was the head of it. It had a head and a back and feet – it was like a person, all covered with grey lichen. Then she lost her head completely. All that remained to her was to pray; she was lost, lost in this awful place, where no one came in the dark except the babies that cried. And she heard her voice rising from whisper to speech, and speech to scream. She shrieked out the holy words, she yelled them as if blaspheming as she groped among tables and chairs and the pleasant things of ordinary life which had become so terrible.

Then came a sudden and an awful answer to her screamed prayer. Once more a pocket of inflammmable gas in the peat on the hearth was reached by the smouldering embers, and the room started into light. She saw the evil eyes of handsome Dick, she saw the little ghostly snowflakes falling thickly outside. And she saw where she was, just opposite the door through which the terrible twins made their entrance. Then the flame went out again, and left her in blackness once more. But she had gained something, for she had her geography now. The centre of the room was bare of furniture, and one swift dart would take her to the door of the landing above the main staircase and into safety. In that gleam she had been able to see the handle of the door, bright-brassed, luminous like a star. She would go straight for it; it was but a matter of a few seconds now.

She took a long breath, partly of relief, partly to satisfy the demands of her galloping heart. But the breath was only half-taken when she was stricken once more into the immobility of nightmare.

There came a little whisper, it was no more than that, from the door opposite which she stood, and through which the twin-babies entered. It was not quite dark outside it, for she could see that the door was opening. And there stood in the opening two little white figures, side by side. They came towards her slowly, shufflingly. She could not see face or form at all distinctly, but the two little white figures were advancing. She knew them to be the ghosts of terror, innocent of the awful doom they were bound to bring, even as she was innocent. With the inconceivable rapidity of thought, she made up her mind what to do. She had not hurt them or laughed at them, and they, they were but babies when the wicked and bloody deed had sent them to their burning death. Surely the spirits of these children would not be inaccessible to the cry of one who was of the same blood as they, who had committed no fault that merited the doom they brought. If she entreated them they might have mercy, they might forbear to bring the curse on her, they might allow her to pass out of the place without blight, without the sentence of death, or the shadow of things worse than death upon her.

It was but for the space of a moment that she hesitated, then she sank down on to her knees, and stretched out her hands towards them.

'Oh, my dears,' she said, 'I only fell asleep. I have done no more wrong than that –'

She paused a moment, and her tender girl's heart thought no more of herself, but only of them, those little innocent spirits on whom so awful a doom was laid, that they should bring death where other children bring laughter, and doom for delight. But all those who had seen them before had dreaded and feared them, or had mocked at them.

Then, as the enlightenment of pity dawned on her, her fear fell from her like the wrinkled sheath that holds the sweet folded buds of Spring.

'Dears, I am so sorry for you,' she said. 'It is not your fault that you must bring me what you must bring, but I am not afraid any longer. I am only sorry for you. God bless you, you poor darlings.'

She raised her head and looked at them. Though it was so dark, she could now see their faces, though all was dim and wavering, like the light of pale flames shaken by a draught. But the faces were not miserable or fierce – they smiled at her with shy little baby smiles. And as she looked they grew faint, fading slowly away like wreaths of vapour in frosty air.

Madge did not at once move when they had vanished, for instead of fear there was wrapped round her a wonderful sense of peace, so happy and serene that she would not willingly stir, and so perhaps disturb it. But before long she got up, and feeling her way, but without any sense of nightmare pressing her on, or frenzy of fear to spur her, she went out of the long gallery, to find Blanche just coming upstairs whistling and swinging her skates.

'How's the leg, dear,' she asked, 'You're not limping any more.'

Till that moment Madge had not thought of it.

'I think it must be all right,' she said, 'I had forgotten it anyhow. Blanche, dear, you won't be frightened for me, will you, but – but I have seen the twins.'

For a moment Blanche's face whitened with terror.

'What?' she said in a whisper.

'Yes, I saw them just now. But they were kind, they smiled at me, and I was so sorry for them. And somehow I am sure I have nothing to fear.'

It seems that Madge was right, for nothing untoward has come to her. Something, her attitude to them, we must suppose, her pity, her sympathy, touched and dissolved and annihilated the curse. Indeed, I was at Church-Peveril only last week, arriving there after dark. Just as I passed the gallery door, Blanche came out.

'Ah, there you are,' she said, 'I've just been seeing the twins. They looked too sweet and stopped nearly ten minutes. Let us have tea at once.'

The Other Bed

I had gone out to Switzerland just before Christmas, expecting, from experience, a month of divinely renovating weather, of skating all day in brilliant sun, and basking in the hot frost of that windless atmosphere. Occasionally, as I knew, there might be a snowfall, which would last perhaps for forty-eight hours at the outside, and would be succeeded by another ten days of cloudless perfection, cold even to zero at night, but irradiated all day long by the unflecked splendour of the sun.

Instead, the climatic conditions were horrible. Day after day a gale screamed through this upland valley that should have been so windless and serene, bringing with it a tornado of sleet that changed to snow by night. For ten days there was no abatement of it, and evening after evening, as I consulted my barometer, feeling sure that the black finger would show that we were coming to the end of these abominations, I found that it had sunk a little lower yet, till it stayed, liked a homing pigeon, on the 'S' of storm. I mention these things in depreciation of the story that follows, in order that the intelligent reader may say at once, if he wishes, that all that occurred was merely a result of the malaise of nerves and digestion that perhaps arose from those storm-bound and disturbing conditions. And now to go back to the beginning again.

I had written to engage a room at the Hôtel Beau Site, and had been agreeably surprised on arrival to find that for the modest sum of twelve francs a day I was allotted a room on the first floor with two beds in it. Otherwise the hotel was quite full. Fearing to be billeted in a twenty-two-franc room, by mistake, I instantly confirmed my arrangements at the bureau. There was no mistake: I had ordered a twelve-franc room and had been give one. The very civil clerk hoped that I was satisfied with it, for otherwise there was nothing vacant. I hastened to say that I was more than satisfied, fearing the fate of Esau.

I arrived about three in the afternoon of a cloudless and glorious day, the last of the series. I hurried down to the rink, having had the prudence to put skates in the forefront of my luggage, and spent a divine but struggling hour or two, coming up to the hotel about sunset. I had letters to write, and after ordering tea to be sent up to my gorgeous apartment, No. 23, on the first floor, I went straight up there.

The door was ajar and – I feel certain I should not even remember this now except in the light of what followed – just as I got close to it, I heard some faint movement inside the room and instinctively knew that my servant was there unpacking. Next moment I was in the room myself, and it was empty. The unpacking had been finished, and everything was neat, orderly, and comfortable. My barometer was on the table, and I observed with dismay that it had gone down nearly half an inch. I did not give another thought to the movement I thought I had heard from outside.

Certainly I had a delightful room for my twelve francs a day. There were, as I have said, two beds in it, on one of which were already laid out my dress-clothes, while night-things were disposed on the other. There were two windows, between which stood a large washing-stand, with plenty of room on it; a sofa with its back on the light stood conveniently near the pipes of central heating, there were a couple of good arm-chairs, a writing table, and, rarest of luxuries, another table, so that every time one had breakfast it was not necessary to pile up a drift of books and papers to make room for the tray. My window looked east, and sunset still flamed on the western faces of the virgin snows, while above, in spite of the dejected barometer, the sky was bare of clouds, and a thin slip of pale crescent moon was swung high among the stars that still burned dimly in these first moments of their kindling. Tea came up for me without delay, and as I ate, I regarded my surroundings with extreme complacency.

Then, quite suddenly and without cause, I saw that the disposition of the beds would never do; I could not possibly sleep in the bed that my servant had chosen for me, and without pause I jumped up, transferred my dress clothes to the other bed, and put my night-things where they had been. It was done breathlessly almost, and not till then did I ask myself why I had done it. I found I had not the slightest idea. I had merely felt that I could not sleep in the other bed. But having made the change I felt perfectly content.

My letters took me an hour or so to finish, and I had yawned and blinked considerably over the last one or two, in part from their inherent dullness, in part from quite natural sleepiness. For I had been in the train for twenty-four hours, and was fresh to these bracing airs which so conduce to appetite, activity, and sleep, and as there was still an hour before I need dress, I lay down on my sofa with a book for excuse, but the intention to slumber as reason. And consciousness ceased as if a tap had been turned off.

Then – I dreamed. I dreamed that my servant came very quietly into the room, to tell me no doubt that it was time to dress. I supposed there were a few minutes to spare yet, and that he saw I was dozing, for, instead of rousing me, he moved quietly about the room, setting things in order. The light appeared to me to be very dim, for I could not see him with any distinctness, indeed, I only knew it was he because it could not be anybody else. Then he paused by my washing-stand, which had a shelf for brushes and razors above it, and I saw him take a razor from its case and begin stropping it; the light was strongly reflected on the blade of the razor. He tried the edge once or twice on his thumb-nail, and then to my horror I saw him trying it on his throat. Instantaneously one of those deafening dream-crashes awoke me, and I saw the door half open, and my servant in the very act of coming in. No doubt the opening of the door had constituted the crash.

I had joined a previously-arrived party of five, all of us old friends, and accustomed to see each other often, and at dinner, and afterwards in intervals of bridge, the conversation roamed agreeably over a variety of topics, rocking-turns and the prospects of weather (a thing of vast importance in Switzerland, and not a commonplace subject) and the performances at the opera, and under what circumstances as revealed in dummy's hand, is it justifiable for a player to refuse to return his partner's original lead in no trumps. Then over whisky and soda and the repeated 'last cigarette,' it veered back via the Zant-zigs to thought transference and the transference of emotion. Here one of the party, Harry Lambert, put forward the much discussed explanation of haunted houses based on this principle. He put it very concisely.

'Everything that happens,' he said, 'whether it is a step we take, or a thought that crosses our mind, makes some change in its immediate material world. Now the most violent and concentrated emotion we can imagine is the emotion that leads a man to take so extreme a step as killing himself or somebody else. I can easily imagine such a deed so eating into the material scene, the room or the haunted heath, where it happens, that its mark lasts an enormous time. The air rings with the cry of the slain and still drips with his blood. It is not everybody who will perceive it, but sensitives will. By the way, I am sure that man who waits on us at dinner is a sensitive.'

It was already late, and I rose.

'Let us hurry him to the scene of a crime,' I said. 'For myself I shall hurry to the scene of sleep.'

Outside the threatening promise of the barometer was already finding fulfilment, and a cold ugly wind was

100

complaining among the pines, and hooting round the peaks, and snow had begun to fall. The night was thickly overcast, and it seemed as if uneasy presences were going to and fro in the darkness. But there was no use in ill augury, and certainly if we were to be house-bound for a few days I was lucky in having so commodious a lodging. I had plenty to occupy myself with indoors, though I should vastly have preferred to be engaged outside, and in the immediate present how good it was to lie free in a proper bed after a cramped night in the train.

I was half-undressed when there came a tap at my door, and the waiter who had served us at dinner came in carrying a bottle of whisky. He was a tall young fellow, and though I had not noticed him at dinner, I saw at once now, as he stood in the glare of the electric light, what Harry had meant when he said he was sure he was a sensitive. There is no mistaking that look: it is exhibited in a peculiar 'inlooking' of the eye. Those eyes, one knows, see further than the surface. . .

'The bottle of whisky for monsieur,' he said, putting it down on the table.

'But I ordered no whisky,' said I.

He looked puzzled.

'Number twenty-three?' he said.

Then he glanced at the other bed.

'Ah, for the other gentleman, without doubt,' he said.

'But there is no other gentleman,' said I. 'I am alone here.'

He took up the bottle again.

'Pardon, monsieur,' he said. 'There must be a mistake. I am new here; I only came today. But I thought –'

'Yes?' said I.

'I thought that number twenty-three had ordered a bottle of whisky,' he repeated. 'Good-night, monsieur, and pardon.'

I got into bed, extinguished the light, and feeling very sleepy and heavy with the oppression, no doubt, of the snow that was coming, expected to fall asleep at once. Instead my mind would not quite go to roost, but kept sleepily stumbling about among the little events of the day, as some tired pedestrian in the dark stumbles over stones instead of lifting his feet. And as I got sleepier it seemed to me that my mind kept moving in a tiny little circle. At one moment it drowsily recollected how I had thought I had heard movement inside my room, at the next it remembered my dream of some figure going stealthily about and stropping a razor, at a third it wondered why this Swiss waiter with the eyes of a 'sensitive' thought that number twenty-three had ordered a bottle of whisky. But at the time I made no guess as to any coherence between these little isolated facts; I only dwelt on them with drowsy persistence. Then a fourth fact came to join the sleepy circle, and I wondered why I had felt a repugnance against using the other bed. But there was no explanation of this forthcoming, either, and the outlines of thought grew more blurred and hazy, until I lost consciousness altogether.

Next morning began the series of awful days, sleet and snow falling relentlessly with gusts of chilly wind, making any out-of-door amusement next to impossible. The snow was too soft for tobogganing, it balled on the skies, and as for the rink it was but a series of pools of slushy snow. This in itself, of course, was quite enough to account for any ordinary depression and heaviness of spirit, but all the time I felt there was something more than that to which I owed the utter blackness that hung over those days. I was beset too by fear that at first was only vague, but which gradually became more definite, until it resolved itself into a fear of number twenty-three and in particular a terror of the other bed. I had no notion why or how I was afraid of it, the thing was perfectly causeless, but the shape and the outline of it grew slowly clearer, as detail after detail of ordinary life, each minute and trivial in itself, carved and moulded this fear, till it became definite. Yet the whole thing was so causeless and childish that I could speak to no one of it; I could but assure myself that it was all a figment of nerves disordered by this unseemly weather.

However, as to the details, there were plenty of them. Once I woke up from strangling nightmare, unable at first to move, but in a panic of terror, believing that I was sleeping in the other bed. More than once, too, awaking before I was called, and getting out of bed to look at the aspect of the morning, I saw with a sense of dreadful misgiving that the bed-clothes on the other bed were strangely disarranged, as if someone had slept there, and smoothed them down afterwards, but not so well as not to give notice of the occupation. So one night I laid a trap, so to speak, for the intruder, of which the real object was to calm my own nervousness (for I still told myself that I was frightened of nothing), and tucked in the sheet very carefully, laying the pillow on the top of it. But in the morning it seemed as if my interference had not been to the taste of the occupant, for there was more impatient disorder than usual in the bed-clothes, and on the pillow was an indentation, round and rather deep, such as we may see any morning in our own beds. Yet by day these things did not frighten me, but it was when I went to bed at night that I quaked at the thought of further developments.

It happened also from time to time that I wanted something brought me, or wanted my servant. On three or four of these occasions my bell was answered by the 'Sensitive,' as we called him, but the Sensitive, I noticed, never came into the room. He would open the door a chink to receive my order, and on returning would again open it a chink to say that my boots, or whatever it was, were at the door. Once I made him come in, but I saw him cross himself as, with a face of icy terror, he stepped into the room, and the sight somehow did not reassure me. Twice also he came up in the evening, when I had not rung at all, even as he came up the first night, and opened the door a chink to say that my bottle of whisky was outside. But the poor fellow was in a state of such bewilderment when I went out and told him that I had not ordered whisky, that I did not press for an explanation. He begged my pardon profusely; he thought a bottle of whisky had been ordered for number twenty-three. It was his mistake, entirely – I should not be charged for it; it must have been the other gentleman. Pardon again; he remembered there was no other gentleman, the other bed was unoccupied.

It was on the night when this happened for the second time that I definitely began to wish that I too was quite certain that the other bed was unoccupied. The ten days of snow and sleet were at an end, and tonight the moon once more, grown from a mere slip to a shining shield, swung serenely among the stars. But though at dinner everyone exhibited an extraordinary change of spirit, with the rising of the barometer and the discharge of this huge snow-fall, the intolerable gloom which had been mine so long but deepened and blackened. The fear was to me now like some statue, nearly finished, modelled by the carving hands of these details, and though it still stood below its moistened sheet, any moment, I felt, the sheet might be twitched away, and I be confronted with it. Twice that evening I had started to go to the bureau, to ask to have a bed made up for me, anywhere, in the billiard-room or the smoking-room, since the hotel was full, but the intolerable childishness of the proceeding revolted me. What was I afraid of? A dream of my own, a mere nightmare? Some fortuitous disarrangement of bed-linen? The fact that a Swiss waiter made mistakes about bottles of whisky? It was an impossible cowardice.

But equally impossible that night were billiards or bridge, or any form of diversion. My only salvation seemed to lie in downright hard work, and soon after dinner I went to my room (in order to make my first real counter-move against fear) and sat down solidly to several hours of proof-correcting, a menial and monotonous employment, but one which is necessary, and engages the entire attention. But first I looked thoroughly round the room, to reassure myself and found all modern and solid; a bright paper of daisies on the wall, a floor parquetted, the hot-water pipes chuckling to themselves in the corner, my bed-clothes turned down for the night, the other bed –

The electric light was burning brightly, and there seemed to me to be a curious stain, as of a shadow, on the lower part of the pillow and the top of the sheet, definite and suggestive, and for a moment I stood there again throttled by a nameless terror. Then taking my courage in my hands I went closer and looked at it. Then I touched it; the sheet, where the stain or shadow was, seemed damp to the hand, so also the pillow. And then I remembered; I had thrown some wet clothes on the bed before dinner. No doubt that was the reason. And fortified by this extremely simple dissipation of my fear, I sat down and began on my proofs. But my fear had been this, that the stain had not in that first moment looked like the mere greyness of water-moistened linen.

From below, at first, came the sound of music, for they were dancing tonight, but I grew absorbed in my work, and only recorded the fact that after a time there was no more music. Steps went along the passages, and I heard the buzz of conversation on landings, and the closing of doors till by degrees the silence became noticeable. The loneliness of night had come.

It was after the silence had become lonely that I made the first pause in my work, and by the watch on my table saw that it was already past midnight. But I had little more to do; another half-hour would see the end of the business, but there were certain notes I had to make for future reference, and my stock of paper was already exhausted. However, I had bought some in the village that afternoon, and it was in the bureau downstairs, where I had left it, when I came in and had subsequently forgotten to bring it upstairs. It would be the work of a minute only to get it.

The electric light had brightened considerably during the last hour, owing no doubt to many burners being put out in the hotel, and as I left the room I saw again the stain on the pillow and sheet of the other bed. I had really forgotten all about it for the last hour, and its presence there came as an unwelcome surprise. Then I remembered the explanation of it, which had struck me before, and for purposes of self-reassurement I again touched it. It was still damp, but – Had I got chilly with my work? For it was warm to the hand. Warm, and surely rather sticky. It did not seem like the touch of the water-damp. And at the same moment I knew I was not alone in the room. There was something there, something silent as yet, and as yet invisible. But it was there.

Now for the consolation of persons who are inclined to be fearful, I may say at once that I am in no way brave, but that terror which, God knows, was real enough, was yet so interesting, that interest over-ruled it. I stood for a moment by the other bed, and, half-consciously only, wiped the hand that had felt the stain, for the touch of it, though all the time I told myself that it was but the touch of the melted snow on the coat I had put there, was unpleasant and unclean. More than that I did not feel, because in the presence of the unknown and the per-haps awful, the sense of curiosity, one of the strongest instincts we have, came to the fore. So, rather eager to get back to my room again, I ran downstairs to get the packet of paper. There was still a light in the bureau, and the Sensitive, on night-duty, I suppose, was sitting there dozing. My entrance did not disturb him, for I had on noiseless felt slippers, and seeing at once the package I was in search of, I took it, and left him still unawakened. That was somehow of a fortifying nature. The Sensitive anyhow could sleep in his hard chair; the occupant of the unoccupied bed was not calling to him tonight.

I closed my door quietly, as one does at night when the house is silent, and sat down at once to open my packet of paper and finish my work. It was wrapped up in an old news-sheet, and struggling with the last of the string that bound it, certain words caught my eye. Also the date at the top of the paper caught my eye, a date nearly a year old, or, to be quite accurate, a date fifty-one weeks old. It was an American paper and what it recorded was this:

'The body of Mr. Silas R. Hume, who committed suicide last week at the Hôtel Beau Site, Moulin sur Chalons, is to be buried at his house in Boston, Mass. The inquest held in Switzerland showed that he cut his throat with a razor, in an attack of delirium tremens induced by drink. In the cupboard of his room were found three dozen empty bottles of Scotch whisky. . .'

So far I had read when without warning the electric light went out, and I was left in, what seemed for the moment, absolute darkness. And again I knew I was not alone, and I knew now who it was who was with me in the room.

Then the absolute paralysis of fear seized me. As if a wind had blown over my head. I felt the hair of it stir and rise a little. My eyes also, I suppose, became accustomed to the sudden darkness, for they could now perceive the shape of the furniture in the room from the light of the starlit sky outside. They saw more too than the mere furniture. There was standing by the wash-stand between the two windows a figure, clothed only in night-garments, and its hands moved among the objects on the shelf above the basin. Then with two steps it made a sort of dive for the other bed, which was in shadow. And then the sweat poured on to my forehead.

Though the other bed stood in shadow I could still see dimly, but sufficiently, what was there. The shape of a head lay on the pillow, the shape of an arm lifted its hand to the electric bell that was close by on the wall, and I fancied I could hear it distantly ringing. Then a moment later came hurrying feet up the stairs and along the passage outside, and a quick rapping at my door.

'Monsieur's whisky, monsieur's whisky,' said a voice just outside. 'Pardon, monsieur, I brought it as quickly as I could.'

The impotent paralysis of cold terror was still on me. Once I tried to speak and failed, and still the gentle tapping went on at the door, and the voice telling someone

107

that his whisky was there. Then at a second attempt, I heard a voice which was mine saying hoarsely:

'For God's sake come in; I am alone with it.'

There was the click of a turned door-handle, and as suddenly as it had gone out a few seconds before, the electric light came back again and the room was in full illumination. I saw a face peer round the corner of the door, but it was at another face I looked, the face of a man shallow and sunken, who lay in the other bed, staring at me with glazed eyes. He lay high in bed, and his throat was cut from ear to ear; and the lower part of the pillow was soaked in blood, and the sheet streamed with it.

Then suddenly that hideous vision vanished, and there was only a sleepy-eyed waiter looking into the room. But below the sleepiness terror was awake, and his voice shook when he spoke.

'Monsieur rang?' he asked.

No, monsieur had not rung. But monsieur made himself a couch in the billiard-room.

The Room in the Tower

It is probable that everybody who is at all a constant dreamer has had at least one experience of an event or a sequence of circumstances which have come to his mind in sleep being subsequently realized in the material world. But, in my opinion, so far from this being a strange thing, it would be far odder if this fulfilment did not occasionally happen, since our dreams are, as a rule, concerned with people whom we know and places with which we are familiar, such as might very naturally occur in the awake and daylit world. True, these dreams are often broken into by some absurd and fantastic incident, which puts them out of court in regard to their subsequent fulfilment, but on the mere calculation of chances, it does not appear in the least unlikely that a dream imagined by anyone who dreams constantly should occasionally come true. Not long ago, for instance, I experienced such a fulfilment of a dream which seems to me in no way remarkable and to have no kind of psychical significance. The manner of it was as follows.

A certain friend of mine, living abroad, is amiable enough to write to me about once in a fortnight. Thus, when fourteen days or thereabout have elapsed since I last heard from him, my mind, probably, either consciously or subconsciously, is expectant of a letter from him. One night last week I dreamed that as I was going upstairs to dress for dinner I heard, as I often heard, the sound of the postman's knock on my front door, and diverted my direction downstairs instead. There, among other correspondence, was a letter from him. Thereafter the fantastic entered, for on opening it I found inside the ace of diamonds, and scribbled across it in his well-known handwriting, 'I am sending you this for safe custody, as you know it is running an unreasonable risk to keep aces in Italy.' The next evening I was just preparing to go upstairs to dress when I heard the postman's knock, and did precisely as I had done in my dream. There, among other letters, was one from my friend. Only it did not contain the ace of diamonds. Had it done so, I should have attached more weight to the matter, which, as it stands, seems to me a perfectly ordinary coincidence. No doubt I consciously or subconsciously expected a letter from him, and this suggested to me my dream. Similarly, the fact that my friend had not written to me for a fortnight suggested to him that he should do so. But occasionally it is not so easy to find such an explanation, and for the following story I can find no explanation at all. It came out of the dark, and into the dark it has gone again.

All my life I have been a habitual dreamer: the nights are few, that is to say, when I do not find on awaking in the morning that some mental experience has been mine, and sometimes, all night long, apparently, a series of the most dazzling adventures befall me. Almost without exception these adventures are pleasant, though often merely trivial. It is of an exception that I am going to speak.

It was when I was about sixteen that a certain dream first came to me, and this is how it befell. It opened with my being set down at the door of a big red-brick house, where, I understood, I was going to stay. The servant who opened the door told me that tea was going on in the garden, and led me through a low dark-panelled hall, with a large open fireplace, on to a cheerful green lawn set round with flower beds. There were grouped about the tea-table a small party of people, but they were all strangers to me except one, who was a school-fellow called Jack Stone, clearly the son of the house, and he

110

introduced me to his mother and father and a couple of sisters. I was, I remember, somewhat astonished to find myself here, for the boy in question was scarcely known to me, and I rather disliked what I knew of him: moreover, he had left school nearly a year before. The afternoon was very hot, and an intolerable oppression reigned. On the far side of the lawn ran a red-brick wall, with an iron gate in its centre, outside which stood a walnut tree. We sat in the shadow of the house opposite a row of long windows, inside which I could see a table with cloth laid, glimmering with glass and silver. This garden front of the house was very long, and at one end of it stood a tower of three storeys, which looked to me much older than the rest of the building.

Before long, Mrs. Stone, who, like the rest of the party, had sat in absolute silence, said to me, 'Jack will show you your room: I have given you the room in the tower.'

Quite inexplicably my heart sank at her words. I felt as if I had known that I should have the room in the tower, and that it contained something dreadful and significant. Jack instantly got up, and I understood that I had to follow him. In silence we passed through the hall, and mounted a great oak staircase with many corners, and arrived at a small landing with two doors set in it. He pushed one of these open for me to enter, and without coming in himself, closed it behind me. Then I knew that my conjecture had been right: there was something awful in the room, and with the terror of nightmare growing swiftly and enveloping me, I awoke in a spasm of terror.

Now that dream or variations on it occurred to me intermittently for fifteen years. Most often it came in exactly this form, the arrival, the tea laid out on the lawn, the deadly silence succeeded by that one deadly sentence, the mounting with Jack Stone up to the room in the tower where horror dwelt, and it always came to a close in the nightmare of terror at that which was in the room, though I never saw what it was. At other times I experienced variations on this same theme. Occasionally, for instance, we would be sitting at dinner in the dining-room, into the windows of which I had looked on the first night when the dream of this house visited me, but wherever we were, there was the same silence, the same sense of dreadful oppression and foreboding. And the silence I knew would always be broken by Mrs. Stone saying to me, 'Jack will show you your room: I have given you the room in the tower.' Upon which (this was invariable) I had to follow him up the oak staircase with many corners, and enter the place that I dreaded more and more each time that I visited it in sleep. Or, again, I would find myself playing cards still in silence in a drawing-room lit with immense chandeliers, that gave a blinding illumination. What the game was I have no idea; what I remember, with a sense of miserable anticipation, was that soon Mrs. Stone would get up and say to me, 'Jack will show you your room: I have given you the room in the tower.' This drawing-room where we played cards was next to the dining-room, and, as I have said, was always brilliantly illuminated, whereas the rest of the house was full of dusk and shadows. And yet, how often, in spite of those bouquets of lights, have I not pored over the cards that were dealt to me, scarcely able for some reason to see them. Their designs, too, were strange: there were no red suits, but all were black, and among them there were certain cards which were black all over. I hated and dreaded those.

As this dream continued to recur, I got to know the greater part of the house. There was a smoking-room beyond the drawing-room, at the end of a passage with a green baize door. It was always very dark there, and as often as I went there I passed somebody whom I could not see in the doorway coming out. Curious developments, too, took place in the characters that peopled the dream as might happen to living persons. Mrs. Stone, for instance, who, when I first saw her, had been black haired, became grey, and instead of rising briskly, as she had done at first when she said, 'Jack will show you your room: I have given you the room in the tower,' got

112

up very feebly, as if the strength was leaving her limbs. Jack also grew up, and became a rather ill-looking young man, with a brown moustache, while one of the sisters ceased to appear, and I understood she was married.

Then it so happened that I was not visited by this dream for six months or more, and I began to hope, in such inexplicable dread did I hold it, that it had passed away for good. But one night after this interval I again found myself being shown out on to the lawn for tea, and Mrs. Stone was not there, while the others were all dressed in black. At once I guessed the reason, and my heart leaped at the thought that perhaps this time I should not have to sleep in the room in the tower, and though we usually all sat in silence, on this occasion the sense of relief made me talk and laugh as I had never yet done. But even then matters were not altogether comfortable, for no one else spoke, but they all looked secretly at each other. And soon the foolish stream of my talk ran dry, and gradually an apprehension worse than anything I had previously known gained on me as the light slowly faded.

Suddenly a voice which I knew well broke the stillness, the voice of Mrs. Stone, saying, 'Jack will show you your room: I have given you the room in the tower.' It seemed to come from near the gate in the red-brick wall that bounded the lawn, and looking up, I saw that the grass outside was sown thick with gravestones. A curious greyish light shone from them, and I could read the lettering on the grave nearest me, and it was, 'In evil memory of Julia Stone.' And as usual Jack got up, and again I followed him through the hall and up the staircase with many corners. On this occasion it was darker than usual, and when I passed into the room in the tower I could only just see the furniture, the position of which was already familiar to me. Also there was a dreadful odour of decay in the room, and I woke screaming.

The dream, with such variations and developments as I have mentioned, went on at intervals for fifteen years. Sometimes I would dream it two or three nights in

succession; once, as I have said, there was an inter-
mission of six months, but taking a reasonable average, I
should say that I dreamed it quite as often as once in a
month. It had, as is plain, something of nightmare about
it, since it always ended in the same appalling terror,
which so far from getting less, seemed to me to gather
fresh fear every time that I experienced it. There was,
too, a strange and dreadful consistency about it. The
characters in it, as I have mentioned, got regularly older,
death and marriage visited this silent family, and I never
in the dream, after Mrs. Stone had died, set eyes on her
again. But it was always her voice that told me that the
room in the tower was prepared for me, and whether we
had tea out on the lawn, or the scene was laid in one of
the rooms overlooking it, I could always see her gravestone standing just outside the iron gate. It was the same,
too, with the married daughter; usually she was not
present, but once or twice she returned again, in company with a man, whom I took to be her husband. He, too,
like the rest of them, was always silent. But, owing to the
constant repetition of the dream, I had ceased to attach,
in my waking hours, any significance to it. I never met
Jack Stone again during all those years, nor did I ever
see a house that resembled this dark house of my dream.
And then something happened.

I had been in London in this year, up till the end of July,
and during the first week in August went down to stay
with a friend in a house he had taken for the summer
months, in the Ashdown Forest district of Sussex. I left
London early, for John Clinton was to meet me at Forest
Row Station, and we were going to spend the day golfing,
and go to his house in the evening. He had his motor with
him, and we set off, about five in the afternoon, after a
thoroughly delightful day, for the drive, the distance
being some ten miles. As it was still so early we did not
have tea at the club house, but waited till we should get
home. As we drove, the weather, which up till then had
been, though hot, deliciously fresh, seemed to me to alter
in quality, and become very stagnant and oppressive,

114

and I felt that indefinable sense of ominous apprehension that I am accustomed to before thunder. John, however, did not share my views, attributing my loss of lightness to the fact that I had lost both my matches. Events proved, however, that I was right, though I do not think that the thunderstorm that broke that night was the sole cause of my depression.

Our way lay through deep high-banked lanes, and before we had gone very far I fell asleep, and was only awakened by the stopping of the motor. And with a sudden thrill, partly of fear but chiefly of curiosity, I found myself standing in the doorway of my house of dream. We went, I half wondering whether or not I was dreaming still, through a low oak-panelled hall, and out on to the lawn, where tea was laid in the shadow of the house. It was set in flower beds, a red-brick wall, with a gate in it, bounded one side, and out beyond that was a space of rough grass with a walnut tree. The façade of the house was very long, and at one end stood a three-storeyed tower, markedly older than the rest.

Here for the moment all resemblance to the repeated dream ceased. There was no silent and somehow terrible family, but a large assembly of exceedingly cheerful persons, all of whom were known to me. And in spite of the horror with which the dream itself had always filled me, I felt nothing of it now that the scene of it was thus reproduced before me. But I felt the intensest curiosity as to what was going to happen.

Tea pursued its cheerful course, and before long Mrs. Clinton got up. And at that moment I think I knew what she was going to say. She spoke to me, and what she said was:

'Jack will show you your room: I have given you the room in the tower.'

At that, for half a second, the horror of the dream took hold of me again. But it quickly passed, and again I felt nothing more than the most intense curiosity. It was not very long before it was amply satisfied.

John turned to me.

'Right up at the top of the house,' he said, 'but I think you'll be comfortable. We're absolutely full up. Would you like to go and see it now? By Jove, I believe that you are right, and that we are going to have a thunderstorm. How dark it has become.'

I got up and followed him. We passed through the hall, and up the perfectly familiar staircase. Then he opened the door, and I went in. And at that moment sheer unreasoning terror again possessed me. I did not know for certain what I feared: I simply feared. Then like a sudden recollection, when one remembers a name which has long escaped the memory, I knew what I feared. I feared Mrs. Stone, whose grave with the sinister inscription, 'In evil memory,' I had so often seen in my dream, just beyond the lawn which lay below my window. And then once more the fear passed so completely that I wondered what there was to fear, and I found myself, sober and quiet and sane, in the room in the tower, the name of which I had so often heard in my dream, and the scene of which was so familiar.

I looked round it with a certain sense of proprietorship, and found that nothing had been changed from the dreaming nights in which I knew it so well. Just to the left of the door was the bed, lengthways along the wall, with the head of it in the angle. In a line with it was the fireplace and a small bookcase; opposite the door the outer wall was pierced by two lattice-paned windows, between which stood the dressing-table, while ranged along the fourth wall was the washing-stand and a big cupboard. My luggage had already been unpacked, for the furniture of dressing and undressing lay orderly on the wash-stand and toilet-table, while my dinner clothes were spread out on the coverlet of the bed. And then, with a sudden start of unexplained dismay, I saw that there were two rather conspicuous objects which I had not seen before in my dreams: one a life-sized oil-painting of Mrs. Stone, the other a black-and-white sketch of Jack Stone, representing him as he had appeared to me only a week before in the last of the series of these repeated dreams, a rather secret and evil-looking man of about thirty. His picture hung between the windows, looking straight across the room to the other portrait, which hung at the side of the bed. At that I looked next, and as I looked I felt once more the horror of nightmare seize me.

It represented Mrs. Stone as I had seen her last in my dreams: old and withered and white haired. But in spite of the evident feebleness of body, a dreadful exuberance and vitality shone through the envelope of flesh, an exuberance wholly malign, a vitality that foamed and frothed with unimaginable evil. Evil beamed from the narrow, leering eyes; it laughed in the demon-like mouth. The whole face was instinct with some secret and appalling mirth; the hands, clasped together on the knee, seemed shaking with suppressed and nameless glee. Then I saw also that it was signed in the left-hand bottom corner, and wondering who the artist could be. I looked more closely, and read the inscription, 'Julia Stone by Julia Stone.'

There came a tap at the door, and John Clinton entered.

'Got everything you want?' he asked.

'Rather more than I want,' said I, pointing to the picture.

He laughed.

'Hard-featured old lady,' he said. 'By herself, too, I remember. Anyhow she can't have flattered herself much.'

'But don't you see?' said I. 'It's scarcely a human face at all. It's the face of some witch, of some devil.'

He looked at it more closely.

'Yes; it isn't very pleasant,' he said. 'Scarcely a bedside manner, eh? Yes; I can imagine getting the nightmare, if I went to sleep with that close by my bed. I'll have it taken down if you like.'

'I really wish you would,' I said.

He rang the bell, and with the help of a servant we detached the picture and carried it out on to the landing, and put it with its face to the wall.

'By Jove, the old lady is a weight,' said John, mopping his forehead. 'I wonder if she had something on her mind.'

The extraordinary weight of the picture had struck me too. I was about to reply, when I caught sight of my own hand. There was blood on it, in considerable quantities, covering the whole palm.

'I've cut myself somehow,' said I.

John gave a little startled exclamation.

'Why, I have too,' he said.

Simultaneously the footman took out his handkerchief and wiped his hand with it. I saw that there was blood also on his handkerchief.

John and I went back into the tower room and washed the blood off; but neither on his hand nor on mine was there the slightest trace of a scratch or cut. It seemed to me that, having ascertained this, we both, by a sort of tacit consent, did not allude to it again. Something in my case had dimly occurred to me that I did not wish to think about. It was but a conjecture, but I fancied that I knew the same thing had occurred to him.

The heat and oppression of the air, for the storm we had expected was still undischarged, increased very much after dinner, and for some time most of the party, among whom were John Clinton and myself, sat outside on the path bounding the lawn, where we had had tea. The night was absolutely dark, and no twinkle of star or moon ray could penetrate the pall of cloud that overset the sky. By degrees our assembly thinned, the women went up to bed, men dispersed to the smoking or billiard room, and by eleven o'clock my host and I were the only two left. All the evening I thought that he had something on his mind, and as soon as we were alone he spoke.

'The man who helped us with the picture had blood on his hand, too, did you notice?' he said. 'I asked him just now if he had cut himself, and he said he supposed he had, but that he could find no mark of it. Now where did that blood come from?'

By dint of telling myself that I was not going to think

about it, I had succeeded in not doing so, and I did not want, especially just at bedtime, to be reminded of it.

'I don't know,' said I, 'and I don't really care so long as the picture of Mrs. Julia Stone is not by my bed.'

He got up.

'But it's odd,' he said. 'Ha! Now you'll see another odd thing.'

A dog of his, an Irish terrier by breed, had come out of the house as we talked. The door behind us into the hall was open, and a bright oblong of light shone across the lawn to the iron gate which led on to the rough grass outside, where the walnut tree stood. I saw that the dog had all his hackles up, bristling with rage and fright; his lips were curled back from his teeth, as if he was ready to spring at something, and he was growling to himself. He took not the slightest notice of his master or me, but stiffly and tensely walked across the grass to the iron gate. There he stood for a moment, looking through the bars and still growling. Then of a sudden his courage seemed to desert him: he gave one long howl, and scuttled back to the house with a curious crouching sort of movement.

'He does that half-a-dozen times a day,' said John. 'He sees something which he both hates and fears.'

I walked to the gate and looked over it. Something was moving on the grass outside, and soon a sound which I could not instantly identify came to my ears. Then I remembered what it was: it was the purring of a cat. I lit a match, and saw the purrer, a big blue Persian, walking round and round in a little circle just outside the gate, stepping high and ecstatically, with tail carried aloft like a banner. Its eyes were bright and shining, and every now and then it put its head down and sniffed at the grass.

I laughed.

'The end of that mystery, I am afraid,' I said. 'Here's a large cat having Walpurgis night all alone.'

'Yes, that's Darius,' said John. 'He spends half the day and all night there. But that's not the end of the dog mystery, for Toby and he are the best of friends, but the beginning of the cat mystery. What's the cat doing there? And why is Darius pleased, while Toby is terror-stricken?'

At that moment I remembered the rather horrible details of my dreams when I saw through the gate, just where the cat was now, the white tombstone with the sinister inscription. But before I could answer the rain began, as suddenly and heavily as if a tap had been turned on, and simultaneously the big cat squeezed through the bars of the gate, and came leaping across the lawn to the house for shelter. Then it sat in the doorway, looking out eagerly into the dark. It spat and struck at John with its paw, as he pushed it in, in order to close the door.

Somehow, with the portrait of Julia Stone in the passage outside, the room in the tower had absolutely no alarm for me, and as I went to bed, feeling very sleepy and heavy, I had nothing more than interest for the curious incident about our bleeding hands, and the conduct of the cat and dog. The last thing I looked at before I put out my light was the square empty space by my bed where the portrait had been. Here the paper was of its original full tint of dark red: over the rest of the walls it had faded. Then I blew out my candle and instantly fell asleep.

My awaking was equally instantaneous, and I sat bolt upright in bed under the impression that some bright light had been flashed in my face, though it was now absolutely pitch dark. I knew exactly where I was, in the room which I had dreaded in dreams, but no horror that I ever felt when asleep approached the fear that now invaded and froze my brain. Immediately after a peal of thunder crackled just above the house, but the probability that it was only a flash of lightning which awoke me gave no reassurance to my galloping heart. Something I knew was in the room with me, and instinctively I put out my right hand, which was nearest the wall, to keep it away. And my hand touched the edge of a picture-frame hanging close to me.

I sprang out of bed, upsetting the small table that stood by it, and I heard my watch, candle, and matches clatter on to the floor. But for the moment there was no need of light, for a blinding flash leaped out of the clouds, and showed me that by my bed again hung the picture of Mrs. Stone. And instantly the room went into blackness again. But in that flash I saw another thing also, namely a figure that leaned over the end of my bed, watching me. It was dressed in some close-clinging white garment, spotted and stained with mould, and the face was that of the portrait.

Overhead the thunder cracked and roared, and when it ceased and the deathly stillness succeeded, I heard the rustle of movement coming nearer me, and, more horrible yet, perceived an odour of corruption and decay. And then a hand was laid on the side of my neck, and close beside my ear I heard quick-taken, eager breathing. Yet I knew that this thing, though it could be perceived by touch, by smell, by eye and by ear, was still not of this earth, but something that had passed out of the body and had power to make itself manifest. Then a voice, already familiar to me, spoke.

'I knew you would come to the room in the tower,' it said. 'I have been long waiting for you. At last you have come. Tonight I shall feast; before long we will feast together.'

And the quick breathing came closer to me; I could feel it on my neck.

At that the terror, which I think had paralysed me for the moment, gave way to the wild instinct of self-preservation. I hit wildly with both arms, kicking out at the same moment, and heard a little animal-squeal, and something soft dropped with a thud beside me. I took a couple of steps forward, nearly tripping up over whatever it was that lay there, and by the merest good-luck found the handle of the door. In another second I ran out on the landing, and had banged the door behind me. Almost at the same moment I heard a door open somewhere below, and John Clinton, candle in hand, came running upstairs.

'What is it?' he said. 'I sleep just below you, and heard a noise as if – Good heavens, there's blood on your shoulder.'

I stood there, so he told me afterwards, swaying from side to side, white as a sheet, with the mark on my shoulder as if a hand covered with blood had been laid there.

'It's in there,' I said, pointing. 'She, you know. The portrait is in there, too, hanging up on the place we took it from.'

At that he laughed.

'My dear fellow, this is mere nightmare,' he said.

He pushed by me, and opened the door, I standing there simply inert with terror, unable to stop him, unable to move.

'Phew! What an awful smell,' he said.

Then there was silence; he had passed out of my sight behind the open door. Next moment he came out again, as white as myself, and instantly shut it.

'Yes, the portrait's there,' he said, 'and on the floor is a thing – a thing spotted with earth, like what they bury people in. Come away, quick, come away.'

How I got downstairs I hardly know. An awful shuddering and nausea of the spirit rather than of the flesh had seized me, and more than once he had to place my feet upon the steps, while every now and then he cast glances of terror and apprehension up the stairs. But in time we came to his dressing-room on the floor below, and there I told him what I have here described.

The sequel can be made short; indeed, some of my readers have perhaps already guessed what it was, if they remember that inexplicable affair of the church-yard at West Fawley, some eight years ago, where an attempt was made three times to bury the body of a certain woman who had committed suicide. On each occasion the coffin was found in the course of a few days again protruding from the ground. After the third attempt, in order that the thing should not be talked about, the body was buried elsewhere in unconsecrated ground. Where it was buried was just outside the iron gate of the garden belonging to the house where this woman had lived. She had committed suicide in a room at the top of the tower in that house. Her name was Julia Stone.

Subsequently the body was again secretly dug up, and the coffin was found to be full of blood.

Mrs. Amworth

The village of Maxley, where, last summer and autumn, these strange events took place, lies on a heathery and pine-clad upland of Sussex. In all England you could not find a sweeter and saner situation. Should the wind blow from the south, it comes laden with the spices of the sea; to the east high downs protect it from the inclemencies of March; and from the west and north the breezes which reach it travel over miles of aromatic forest and heather. The village itself is insignificant enough in point of population, but rich in amenities and beauty. Half-way down its single street, with its broad road and spacious areas of grass on each side, stands the little Norman Church and the antique graveyard long disused: for the rest there are a dozen small, sedate Georgian houses, red-bricked and long-windowed, each with a square of flower-garden in front, and an ampler strip behind; a score of shops, and a couple of score of thatched cottages belonging to labourers on neighbouring estates, complete the entire cluster of its peaceful habitations. The general peace, however, is sadly broken on Saturdays and Sundays, for we lie on one of the main roads between London and Brighton and our quiet street becomes a race-course for flying motor-cars and bicycles. A notice just outside the village begging them to go slowly only seems to encourage them to accelerate their speed, for the road lies open and straight, and there is really no reason why they should do otherwise. By way of protest, therefore, the ladies of Maxley cover their noses and mouths with their handkerchiefs as they

124

see a motor-car approaching, though, as the street is asphalted, they need not really take these precautions against dust. But late on Sunday night the horde of scorchers has passed, and we settle down again to five days of cheerful and leisurely seclusion. Railway strikes which agitate the country so much leave us undisturbed because most of the inhabitants of Maxley never leave it at all.

I am the fortunate possessor of one of these small Georgian houses, and consider myself no less fortunate in having so interesting and stimulating a neighbour as Francis Urcombe, who, the most confirmed of Maxleyites, has not slept away from his house, which stands just opposite to mine in the village street, for nearly two years, at which date, though still in middle life, he resigned his Physiological Professorship at Cambridge University and devoted himself to the study of those occult and curious phenomena which seem equally to concern the physical and the psychical sides of human nature. Indeed his retirement was not unconnected with his passion for the strange uncharted places that lie on the confines and borders of science, the existence of which is so stoutly denied by the more materialistic minds, for he advocated that all medical students should be obliged to pass some sort of examination in mesmerism, and that one of the tripos papers should be designed to test their knowledge in such subjects as appearances at time of death, haunted houses, vampirism, automatic writing, and possession.

'Of course they wouldn't listen to me,' ran his account of the matter, 'for there is nothing that these seats of learning are so frightened of as knowledge, and the road to knowledge lies in the study of things like these. The functions of the human frame are, broadly speaking, known. They are a country, anyhow, that has been charted and mapped out. But outside that lie huge tracts of undiscovered country, which certainly exists, and the real pioneers of knowledge are those who, at the cost of being derided as credulous and superstitious, want to

125

push on into those misty and probably perilous places. I felt that I could be of more use by setting out without compass or knapsack into the mists than by sitting in a cage like a canary and chirping about what was known. Besides, teaching is very bad for a man who knows himself only to be a learner: you only need to be a self-conceited ass to teach.'

Here, then, in Francis Urcombe, was a delightful neighbour to one who, like myself, has an uneasy and burning curiosity about what he called the 'misty and perilous places'; and this last spring we had a further and most welcome addition to our pleasant little community, in the person of Mrs. Amworth, widow of an Indian civil servant. Her husband had been a judge in the Northwest Provinces, and after his death at Peshawar she came back to England, and after a year in London found herself starving for the ampler air and sunshine of the country to take the place of the fogs and griminess of town. She had, too, a special reason for settling in Maxley, since her ancestors up till a hundred years ago had long been native to the place, and in the old churchyard, now disused, are many gravestones bearing her maiden name of Chaston. Big and energetic, her vigorous and genial personality speedily woke Maxley up to a higher degree of sociality than it had ever known. Most of us were bachelors or spinsters or elderly folk not much inclined to exert ourselves in the expense and effort of hospitality, and hitherto the gaiety of a small tea-party, with bridge afterwards and goloshes (when it was wet) to trip home again for a solitary dinner, was about the climax of our festivities. But Mrs. Amworth showed us a more gregarious way, and set an example of luncheon-parties and little dinners, which we began to follow. On other nights when no such hospitality was on foot, a lone man like myself found it pleasant to know that a call on the telephone to Mrs. Amworth's house not a hundred yards off, and an inquiry as to whether I might come over after dinner for a game of piquet before bed-time, would probably evoke a response of welcome. There she would be, with a comrade-like eagerness for companionship, and there was a glass of port and a cup of coffee and a cigarette and a game of piquet. She played the piano, too, in a free and exuberant manner, and had a charming voice and sang to her own accompaniment; and as the days grew long and the light lingered late, we played our game in her garden, which in the course of a few months she had turned from being a nursery for slugs and snails into a glowing patch of luxuriant blossoming. She was always cheery and jolly; she was interested in everything, and in music, in gardening, in games of all sorts was a competent performer. Everybody (with one exception) liked her, everybody felt her to bring with her the tonic of a sunny day. That one exception was Francis Urcombe; he, though he confessed he did not like her, acknowledged that he was vastly interested in her. This always seemed strange to me, for pleasant and jovial as she was, I could see nothing in her that could call forth conjecture or intrigued surmise, so healthy and unmysterious a figure did she present. But of the genuineness of Urcombe's interest there could be no doubt; one could see him watching and scrutinising her. In matter of age, she frankly volunteered the information that she was forty-five; but her briskness, her activity, her unravaged skin, her coal-black hair, made it difficult to believe that she was not adopting an unusual device, and adding ten years on to her age instead of subtracting them.

Often, also, as our quite unsentimental friendship ripened, Mrs. Amworth would ring me up and propose her advent. If I was busy writing, I was to give her, so we definitely bargained, a frank negative, and in answer I could hear her jolly laugh and her wishes for a successful evening of work. Sometimes, before her proposal arrived, Urcombe would already have stepped across from his house opposite for a smoke and a chat, and he, hearing who my intending visitor was, always urged me to beg her to come. She and I should play our piquet, said he, and he would look on, if we did not object, and learn something of the game. But I doubt whether he paid much attention to it, for nothing could be clearer than that, under that penthouse of forehead and thick eyebrows, his attention was fixed not on the cards, but on one of the players. But he seemed to enjoy an hour spent thus, and often, until one particular evening in July, he would watch her with the air of a man who has some deep problem in front of him. She, enthusiastically keen about our game, seemed not to notice his scrutiny. Then came that evening, when, as I see in the light of subsequent events, began the first twitching of the veil that hid the secret horror from my eyes. I did not know it then, though I noticed that thereafter, if she rang up to propose coming round, she always asked not only if I was at leisure, but whether Mr. Urcombe was with me. If so, she said, she would not spoil the chat of two old bachelors, and laughingly wished me good night.

Urcombe, on this occasion, had been with me for some half-hour before Mrs. Amworth's appearance, and had been talking to me about the mediaeval superstitions concerning vampirism, one of those borderland subjects which he declared had not been sufficiently studied before it had been consigned by the medical profession to the dust-heap of exploded superstitions. There he sat, grim and eager, tracing, with that pellucid clearness which had made him in his Cambridge days so admirable a lecturer, the history of those mysterious visitations. In all these there were the same general features: one of those ghoulish spirits took up its abode in a living man or woman, conferring supernatural powers of batlike flight and glutting itself with nocturnal blood-feasts. When its host died it continued to dwell in the corpse, which remained undecayed. By day it rested, by night it left the grave and went on its awful errands. No European country in the Middle Ages seemed to have escaped them; earlier yet, parallels were to be found, in Roman and Greek and in Jewish history.

'It's a large order to set all that evidence aside as being moonshine,' he said. 'Hundreds of totally independent witnesses in many ages have testified to the occurrence of these phenomena, and there's no explanation known to me which covers all the facts. And if you feel inclined to say, "Why, then, if these are facts, do we not come across them now?" there are two answers I can make you. One is that there were diseases known in the Middle Ages, such as the black death, which were certainly existent then and which have become extinct since, but for that reason we do not assert that such diseases never existed. Just as the black death visited England and decimated the population of Norfolk, so here in this very district about three hundred years ago there was certainly an outbreak of vampirism, and Maxley was the centre of it. My second answer is even more convincing, for I tell you that vampirism is by no means extinct now. An outbreak of it certainly occurred in India a year or two ago.'

At that moment I heard my knocker plied in the cheerful and peremptory manner in which Mrs. Amworth is accustomed to announce her arrival, and I went to the door to open it.

'Come in at once,' I said, 'and save me from having my blood curdled. Mr. Urcombe has been trying to alarm me.'

Instantly her vital, voluminous presence seemed to fill the room.

'Ah, but how lovely!' she said. 'I delight in having my blood curdled. Go on with your ghost story, Mr. Urcombe. I adore ghost stories.'

I saw that, as his habit was, he was intently observing her.

'It wasn't a ghost story exactly,' said he. 'I was only telling our host how vampirism was not extinct yet. I was saying that there was an outbreak of it in India only a few years ago.'

There was a more than perceptible pause, and I saw that, if Urcombe was observing her, she on her side was observing him with fixed eye and parted mouth. Then her jolly laugh invaded that rather tense silence.

'Oh, what a shame!' she said. 'You're not going to curdle my blood at all. Where did you pick up such a tale, Mr. Urcombe? I have lived for years in India and never heard a rumour of such a thing. Some story-teller in the bazaars must have invented it: they are famous at that.'

I could see that Urcombe was on the point of saying something further, but checked himself.

'Ah! Very likely that was it,' he said.

But something had disturbed our usual peaceful sociability that night, and something had damped Mrs. Amworth's usual high spirits. She had no gusto for her piquet, and left after a couple of games. Urcombe had been silent too, indeed he hardly spoke again till she departed.

'That was unfortunate,' he said, 'for the outbreak of – of a very mysterious disease, let us call it, took place at Peshawar, where she and her husband were. And –'

'Well?' I asked.

'He was one of the victims of it,' said he. 'Naturally I had quite forgotten that when I spoke.'

The summer was unreasonably hot and rainless, and Maxley suffered much from drought, and also from a plague of big black night-flying gnats, the bite of which was very irritating and virulent. They came sailing in of an evening, settling on one's skin so quietly that one perceived nothing till the sharp stab announced that one had been bitten. They did not bite one's hands or face, but chose always the neck and throat for their feeding-ground, and most of us, as the poison spread, assumed a temporary goitre. Then about the middle of August appeared the first of those mysterious cases of illness which our local doctor attributed to the long-continued heat coupled with the bite of these venomous insects. The patient was a boy of sixteen or seventeen, the son of Mrs. Amworth's gardener, and the symptoms were an anaemic pallor and a languid prostration, accompanied by great drowsiness and an abnormal appetite. He had, too, on his throat two small punctures where, so Dr. Ross conjectured, one of these great gnats had bitten him. But the odd thing was that there was no swelling or inflammation round the place where he had been bitten. The heat at this time had begun to abate, but the cooler weather failed to restore him, and the boy, in spite of the quantity of good food which he so ravenously swallowed, wasted away to a skin-clad skeleton.

I met Dr. Ross in the street one afternoon about this time, and in answer to my inquiries about his patient he said that he was afraid the boy was dying. The case, he confessed, completely puzzled him: some obscure form of pernicious anaemia was all he could suggest. But he wondered whether Mr. Urcombe would consent to see the boy, on the chance of his being able to throw some new light on the case; and since Urcombe was dining with me that night, I proposed to Dr. Ross to join us. He could not do this, but said he would look in later. When he came, Urcombe at once consented to put his skill at the other's disposal, and together they went off at once. Being thus shorn of my sociable evening, I telephoned to Mrs. Amworth to know if I might inflict myself on her for an hour. Her answer was a welcoming affirmative, and between piquet and music the hour lengthened itself into two. She spoke of the boy who was lying so desperately and mysteriously ill, and told me that she had often been to see him, taking him nourishing and delicate food. But today – and her kind eyes moistened as she spoke – she was afraid she had paid her last visit. Knowing the antipathy between her and Urcombe, I did not tell her that he had been called into consultation; and when I returned home she accompanied me to my door, for the sake of a breath of night air, and in order to borrow a magazine which contained an article on gardening which she wished to read.

'Ah, this delicious night air,' she said, luxuriously sniffing in the coolness. 'Night air and gardening are the great tonics. There is nothing so stimulating as bare contact with rich mother earth. You are never so fresh as when you have been grubbing in the soil – black hands, black nails, and boots covered with mud.' She gave her great jovial laugh.

'I'm a glutton for air and earth,' she said. 'Positively I look forward to death, for then I shall be buried and have the kind earth all round me. No leaden caskets for me – I have given explicit directions. But what shall I do about air? Well, I suppose one can't have everything. The magazine? A thousand thanks, I will faithfully return it. Good night: garden and keep your windows open, and you won't have anaemia.'

'I always sleep with my windows open,' said I.

I went straight up to my bedroom, of which one of the windows looks out over the street, and as I undressed I thought I heard voices talking outside not far away. But I paid no particular attention, put out my lights, and falling asleep plunged into the depths of a most horrible dream, distortedly suggested no doubt, by my last words with Mrs. Amworth. I dreamed that I woke, and found that both my bedroom windows were shut. Half-suffocating I dreamed that I sprang out of bed, and went across to open them. The blind over the first was drawn down, and pulling it up I saw, with the indescribable horror of incipient nightmare, Mrs. Amworth's face suspended close to the pane in the darkness outside, nodding and smiling at me. Pulling down the blind again to keep that terror out, I rushed to the second window on the other side of the room, and there again was Mrs. Amworth's face. Then the panic came upon me in full blast; here was I suffocating in the airless room, and whichever window I opened Mrs. Amworth's face would float in, like those noiseless black gnats that bit before one was aware. The nightmare rose to screaming point, and with strangled yells I awoke to find my room cool and quiet with both windows open and blinds up and a half-moon high in its course, casting an oblong of tranquil light on the floor. But even when I was awake the horror persisted, and I lay tossing and turning. I must have slept long before the nightmare seized me, for now it was nearly day, and soon in the east the drowsy eyelids of morning began to lift.

I was scarcely downstairs next morning – for after the dawn I slept late – when Urcombe rang up to know if he might see me immediately. He came in, grim and preoccupied, and I noticed that he was pulling on a pipe that was not even filled.

'I want your help,' he said, 'and so I must tell you first of all what happened last night. I went round with the little doctor to see his patient, and found him just alive, but scarcely more. I instantly diagnosed in my own mind what this anaemia, unaccountable by any other explanation, meant. The boy is the prey of a vampire.'

He put his empty pipe on the breakfast-table, by which I had just sat down, and folded his arms, looking at me steadily from under his overhanging brows.

'Now about last night,' he said. 'I insisted that he should be moved from his father's cottage into my house. As we were carrying him on a stretcher, whom should we meet but Mrs. Amworth? She expressed shocked surprise that we were moving him. Now why do you think she did that?'

With a start of horror, as I remembered my dream the night before, I felt an idea come into my mind so preposterous and unthinkable that I instantly turned it out again.

'I haven't the smallest idea,' I said.

'Then listen, while I tell you about what happened later. I put out all lights in the room where the boy lay, and watched. One window was a little open, for I had forgotten to close it, and about midnight I heard something outside, trying apparently to push it farther open. I guessed who it was – yes, it was full twenty feet from the ground – and I peeped round the corner of the blind. Just outside was the face of Mrs. Amworth and her hand was on the frame of the window. Very softly I crept close, and then banged the window down, and I think I just caught the tip of one of her fingers.'

'But it's impossible,' I cried. 'How could she be floating in the air like that? And what had she come for? Don't tell me such –'

Once more, with closer grip, the remembrance of my nightmare seized me.

'I am telling you what I saw,' said he. 'And all night long, until it was nearly day, she was fluttering outside, like some terrible bat, trying to gain admittance. Now put together various things I have told you.'

He began checking them off on his fingers.

'Number one,' he said: 'there was an outbreak of disease similar to that which this boy is suffering from at Peshawar, and her husband died of it. Number two: Mrs. Amworth protested against my moving the boy to my house. Number three: she, or the demon that inhabits her body, a creature powerful and deadly, tries to gain admittance. And add this, too: in mediaeval times there was an epidemic of vampirism here at Maxley. The vampire, so the accounts run, was found to be Elizabeth Chaston... I see you remember Mrs. Amworth's maiden name. Finally, the boy is stronger this morning. He would certainly not have been alive if he had been visited again. And what do you make of it?'

There was a long silence, during which I found this incredible horror assuming the hues of reality.

'I have something to add,' I said, 'which may or may not bear on it. You say that the – the spectre went away shortly before dawn.'

'Yes.'

I told him of my dream, and he smiled grimly.

'Yes, you did well to awake,' he said. 'That warning came from your subconscious self, which never wholly slumbers, and cried out to you of deadly danger. For two reasons, then, you must help me: one to save others, the second to save yourself.'

'What do you want me to do?' I asked.

'I want you first of all to help me in watching this boy, and ensuring that she does not come near him. Eventually I want you to help me in tracking the thing down,

134

in exposing and destroying it. It is not human: it is an incarnate fiend. What steps we shall have to take I don't yet know.'

It was now eleven of the forenoon, and presently I went across to his house for a twelve-hour vigil while he slept, to come on duty again that night, so that for the next twenty-four hours either Urcombe or myself was always in the room where the boy, now getting stronger every hour, was lying. The day following was Saturday and a morning of brilliant, pellucid weather, and already when I went across to his house to resume my duty the stream of motors down to Brighton had begun. Simultaneously I saw Urcombe with a cheerful face, which boded good news of his patient, coming out of his house, and Mrs. Amworth, with a gesture of salutation to me and a basket in her hand, walking up the broad strip of grass which bordered the road. There we all three met. I noticed (and saw that Urcombe noticed it too) that one finger of her left hand was bandaged.

'Good morning to you both,' said she. 'And I hear your patient is doing well, Mr. Urcombe. I have come to bring him a bowl of jelly, and to sit with him for an hour. He and I are great friends. I am overjoyed at his recovery.'

Urcombe paused a moment, as if making up his mind, and then shot out a pointing finger at her.

'I forbid that,' he said. 'You shall not sit with him or see him. And you know the reason as well as I do.'

I have never seen so horrible a change pass over a human face as that which now blanched hers to the colour of a grey mist. She put up her hand as if to shield herself from that pointing finger, which drew the sign of the cross in the air, and shrank back cowering on to the road. There was a wild hoot from a horn, a grinding of brakes, a shout – too late – from a passing car, and one long scream suddenly cut short. Her body rebounded from the roadway after the first wheel had gone over it, and the second followed. It lay there, quivering and twitching, and was still.

She was buried three days afterwards in the cemetery

outside Maxley, in accordance with the wishes she had told me that she had devised about her interment, and the shock which her sudden and awful death had caused to the little community began by degrees to pass off. To two people only, Urcombe and myself, the horror of it was mitigated from the first by the nature of the relief that death brought; but, naturally enough, we kept our own counsel, and no hint of what greater horror had been thus averted was ever let slip. But, oddly enough, so it seemed to me, he was still not satisfied about something in connection with her, and would give no answer to my questions on the subject. Then as the days of a tranquil mellow September and the October that followed began to drop away like the leaves of the yellowing trees, his uneasiness relaxed. But before the entry of November the seeming tranquillity broke into hurricane.

I had been dining one night at the far end of the village, and about eleven o'clock was walking home again. The moon was of an unusual brilliance, rendering all that it shone on as distinct as in some etching. I had just come opposite the house which Mrs. Amworth had occupied, where there was a board up telling that it was to let, when I heard the click of her front gate, and next moment I saw, with a sudden chill and quaking of my very spirit, that she stood there. Her profile, vividly illuminated, was turned to me, and I could not be mistaken in my identification of her. She appeared not to see me (indeed the shadow of the yew hedge in front of her garden enveloped me in its blackness) and she went swiftly across the road, and entered the gate of the house directly opposite. There I lost sight of her completely.

My breath was coming in short pants as if I had been running – and now indeed I ran, with fearful backward glances, along the hundred yards that separated me from my house and Urcombe's. It was to his that my flying steps took me, and next minute I was within.

'What have you come to tell me?' he asked. 'Or shall I guess?'

'You can't guess,' said I.

'No; it's no guess. She has come back and you have seen her. Tell me about it.'

I gave him my story.

'That's Major Pearsall's house,' he said. 'Come back with me there at once.'

'But what can we do?' I asked.

'I've no idea. That's what we have got to find out.'

A minute later, we were opposite the house. When I had passed it before, it was all dark; now lights gleamed from a couple of windows upstairs. Even as we faced it, the front door opened, and next moment Major Pearsall emerged from the gate. He saw us and stopped.

'I'm on my way to Dr. Ross,' he said quickly. 'My wife has been taken suddenly ill. She had been in bed an hour when I came upstairs, and I found her white as a ghost and utterly exhausted. She had been to sleep, it seemed – but you will excuse me.'

'One moment, Major,' said Urcombe. 'Was there any mark on her throat?'

'How did you guess that?' said he. 'There was: one of those beastly gnats must have bitten her twice there. She was streaming with blood.'

'And there's some one with her?' asked Urcombe.

'Yes, I roused her maid.'

He went off, and Urcombe turned to me. 'I know now what we have to do,' he said. 'Change your clothes, and I'll join you at your house.'

'What is it?' I asked.

'I'll tell you on our way. We're going to the cemetery.'

He carried a pick, a shovel, and a screw-driver when he rejoined me, and wore round his shoulders a long coil of rope. As we walked, he gave me the outlines of the ghastly hour that lay before us.

'What I have to tell you,' he said, 'will seem to you now too fantastic for credence, but before dawn we shall see whether it outstrips reality. By a most fortunate happening, you saw the spectre, the astral body, whatever you choose to call it, of Mrs. Amworth, going on its grisly business, and therefore, beyond doubt, the vampire spirit which abode in her during life animates her again in death. That is not exceptional – indeed, all these weeks since her death I have been expecting it. If I am right, we shall find her body undecayed and untouched by corruption.'

'But she has been dead nearly two months,' said I.

'If she had been dead two years it would still be so, if the vampire has possession of her. So remember: whatever you see done, it will be done not to her, who in the natural course would now be feeding the grasses above her grave, but to a spirit of untold evil and malignancy, which gives a phantom life to her body.'

'But what shall I see done?' said I.

'I will tell you. We know that now, at this moment, the vampire clad in her mortal semblance is out; dining out. But it must get back before dawn, and it will pass into the material form that lies in her grave. We must wait for that, and then with your help I shall dig up her body. If I am right, you will look on her as she was in life, with the full vigour of the dreadful nutriment she has received pulsing in her veins. And then, when dawn has come, and the vampire cannot leave the lair of her body, I shall strike her with this' – and he pointed to his pick – 'through the heart, and she, who comes to life again only with the animation the fiend gives her, she and her hellish partner will be dead indeed. Then we must bury her again, delivered at last.'

We had come to the cemetery, and in the brightness of the moonshine there was no difficulty in identifying her grave. It lay some twenty yards from the small chapel, in the porch of which, obscured by shadow, we concealed ourselves. From there we had a clear and open sight of the grave, and now we must wait till its infernal visitor returned home. The night was warm and windless, yet even if a freezing wind had been raging I think I should have felt nothing of it, so intense was my preoccupation as to what the night and dawn would bring. There was a bell in the turret of the chapel, that struck the quarters of the hour, and it amazed me to find how swiftly the chimes succeeded one another.

The moon had long set, but a twilight of stars shone in a clear sky, when five o'clock of the morning sounded from the turret. A few minutes more passed, and then I felt Urcombe's hand softly nudging me; and looking out in the direction of his pointing finger, I saw that the form of a woman, tall and large in build, was approaching from the right. Noiselessly, with a motion more of gliding and floating than walking, she moved across the cemetery to the grave which was the centre of our observation. She moved round it as if to be certain of its identity, and for a moment stood directly facing us. In the greyness to which now my eyes had grown accustomed, I could easily see her face, and recognise its features.

She drew her hand across her mouth as if wiping it, and broke into a chuckle of such laughter as made my hair stir on my head. Then she leaped on to the grave, holding her hands high above her head, and inch by inch disappeared into the earth. Urcombe's hand was laid on my arm, in an injunction to keep still, but now he removed it.

'Come,' he said.

With pick and shovel and rope we went to the grave. The earth was light and sandy, and soon after six struck we had delved down to the coffin lid. With his pick he loosened the earth round it, and, adjusting the rope through the handles by which it had been lowered, we tried to raise it. This was a long and laborious business, and the light had begun to herald day in the east before we had it out, and lying by the side of the grave. With his screw-driver he loosed the fastenings of the lid, and slid it aside, and standing there we looked on the face of Mrs. Amworth. The eyes, once closed in death, were open, the cheeks were flushed with colour, the red, full-lipped mouth seemed to smile.

'One blow and it is all over,' he said. 'You need not look.'

Even as he spoke he took up the pick again, and, laying

the point of it on her left breast, measured his distance. And though I knew what was coming I could not look away. . .

He grasped the pick in both hands, raised it an inch or two for the taking of his aim, and then with full force brought it down on her breast. A fountain of blood, though she had been dead so long, spouted high in the air, falling with the thud of a heavy splash over the shroud, and simultaneously from those red lips came one long, appalling cry, swelling up like some hooting siren, and dying away again. With that, instantaneous as a lightning flash, came the touch of corruption on her face, the colour of it faded to ash, the plump cheeks fell in, the mouth dropped.

'Thank God that's over,' said he, and without pause slipped the coffin lid back into its place.

Day was coming fast now, and, working like men possessed, we lowered the coffin into its place again, and shovelled the earth over it. . . The birds were busy with their earliest pipings as we went back to Maxley.

'And No Bird Sings'

The red chimneys of the house for which I was bound were visible from just outside the station at which I had alighted, and, so the chauffeur told me, the distance was not more than a mile's walk if I took the path across the fields. It ran straight till it came to the edge of that wood yonder, which belonged to my host, and above which his chimneys were visible. I should find a gate in the paling of this wood, and a track traversing it, which debouched close to his garden. So, on this adorable afternoon of early May, it seemed a waste of time to do other than walk through meadows and woods, and I set off on foot, while the motor carried my traps.

It was one of those golden days which every now and again leak out of paradise and drip to earth. Spring had been late in coming, but now it was here with a burst, and the whole world was boiling with the sap of life. Never have I seen such a wealth of spring flowers, or such vividness of green, or heard such melodious business among the birds in the hedgerows; this walk through the meadows was a jubilee of festal ecstasy. And best of all, so I promised myself, would be the passage through the wood newly fledged with milky green that lay just ahead. There was the gate, just facing me, and I passed through it into the dappled lights and shadows of the grass-grown track.

Coming out of the brilliant sunshine was like entering a dim tunnel; one had the sense of being suddenly withdrawn from the brightness of the spring into some subaqueous cavern. The tree-tops formed a green roof overhead, excluding the light to a remarkable degree. I moved in a world of shifting obscurity. Presently as the trees grew more scattered, their place was taken by a thick growth of hazels, which met over the path, and then, the ground sloping downwards, I came upon an open clearing, covered with bracken and heather, and studded with birches. But though now I walked once more beneath the luminous sky, with the sunlight pouring down, it seemed to have lost its effulgence. The brightness – was it some odd optical illusion? – was veiled as if it came from crape. Yet there was the sun still well above the tree-tops in an unclouded heaven, but for all that the light was that of a stormy winter's day, without warmth or brilliance. It was oddly silent too; I had thought that the bushes and trees would be ringing with the song of mating-birds, but listening, I could hear no note of any sort, neither the fluting of thrush or blackbird, nor the cheerful whirr of the chaffinch, nor the cooing wood-pigeon, nor the strident clamour of the jay. I paused to verify this odd silence; there was no doubt about it. It was rather eerie, rather uncanny, but I supposed the birds knew their own business best, and if they were too busy to sing it was their affair.

As I went on it struck me also that since entering the wood I had not seen a bird of any kind; and now, as I crossed the clearing, I kept my eyes alert for them, but fruitlessly, and soon I entered the further belt of thick trees which surrounded it. Most of them I noticed were beeches, growing very close to each other, and the ground beneath them was bare but for the carpet of fallen leaves, and a few thin bramble-bushes. In this curious dimness and thickness of the trees, it was impossible to see far to right or left of the path, and now, for the first time since I had left the open, I heard some sound of life. There came the rustle of leaves from not far away, and I thought to myself that a rabbit, anyhow, was moving. But somehow it lacked the staccato patter of a small animal; there was a certain stealthy heaviness about it, as if something much larger were stealing along and desirous of not being heard. I paused again to see what might emerge, but instantly the sound ceased. Simultaneously I was conscious of some faint but very foul odour reaching me, a smell choking and corrupt, yet somehow pungent, more like the odour of something alive rather than rotting. It was peculiarly sickening, and not wanting to get any closer to its source, I went on my way.

Before long I came to the edge of the wood; straight in front of me was a strip of meadow-land, and beyond an iron gate between two brick walls, through which I had a glimpse of lawn and flower-beds. To the left stood the house, and over house and garden there poured the amazing brightness of the declining afternoon.

Hugh Granger and his wife were sitting out on the lawn, with the usual pack of assorted dogs: a Welsh collie, a yellow retriever, a fox-terrier, and a Pekinese. Their protest at my intrusion gave way to the welcome of recognition, and I was admitted into the circle. There was much to say, for I had been out of England for the last three months, during which time Hugh had settled into this little estate left him by a recluse uncle, and he and Daisy had been busy during the Easter vacation with getting into the house. Certainly it was a most attractive legacy; the house, through which I was presently taken, was a delightful little Queen Anne manor, and its situation on the edge of this heather-clad Surrey ridge quite superb. We had tea in a small panelled parlour overlooking the garden, and soon the wider topics narrowed down to those of the day and the hour. I had walked, had I, asked Daisy, from the station: did I go through the wood, or follow the path outside it?

The question she thus put to me was given trivially enough; there was no hint in her voice that it mattered a straw to her which way I had come. But it was quite clearly borne in upon me that not only she but Hugh also listened intently for my reply. He had just lit a match for his cigarette, but held it unapplied till he heard my answer. Yes, I had gone through the wood; but now, though I had received some odd impressions in the wood, it seemed quite ridiculous to mention what they were. I could not soberly say that the sunshine there was of very poor quality, and that at one point in my traverse I had smelt a most iniquitous odour. I had walked through the wood; that was all I had to tell them.

I had known both my host and hostess for a tale of many years, and now, when I felt that there was nothing except purely fanciful stuff that I could volunteer about my experiences there, I noticed that they exchanged a swift glance, and could easily interpret it. Each of them signalled to the other an expression of relief; they told each other (so I construed their glance) that I, at any rate, had found nothing unusual in the wood, and they were pleased at that. But then, before any real pause had succeeded to my answer that I had gone through the wood, I remembered that strange absence of bird-song and birds, and as that seemed an innocuous observation in natural history, I thought I might as well mention it.

'One odd thing struck me,' I began (and instantly I saw the attention of both riveted again), 'I didn't see a single bird or hear one from the time I entered the wood to when I left it.'

Hugh lit his cigarette.

'I've noticed that too,' he said, 'and it's rather puzzling. The wood is certainly a bit of primeval forest, and one would have thought that hosts of birds would have nested in it from time immemorial. But, like you, I've never heard or seen one in it. And I've never seen a rabbit there either.'

'I thought I heard one this afternoon,' said I. 'Something was moving in the fallen beech leaves.'

'Did you see it?' he asked.

I recollected that I had decided that the noise was not quite the patter of a rabbit.

'No, I didn't see it,' I said, 'and perhaps it wasn't one. It sounded, I remember, more like something larger.'

Once again and unmistakably a glance passed between Hugh and his wife, and she rose.

144

'I must be off,' she said. 'Post goes out at seven, and I lazed all morning. What are you two going to do?'

'Something out of doors, please,' said I. 'I want to see the domain.'

Hugh and I accordingly strolled out again with the cohort of dogs. The domain was certainly very charming; a small lake lay beyond the garden, with a reed bed vocal with warblers, and a tufted margin into which coots and moorhens scudded at our approach. Rising from the end of that was a high heathery knoll full of rabbit holes, which the dogs nosed at with joyful expectations, and there we sat for a while overlooking the wood which covered the rest of the estate. Even now, in the blaze of the sun near to its setting, it seemed to be in shadow, though like the rest of the view it should have basked in brilliance, for not a cloud flecked the sky and the level rays enveloped the world in a crimson splendour. But the wood was grey and darkling. Hugh, also, I was aware, had been looking at it, and now, with an air of breaking into a disagreeable topic, he turned to me.

'Tell me,' he said, 'does anything strike you about that wood?'

'Yes: it seems to lie in shadow.'

He frowned.

'But it can't, you know,' he said. 'Where does the shadow come from? Not from outside, for sky and land are on fire.'

'From inside, then?' I asked.

He was silent a moment.

'There's something queer about it,' he said at length. 'There's something there, and I don't know what it is. Daisy feels it too; she won't ever go into the wood, and it appears that birds won't either. Is it just the fact that, for some unexplained reason, there are no birds in it that has set all our imaginations at work?'

I jumped up.

'Oh, it's all rubbish,' I said. 'Let's go through it now and find a bird. I bet you I find a bird.'

'Sixpence for every bird you see,' said Hugh.

We went down the hillside and walked round the wood till we came to the gate where I had entered that afternoon. I held it open after I had gone in for the dogs to follow. But there they stood, a yard or so away, and none of them moved.

'Come on, dogs,' I said, and Fifi, the fox-terrier, came a step nearer and then, with a little whine, retreated again.

'They always do that,' said Hugh; 'not one of them will set foot inside the wood. Look!'

He whistled and called, he cajoled and scolded, but it was no use. There the dogs remained, with little apologetic grins and signallings of tails, but quite determined not to come.

'But why?' I asked.

'Same reason as the birds, I suppose, whatever that happens to be. There's Fifi, for instance, the sweetest-tempered little lady; once I tried to pick her up and carry her in, and she snapped at me. They'll have nothing to do with the wood; they'll trot round outside it and go home.'

We left them there and, in the sunset light which was now beginning to fade, began the passage. Usually the sense of eeriness disappears if one has a companion, but now to me, even with Hugh walking by my side, the place seemed even more uncanny than it had done that afternoon, and a sense of intolerable uneasiness, that grew into a sort of waking nightmare, obsessed me. I had thought before that the silence and loneliness of it had played tricks with my nerves; but with Hugh here it could not be that, and indeed I felt that it was not any such notion that lay at the root of this fear, but rather the conviction that there was some presence lurking there, invisible as yet, but permeating the gathered gloom. I could not form the slightest idea of what it might be, or whether it was material or ghostly; all I could diagnose of it from my own sensations was that it was evil and antique.

As we came to the open ground in the middle of the wood, Hugh stopped, and though the evening was cool I noticed that he mopped his forehead.

'Pretty nasty,' he said. 'No wonder the dogs don't like it. How do you feel about it?'

Before I could answer he shot out his hand, pointing to the belt of trees that lay beyond.

'What's that?' he said in whisper.

I followed his finger, and for one half-second thought I saw against the black of the wood some vague flicker, grey or faintly luminous. It waved as if it had been the head and forepart of some huge snake rearing itself, but it instantly disappeared, and my glimpse had been so momentary that I could not trust my impression.

'It's gone,' said Hugh, still looking in the direction he had pointed; and as we stood there I heard again what I had heard that afternoon, a rustle among the fallen beech-leaves. But there was no wind nor breath of breeze astir.

He turned to me.

'What on earth was it?' he said. 'It looked like some enormous slug standing up. Did you see it?'

'I'm not sure whether I did or not,' I said. 'I think I just caught sight of what you saw.'

'But what was it?' he said again. 'Was it a real material creature, or was it –'

'Something ghostly, do you mean?' I asked.

'Something half-way between the two,' he said. 'I'll tell you what I mean afterwards, when we've got out of this place.'

The thing, whatever it was, had vanished among the trees to the left of where our path lay, and in silence we walked across the open till we came to where it entered tunnel-like among the trees. Frankly I hated and feared the thought of plunging into that darkness with the knowledge that not so far off there was something the nature of which I could not ever so faintly conjecture, but which, I now made no doubt, was that which filled the wood with some nameless terror. Was it material, was it ghostly, or was it (and now some inkling of what Hugh meant began to form itself into my mind) some being

147

that lay on the borderland between the two? Of all the sinister possibilities that appeared the most terrifying.

As we entered the trees again I perceived that reek, alive and yet corrupt, which I had smelt before, but now it was far more potent, and we hurried on, choking with the odour that I now guessed to be not the putrescence of decay, but the living substance of that which crawled and reared itself in the darkness of the wood where no bird would shelter. Somewhere among those trees lurked the reptilian thing that defied and yet compelled credence.

It was a blessed relief to get out of that dim tunnel into the wholesome air of the open and the clear light of evening. Within doors, when we returned, windows were curtained and lamps lit. There was a hint of frost, and Hugh put a match to the fire in his room, where the dogs, still a little apologetic, hailed us with thumpings of drowsy tails.

'And now we've got to talk,' said he, 'and lay our plans, for whatever it is that is in the wood we've got to make an end of it. And, if you want to know what I think it is, I'll tell you.'

'Go ahead,' said I.

'You may laugh at me, if you like,' he said, 'but I believe it's an elemental. That's what I meant when I said it was a being half-way between the material and the ghostly. I never caught a glimpse of it till this afternoon; I only felt there was something horrible there. But now I've seen it, and it's like what spiritualists and that sort of folk describe as an elemental. A huge phosphorescent slug is what they tell us of it, which at will can surround itself with darkness.'

Somehow, now safe within doors, in the cheerful light and warmth of the room, the suggestion appeared merely grotesque. Out there in the darkness of that uncomfortable wood something within me had quaked, and I was prepared to believe any horror, but now common sense revolted.

'But you don't mean to tell me you believe in such

rubbish?' I said. 'You might as well say it was a unicorn. What is an elemental, anyway? Who has ever seen one except the people who listen to raps in the darkness and say they are made by their aunts?'

'What is it, then?' he asked.

'I should think it is chiefly our own nerves,' I said. 'I frankly acknowledge I got the creeps when I went through the wood first, and I got them much worse when I went through it with you. But it was just nerves; we are frightening ourselves and each other.'

'And are the dogs frightening themselves and each other?' he asked. 'And the birds?'

That was rather harder to answer; in fact, I gave it up.

Hugh continued.

'Well, just for the moment we'll suppose that something else, not ourselves, frightened us and the dogs and the birds,' he said, 'and that we did see something like a huge phosphorescent slug. I won't call it an elemental, if you object to that; I'll call it It. There's another thing, too, which the existence of It would explain.'

'What's that?' I asked.

'Well, It is supposed to be some incarnation of evil; it is a corporeal form of the devil. It is not only spiritual, it is material to this extent – that it can be seen, bodily in form, and heard, and, as you noticed, smelt, and, God forbid, handled. It has to be kept alive by nourishment. And that explains perhaps why, every day since I have been here, I've found on that knoll we went up some half-dozen dead rabbits.'

'Stoats and weasels,' said I.

'No, not stoats and weasels. Stoats kill their prey and eat it. These rabbits have not been eaten; they've been drunk.'

'What on earth do you mean?' I asked.

'I examined several of them. There was just a small hole in their throats, and they were drained of blood. Just skin and bones, and a sort of grey mash of fibre, like – like the fibre of an orange which has been sucked. Also there was a horrible smell lingering on them. And was the thing you had a glimpse of like a stoat or a weasel?'

There came a rattle at the handle of the door.

'Not a word to Daisy,' said Hugh as she entered.

'I heard you come in,' she said. 'Where did you go?'

'All round the place,' said I, 'and came back through the wood. It is odd; not a bird did we see; but that is partly accounted for because it was dark.'

I saw her eyes search Hugh's, but she found no communication there. I guessed that he was planning some attack on It next day, and he did not wish her to know that anything was afoot.

'The wood's unpopular,' he said. 'Birds won't go there, dogs won't go there, and Daisy won't go there. I'm bound to say I share the feeling too, but having braved its terrors in the dark I've broken the spell.'

'All quiet, was it?' asked she.

'Quiet wasn't the word for it. The smallest pin could have been heard dropping half a mile off.'

We talked over our plans that night after she had gone up to bed. Hugh's story about the sucked rabbits was rather horrible, and though there was no certain connection between those empty rinds of animals and what we had seen, there seemed a certain reasonableness about it. But anything, as he pointed out, which could feed like that was clearly not without its material side – ghosts did not have dinner, and if it was material it was vulnerable.

Our plans, therefore, were very simple; we were going to tramp through the wood, as one walks up patridges in a field of turnips, each with a shotgun and a supply of cartridges. I cannot say that I looked forward to the expedition, for I hated the thought of getting into closer quarters with that mysterious denizen of the woods; but there was a certain excitement about it, sufficient to keep me awake a long time, and when I got to sleep to cause very vivid and awful dreams.

The morning failed to fulfil the promise of the clear sunset; the sky was lowering and cloudy and a fine rain

150

was falling. Daisy had shopping errands which took her into the little town, and as soon as she had set off we started on our business. The yellow retriever, mad with joy at the sight of guns, came bounding with us across the garden, but on our entering the wood he slunk back home again.

The wood was roughly circular in shape, with a diameter perhaps of half a mile. In the centre, as I have said, there was an open clearing about a quarter of a mile across, which was thus surrounded by a belt of thick trees and copse a couple of hundred yards in breadth. Our plan was first to walk together up the path which led through the wood, with all possible stealth, hoping to hear some movement on the part of what we had come to seek. Failing that, we had settled to tramp through the wood at the distance of some fifty yards from each other in a circular track; two or three of these circuits would cover the whole ground pretty thoroughly. Of the nature of our quarry, whether it would try to steal away from us, or possibly attack, we had no idea; it seemed, however, yesterday to have avoided us.

Rain had been falling steadily for an hour when we entered the wood; it hissed a little in the tree-tops overhead; but so thick was the cover that the ground below was still not more than damp. It was a dark morning outside; here you would say that the sun had already set and that night was falling. Very quietly we moved up the grassy path, where our footfalls were noiseless, and once we caught a whiff of that odour of live corruption; but though we stayed and listened not a sound of anything stirred except the sibilant rain over our heads. We went across the clearing and through to the far gate, and still there was no sign.

'We'll be getting into the trees, then,' said Hugh. 'We had better start where we got that whiff of it.'

We went back to the place, which was towards the middle of the encompassing trees. The odour still lingered on the windless air.

'Go on about fifty yards,' he said, 'and then we'll go in.

If either of us comes on the track of it we'll shout to each other.'

I walked on down the path till I had gone the right distance, signalled to him, and we stepped in among the trees.

I have never known the sensation of such utter loneliness. I knew that Hugh was walking parallel with me, only fifty yards away, and if I hung on my step I could faintly hear his tread among the beech-leaves. But I felt as if I was quite sundered in this dim place from all companionship of man; the only live thing that lurked here was that monstrous mysterious creature of evil. So thick were the trees that I could not see more than a dozen yards in any direction; all places outside the wood seemed infinitely remote, and infinitely remote also everything that had occurred to me in normal human life. I had been whisked out of all wholesome experiences into this antique and evil place. The rain had ceased, it whispered no longer in the tree-tops, testifying that there did exist a world and a sky outside, and only a few drops from above pattered on the beech-leaves.

Suddenly I heard the report of Hugh's gun, followed by his shouting voice.

'I've missed it,' he shouted; 'it's coming your direction.'

I heard him running towards me, the beech-leaves rustling, and no doubt his footsteps drowned a stealthier noise that was close to me. All that happened now, until once more I heard the report of Hugh's gun, happened, I suppose, in less than a minute. If it had taken much longer I do not imagine I should be telling it today.

I stood there then, having heard Hugh's shout, with my gun cocked, and ready to put to my shoulder, and I listened to his running footsteps. But still I saw nothing to shoot at and heard nothing. Then between two beech trees, quite close to me, I saw what I can only describe as a ball of darkness. It rolled very swiftly towards me over the few yards that separated me from it, and then, too late, I heard the dead beech-leaves rustling below it.

Just before it reached me, my brain realized what it was, or what it might be, but before I could raise my gun to shoot at that nothingness it was upon me. My gun was twitched out of my hand, and I was enveloped in this blackness, which was the very essence of corruption. It knocked me off my feet, and I sprawled flat on my back, and upon me, as I lay there, I felt the weight of this invisible assailant.

I groped wildly with my hands and they clutched something cold and slimy and hairy. They slipped off it, and next moment there was laid across my shoulder and neck something which felt like an india-rubber tube. The end of it fastened on to my neck like a snake, and I felt the skin rise beneath it. Again, with clutching hands, I tried to tear that obscene strength away from me, and as I struggled with it I heard Hugh's footsteps close to me through this layer of darkness that hid everything.

My mouth was free, and I shouted at him.

'Here, here!' I yelled. 'Close to you, where it is darkest.'

I felt his hands on mine, and that added strength detached from my neck that sucker that pulled at it. The coil that lay heavy on my legs and chest writhed and struggled and relaxed. Whatever it was that our four hands held, slipped out of them, and I saw Hugh standing close to me. A yard or two off, vanishing among the beech trunks, was that blackness which had poured over me. Hugh put up his gun, and with his second barrel fired at it.

The blackness dispersed, and there, wriggling and twisting like a huge worm lay what we had come to find. It was alive still, and I picked up my gun which lay by my side and fired two more barrels into it. The writhings dwindled into mere shudderings and shakings, and then it lay still.

With Hugh's help I got to my feet, and we both reloaded before going nearer. On the ground there lay a monstrous thing, half slug, half worm. There was no head to it; it ended in a blunt point with an orifice. In colour it was grey, covered with sparse black hairs; its length, I suppose, was some four feet, its thickness at the broadest part was that of a man's thigh, tapering towards each end. It was shattered by shot at its middle. There were stray pellets which had hit it elsewhere, and from the holes they had made there oozed not blood, but some grey viscous matter.

As we stood there some swift process of disintegration and decay began. It lost outline, it melted, it liquified, and in a minute more we were looking at a mass of stained and coagulated beech-leaves. Again and quickly that liquor of corruption faded, and there lay at our feet no trace of what had been there. The overpowering odour passed away, and there came from the ground just the sweet savour of wet earth in springtime, and from above the glint of a sunbeam piercing the clouds. Then a sudden pattering among the dead leaves sent my heart into my mouth again, and I cocked my gun. But it was only Hugh's yellow retriever who had joined us.

We looked at each other.

'You're not hurt?' he said.

I held my chin up.

'Not a bit,' I said. 'The skin's not broken, is it?'

'No; only a round red mark. My God, what was it? What happened?'

'Your turn first,' said I. 'Begin at the beginning.'

'I came upon it quite suddenly,' he said. 'It was lying coiled like a sleeping dog behind a big beech. Before I could fire, it slithered off in the direction where I knew you were. I got a snapshot at it among the trees, but I must have missed, for I heard it rustling away. I shouted to you and ran after it. There was a circle of absolute darkness on the ground, and your voice came from the middle of it. I couldn't see you at all, but I clutched at the blackness and my hands met yours. They met something else too.'

We got back to the house and had put the guns away before Daisy came home from her shopping. We had also scrubbed and brushed and washed. She came into the smoking-room.

'You lazy folk,' she said. 'It has cleared up, and why are you still indoors? Let's go out at once.'

I got up.

'Hugh has told me you've got a dislike of the wood,' I said, 'and it's a lovely wood. Come and see; he and I will walk on each side of you and hold your hands. The dogs shall protect you as well.'

'But not one of them will go a yard into the wood,' said she.

'Oh yes, they will. At least, we'll try them. You must promise to come if they do.'

Hugh whistled them up, and down we went to the gate. They sat panting for it to be opened, and scuttled into the thickets in pursuit of interesting smells.

'And who says there are no birds in it?' said Daisy. 'Look at that robin! Why, there are two of them. Evidently house-hunting.'

Mr. Tilly's Séance

Mr. Tilly had only the briefest moment for reflection, when, as he slipped and fell on the greasy wood pavement at Hyde Park Corner, which he was crossing at a smart trot, he saw the huge traction-engine with its grooved ponderous wheels towering high above him.

'Oh, dear! oh, dear!' he said petulantly, 'it will certainly crush me quite flat, and I shan't be able to be at Mrs. Cumberbatch's séance! Most provoking! A-ow!'

The words were hardly out of his mouth, when the first half of his horrid anticipations was thoroughly fulfilled. The heavy wheels passed over him from head to foot and flattened him completely out. Then the driver (too late) reversed his engine and passed over him again, and finally lost his head, whistled loudly and stopped. The policeman on duty at the corner turned quite faint at the sight of the catastrophe, but presently recovered sufficiently to hold up the traffic, and ran to see what on earth could be done. It was all so much 'up' with Mr. Tilly that the only thing possible was to get the hysterical engine-driver to move clear. Then the ambulance from the hospital was sent for, and Mr. Tilly's remains, detached with great difficulty from the road (so firmly had they been pressed into it), were reverently carried away into the mortuary. . .

Mr. Tilly during this had experienced one moment's excruciating pain, resembling the severest neuralgia as his head was ground beneath the wheel, but almost before he realised it, the pain was past, and he found himself, still rather dazed, floating or standing (he did

not know which) in the middle of the road. There had
been no break in his consciousness; he perfectly recollected slipping, and wondered how he had managed to
save himself. He saw the arrested traffic, the policeman
with white wan face making suggestions to the gibbering
engine-driver, and he received the very puzzling impression that the traction engine was all mixed up with him.
He had a sensation of red-hot coals and boiling water
and rivets all around him, but yet no feeling of scalding
or burning or confinement. He was, on the contrary,
extremely comfortable, and had the most pleasant consciousness of buoyancy and freedom. Then the engine
puffed and the wheels went round, and immediately, to
his immense surprise, he perceived his own crushed
remains, flat as a biscuit, lying on the roadway. He identified them for certain by his clothes, which he had put
on for the first time that morning, and one patent leather
boot which had escaped demolition.

'But what on earth has happened?' he said. 'Here am
I, and yet that poor pressed flower of arms and legs is
me – or rather I – also. And how terribly upset the
driver looks. Why, I do believe that I've been run over! It
did hurt for a moment, now I come to think of it. . . My
good man, where are you shoving to? Don't you see me?'

He addressed these two questions to the policeman,
who appeared to walk right through him. But the man
took no notice, and calmly came out on the other side: it
was quite evident that he did not see him, or apprehend
him in any way.

Mr. Tilly was still feeling rather at sea amid these
unusual occurrences, and there began to steal into his
mind a glimpse of the fact which was so obvious to the
crowd which formed an interested but respectful ring
round his body. Men stood with bared heads; women
screamed and looked away and looked back again.

'I really believe I'm dead,' said he. 'That's the only
hypothesis which will cover the facts. But I must feel
more certain of it before I do anything. Ah! Here they
come with the ambulance to look at me. I must be

terribly hurt, and yet I don't feel hurt. I should feel hurt surely if I was hurt. I must be dead.'

Certainly it seemed the only thing for him to be, but he was far from realising it yet. A lane had been made through the crowd for the stretcher-bearers, and he found himself wincing when they began to detach him from the road.

'Oh, do take care!' he said. 'That's the sciatic nerve protruding there surely, isn't it? A-ow! No, it didn't hurt after all. My new clothes, too: I put them on today for the first time. What bad luck! Now you're holding my leg upside down. Of course all my money comes out of my trouser pocket. And there's my ticket for the séance; I must have that: I may use it after all.'

He tweaked it out of the fingers of the man who had picked it up, and laughed to see the expression of amazement on his face as the card suddenly vanished. That gave him something fresh to think about, and he pondered for a moment over some touch of association set up by it.

'I have it,' he thought. 'It is clear that the moment I came into connection with that card, it became invisible. I'm invisible myself (of course to the grosser sense), and everything I hold becomes invisible. Most interesting! That accounts for the sudden appearances of small objects at a séance. The spirit has been holding them, and as long as he holds them they are invisible. Then he lets go, and there's the flower or the spirit-photograph on the table. It accounts, too, for the sudden disappearances of such objects. The spirit has taken them, though the scoffers say that the medium has secreted them about his person. It is true that when searched he sometimes appears to have done so; but, after all, that may be a joke on the part of the spirit. Now, what am I to do with myself. . . . Let me see, there's the clock. It's just half-past ten. All this has happened in a few minutes, for it was a quarter past when I left my house. Half-past ten now: what does that mean exactly? I used to know what it meant, but now it seems nonsense. Ten what? Hours, is it? What's an hour?'

This was very puzzling. He felt that he used to know what an hour and a minute meant, but the perception of that, naturally enough, had ceased with his emergence from time and space into eternity. The conception of time was like some memory which, refusing to record itself on the consciousness, lies perdu in some dark corner of the brain, laughing at the efforts of the owner to ferret it out. While he still interrogated his mind over this lapsed perception, he found that space as well as time had similarly grown obsolete for him, for he caught sight of his friend Miss Ida Soulsby, who he knew was to be present at the séance for which he was bound, hurrying with bird-like steps down the pavement opposite. Forgetting for the moment that he was a disembodied spirit, he made the effort of will which in his past human existence would have set his legs in pursuit of her, and found that the effort of will alone was enough to place him at her side.

'My dear Miss Soulsby,' he said, 'I was on my way to Mrs. Cumberbatch's house when I was knocked down and killed. It was far from unpleasant, a moment's headache –'

So far his natural volubility had carried him before he recollected that he was invisible and inaudible to those still closed in by the muddy vesture of decay, and stopped short. But though it was clear that what he said was inaudible to Miss Soulsby's rather large intelligent-looking ears, it seemed that some consciousness of his presence was conveyed to her finer sense, for she looked suddenly startled, a flush rose to her face, and he heard her murmur, 'Very odd. I wonder why I received so vivid an impression of dear Teddy.'

That gave Mr. Tilly a pleasant shock. He had long admired the lady, and here she was alluding to him in her supposed privacy as 'dear Teddy.' That was followed by a momentary regret that he had been killed: he would have liked to have been possessed of this information before, and have pursued the primrose path of dalliance down which it seemed to lead. (His intentions, of course, would, as always, have been strictly honourable: the path of dalliance would have conducted them both, if she consented, to the altar, where the primroses would have been exchanged for orange blossom.) But his regret was quite short-lived; though the altar seemed inaccessible, the primrose path might still be open, for many of the spiritualistic circle in which he lived were on most affectionate terms with their spiritual guides and friends who, like himself, had passed over. From a human point of view these innocent and even elevating flirtations had always seemed to him rather bloodless; but now, looking on them from the far side, he saw how charming they were, for they gave him the sense of still having a place and an identity in the world he had just quitted. He pressed Miss Ida's hand (or rather put himself into the spiritual condition of so doing), and could vaguely feel that it had some hint of warmth and solidity about it. This was gratifying, for it showed that though he had passed out of the material plane, he could still be in touch with it. Still more gratifying was it to observe that a pleased and secret smile overspread Miss Ida's fine features as he gave this token of his presence: perhaps she only smiled at her own thoughts, but in any case it was he who had inspired them. Encouraged by this, he indulged in a slightly more intimate token of affection, and permitted himself a respectful salute, and saw that he had gone too far, for she said to herself, 'Hush, hush!' and quickened her pace, as if to leave these amorous thoughts behind.

He felt that he was beginning to adjust himself to the new conditions in which he would now live, or, at any rate, was getting some sort of inkling as to what they were. Time existed no more for him, nor yet did space, since the wish to be at Miss Ida's side had instantly transported him there, and with a view to testing this further he wished himself back in his flat. As swiftly as the change of scene in a cinematograph show he found himself there, and perceived that the news of his death must have reached his servants, for his cook and parlour-maid, with excited faces, were talking over the event.

'Poor little gentleman,' said his cook. 'It seems a shame, it does. He never hurt a fly, and to think of one of those great engines laying him out flat. I hope they'll take him to the cemetery from the hospital: I never could bear a corpse in the house.'

The great strapping parlour-maid tossed her head.

'Well, I'm not sure that it doesn't serve him right,' she observed. 'Always messing about with spirits he was, and the knockings and concertinas was awful sometimes when I've been laying out supper in the dining-room. Now perhaps he'll come himself and visit the rest of the loonies. But I'm sorry all the same. A less troublesome little gentleman never stepped. Always pleasant, too, and wages paid to the day.'

These regretful comments and encomiums were something of a shock to Mr. Tilly. He had imagined that his excellent servants regarded him with a respectful affection, as befitted some sort of demigod, and the rôle of the poor little gentleman was not at all to his mind. This revelation of their true estimate of him, although what they thought of him could no longer have the smallest significance, irritated him profoundly.

'I never heard such impertinence,' he said (so he thought) quite out loud, and still intensely earthbound, was astonished to see that they had no perception whatever of his presence. He raised his voice, replete with extreme irony, and addressed his cook.

'You may reserve your criticism on my character for your saucepans,' he said. 'They will no doubt appreciate them. As regards the arrangements for my funeral, I have already provided for them in my will, and do not propose to consult your convenience. At present –'

'Lor'!' said Mrs. Inglis, 'I declare I can almost hear his voice, poor little fellow. Husky it was, as if he would do better by clearing his throat. I suppose I'd best be making a black bow to my cap. His lawyers and what not will be here presently.'

161

Mr. Tilly had no sympathy with this suggestion. He was immensely conscious of being quite alive, and the idea of his servants behaving as if he were dead, especially after the way in which they had spoken about him, was very vexing. He wanted to give them some striking evidence of his presence and his activity, and he banged his hand angrily on the dining-room table, from which the breakfast equipage had not yet been cleared. Three tremendous blows he gave it, and was rejoiced to see that his parlour-maid looked startled. Mrs. Inglis's face remained perfectly placid.

'Why, if I didn't hear a sort of rapping sound,' said Miss Talton. 'Where did it come from?'

'Nonsense! You've the jumps, dear,' said Mrs. Inglis, picking up a remaining rasher of bacon on a fork, and putting it into her capacious mouth.

Mr. Tilly was delighted at making any impression at all on either of these impercipient females.

'Talton!' he called at the top of his voice.

'Why, what's that?' said Talton. 'Almost hear his voice, do you say, Mrs. Inglis? I declare I did hear his voice then.'

'A pack o' nonsense, dear,' said Mrs. Inglis placidly. 'That's a prime bit of bacon, and there's a good cut of it left. Why, you're all of a tremble! It's your imagination.'

Suddenly it struck Mr. Tilly that he might be employing himself much better than, with such extreme exertion, managing to convey so slight a hint of his presence to his parlour-maid, and that the séance at the house of the medium, Mrs. Cumberbatch, would afford him much easier opportunities of getting through to the earth-plane again. He gave a couple more thumps to the table and, wishing himself at Mrs. Cumberbatch's, nearly a mile away, scarcely heard the faint scream of Talton at the sound of his blows before he found himself in West Norfolk Street.

He knew the house well, and went straight to the drawing-room, which was the scene of the séances he had so often and so eagerly attended. Mrs. Cumberbatch, who had a long spoon-shaped face, had already pulled down the blinds, leaving the room in total darkness except for the glimmer of the night-light which, under a shade of ruby-glass, stood on the chimney-piece in front of the coloured photograph of Cardinal Newman. Round the table were seated Miss Ida Soulsby, Mr. and Mrs. Meriott (who paid their guineas at least twice a week in order to consult their spiritual guide Abibel and received mysterious advice about their indigestion and investments), and Sir John Plaice, who was much interested in learning the details of his previous incarnation as a Chaldean priest, completed the circle. His guide, who revealed to him his sacerdotal career, was playfully called Mespot. Naturally many other spirits visited them, for Miss Soulsby had no less than three guides in her spiritual household, Sapphire, Semiramis, and Sweet William, while Napoleon and Plato were not infrequent guests. Cardinal Newman, too, was a great favourite, and they encouraged his presence by the singing in unison of 'Lead, kindly Light': he could hardly ever resist that. . .

Mr. Tilly observed with pleasure that there was a vacant seat by the table which no doubt had been placed there for him. As he entered, Mrs. Cumberbatch peered at her watch.

'Eleven o'clock already,' she said, 'and Mr. Tilly is not here yet. I wonder what can have kept him. What shall we do, dear friends? Abibel gets very impatient sometimes if we keep him waiting.'

Mr. and Mrs. Meriott were getting impatient too, for he terribly wanted to ask about Mexican oils, and she had a very vexing heartburn.

'And Mespot doesn't like waiting either,' said Sir John, jealous for the prestige of his protector, 'not to mention Sweet William.'

Miss Soulsby gave a little silvery laugh.

'Oh, but my Sweet William's so good and kind,' she said; 'besides, I have a feeling, quite a psychic feeling, Mrs. Cumberbatch, that Mr. Tilly is very close.'

'So I am,' said Mr. Tilly.

'Indeed, as I walked here,' continued Miss Soulsby, 'I felt that Mr. Tilly was somewhere quite close to me. Dear me, what's that?'

Mr. Tilly was so delighted at being sensed, that he could not resist giving a tremendous rap on the table, in a sort of pleased applause. Mrs. Cumberbatch heard it too.

'I'm sure that's Abibel come to tell us that he is ready,' she said. 'I know Abibel's knock. A little patience, Abibel. Let's give Mr. Tilly three minutes more and then begin. Perhaps, if we put up the blinds, Abibel will understand we haven't begun.'

This was done, and Miss Soulsby glided to the window, in order to make known Mr. Tilly's approach, for he always came along the opposite pavement and crossed over by the little island in the river of traffic. There was evidently some lately published news, for the readers of early editions were busy, and she caught sight of one of the advertisement-boards bearing in large letters the announcement of a terrible accident at Hyde Park Corner. She drew in her breath with a hissing sound and turned way, unwilling to have her psychic tranquillity upset by the intrusion of painful incidents. But Mr. Tilly, who had followed her to the window and saw what she had seen, could hardly restrain a spiritual whoop of exultation.

'Why, it's all about me!' he said. 'Such large letters, too. Very gratifying. Subsequent editions will no doubt contain my name.'

He gave another loud rap to call attention to himself, and Mrs. Cumberbatch, sitting down in her antique chair which had once belonged to Madame Blavatsky, again heard.

'Well, if that isn't Abibel again,' she said. 'Be quiet, naughty. Perhaps we had better begin.'

She recited the usual invocation to guides and angels, and leaned back in her chair. Presently she began to twitch and mutter, and shortly afterwards with several loud snorts, relapsed into cataleptic immobility. There

164

she lay, stiff as a poker, a port of call, so to speak, for any voyaging intelligence. With pleased anticipation Mr. Tilly awaited their coming. How gratifying if Napoleon, with whom he had so often talked, recognised him and said, 'Pleased to see you, Mr. Tilly. I perceive you have joined us . . .' The room was dark except for the ruby-shaded lamp in front of Cardinal Newman, but to Mr. Tilly's emancipated perceptions the withdrawal of mere material light made no difference, and he idly wondered why it was generally supposed that disembodied spirits like himself produced their most powerful efforts in the dark. He could not imagine the reason for that, and, what puzzled him still more, there was not to his spiritual perception any sign of those colleagues of his (for so he might now call them) who usually attended Mrs. Cumberbatch's séances in such gratifying numbers. Though she had been moaning and muttering a long time now, Mr. Tilly was in no way conscious of the presence of Abibel and Sweet William and Sapphire and Napoleon. 'They ought to be here by now,' he said to himself.

But while he still wondered at their absence, he saw to his amazed disgust that the medium's hand, now covered with a black glove, and thus invisible to ordinary human vision in the darkness, was groping about the table and clearly searching for the megaphone-trumpet which lay there. He found that he could read her mind with the same ease, though far less satisfaction, as he had read Miss Ida's half an hour ago, and knew that she was intending to apply the trumpet to her own mouth and pretend to be Abibel or Semiramis or somebody, whereas she affirmed that she never touched the trumpet herself. Much shocked at this, he snatched up the trumpet himself, and observed that she was not in trance at all, for she opened her sharp black eyes, which always reminded him of buttons covered with American cloth, and gave a great gasp.

'Why, Mr. Tilly!' she said. 'On the spiritual plane too!'

The rest of the circle was now singing 'Lead, kindly

Light' in order to encourage Cardinal Newman, and this conversation was conducted under cover of the hoarse crooning voices. But Mr. Tilly had the feeling that though Mrs. Cumberbatch saw and heard him as clearly as he saw her, he was quite imperceptible to the others.

'Yes, I've been killed,' he said, 'and I want to get into touch with the material world. That's why I came here. But I want to get into touch with other spirits too, and surely Abibel or Mespot ought to be here by this time.'

He received no answer, and her eyes fell before his like those of a detected charlatan. A terrible suspicion invaded his mind.

'What? Are you a fraud, Mrs. Cumberbatch?' he asked. 'Oh, for shame! Think of all the guineas I have paid you.'

'You shall have them all back,' said Mrs. Cumberbatch. 'But don't tell of me.'

She began to whimper, and he remembered that she often made that sort of sniffling noise when Abibel was taking possession of her.

'That usually means that Abibel is coming,' he said, with withering sarcasm. 'Come along, Abibel: we're waiting.'

'Give me the trumpet,' whispered the miserable medium. 'Oh, please give me the trumpet!'

'I shall do nothing of the kind,' said Mr. Tilly indignantly. 'I would sooner use it myself.'

She gave a sob of relief.

'Oh, do, Mr. Tilly!' she said. 'What a wonderful idea! It will be most interesting to everybody to hear you talk just after you've been killed and before they know. It would be the making of me! And I'm not a fraud, at least not altogether. I do have spiritual perceptions sometimes; spirits do communicate through me. And when they won't come through it's a dreadful temptation to a poor woman to – to supplement them by human agency. And how could I be seeing and hearing you now, and be able to talk to you – so pleasantly, I'm sure – if I hadn't super-normal powers? You've been killed, so you assure

166

me, and yet I can see and hear you quite plainly. Where did it happen, may I ask, if it's not a painful subject?'

'Hyde Park Corner, half an hour ago,' said Mr. Tilly. 'No, it only hurt for a moment, thanks. But about your other suggestion –'

While the third verse of 'Lead, kindly Light' was going on, Mr. Tilly applied his mind to this difficult situation. It was quite true that if Mrs. Cumberbatch had no power of communication with the unseen she could not possibly have seen him. But she evidently had, and had heard him too, for their conversation had certainly been conducted on the spirit plane, with perfect lucidity. Naturally, now that he was a genuine spirit, he did not want to be mixed up in fraudulent mediumship, for he felt that such a thing would seriously compromise him on the other side, where, probably, it was widely known that Mrs. Cumberbatch was a person to be avoided. But, on the other hand, having so soon found a medium through whom he could communicate with his friends, it was hard to take a high moral view, and say that he would have nothing whatever to do with her.

'I don't know if I trust you,' he said. 'I shouldn't have a moment's peace if I thought that you would be sending all sorts of bogus messages from me to the circle, which I wasn't responsible for at all. You've done it with Abibel and Mespot. How can I know that when I don't choose to communicate through you, you won't make up all sorts of piffle on your own account?'

She positively squirmed in her chair.

'Oh, I'll turn over a new leaf,' she said. 'I will leave all that sort of thing behind me. And I am a medium. Look at me! Aren't I more real to you than any of the others? Don't I belong to your plane in a way that none of the others do? I may be occasionally fraudulent, and I can no more get Napoleon here than I can fly, but I'm genuine as well. Oh, Mr. Tilly, be indulgent to us poor human creatures! It isn't so long since you were one of us yourself.'

The mention of Napoleon, with the information that

Mrs. Cumberbatch had never been controlled by that great creature, wounded Mr. Tilly again. Often in this darkened room he had held long colloquies with him, and Napoleon had given him most interesting details of his life on St. Helena, which, so Mr. Tilly had found, were often borne out by Lord Rosebery's pleasant volume *The Last Phase*. But now the whole thing wore a more sinister aspect, and suspicion as solid as certainty bumped against his mind.

'Confess!' he said. 'Where did you get all that Napoleon talk from? You told us you had never read Lord Rosebery's book, and allowed us to look through your library to see that it wasn't there. Be honest for once, Mrs. Cumberbatch.'

She suppressed a sob.

'I will,' she said. 'The book was there all the time. I put it into an old cover called "Elegant Extracts. . ." But I'm not wholly a fraud. We're talking together, you a spirit and I a mortal female. They can't hear us talk. But only look at me, and you'll see. . . You can talk to them through me, if you'll only be so kind. I don't often get in touch with a genuine spirit like yourself.'

Mr. Tilly glanced at the other sitters and then back to the medium, who, to keep the others interested, was making weird gurgling noises like an undervitalised syphon. Certainly she was far clearer to him than were the others, and her argument that she was able to see and hear him had great weight. And then a new and curious perception came to him. Her mind seemed spread out before him like a pool of slightly muddy water, and he figured himself as standing on a head-board above it, perfectly able, if he chose, to immerse himself in it. The objection to so doing was its muddiness, its materiality; the reason for so doing was that he felt that then he would be able to be heard by the others, possibly to be seen by them, certainly to come into touch with them. As it was, the loudest bangs on the table were only faintly perceptible.

'I'm beginning to understand,' he said.

'Oh, Mr. Tilly! Just jump in like a kind good spirit,' she said. 'Make your own test-conditions. Put your hand over my mouth to make sure that I'm not speaking, and keep hold of the trumpet.'

'And you'll promise not to cheat any more?' he asked.

'Never!'

He made up his mind.

'All right then,' he said, and, so to speak, dived into her mind.

He experienced the oddest sensation. It was like passing out of some fine, sunny air into the stuffiest of unventilated rooms. Space and time closed over him again: his head swam, his eyes were heavy. Then, with the trumpet in one hand, he laid the other firmly over her mouth. Looking round, he saw that the room seemed almost completely dark, but that the outline of the figures sitting round the table had vastly gained in solidity.

'Here I am!' he said briskly.

Miss Soulsby gave a startled exclamation.

'That's Mr. Tilly's voice!' she whispered.

'Why, of course it is,' said Mr. Tilly. 'I've just passed over at Hyde Park Corner under a traction engine. . .'

He felt the dead weight of the medium's mind, her conventional conceptions, her mild, unreal piety pressing in on him from all sides, stifling and confusing him. Whatever he said had to pass through muddy water. . .

'There's a wonderful feeling of joy and lightness,' he said. 'I can't tell you of the sunshine and happiness. We're all very busy and active, helping others. And it's such a pleasure, dear friends, to be able to get into touch with you all again. Death is not death: it is the gate of life. . .'

He broke off suddenly.

'Oh, I can't stand this,' he said to the medium. 'You make me talk such twaddle. Do get your stupid mind out of the way. Can't we do anything in which you won't interfere with me so much?'

'Can you give us some spirit lights round the room?' suggested Mrs. Cumberbatch in a sleepy voice. 'You have come through beautifully, Mr. Tilly. It's too dear of you!'

'You're sure you haven't arranged some phosphorescent patches already!' asked Mr. Tilly suspiciously.

'Yes, there are one or two near the chimney-piece,' said Mrs. Cumberbatch, 'but none anywhere else. Dear Mr. Tilly, I swear there are not. Just give us a nice star with long rays on the ceiling!'

Mr. Tilly was the most good-natured of men, always willing to help an unattractive female in distress, and whispering to her, 'I shall require the phosphorescent patches to be given into my hands after the séance,' he proceeded, by the mere effort of his imagination, to light a beautiful big star with red and violet rays on the ceiling. Of course it was not nearly as brilliant as his own conception of it, for its light had to pass through the opacity of the medium's mind, but it was still a most striking object, and elicited gasps of applause from the company. To enhance the effect of it he intoned a few very pretty lines about a star by Adelaide Anne Procter, whose poems had always seemed to him to emanate from the top-most peak of Parnassus.

'Oh, thank you, Mr. Tilly!' whispered the medium. 'It was lovely! Would a photograph of it be permitted on some future occasion, if you would be so kind as to reproduce it again?'

'Oh, I don't know,' said Mr. Tilly irritably. 'I want to get out. I'm very hot and uncomfortable. And it's all so cheap.'

'Cheap?' ejaculated Mrs. Cumberbatch.

'Why, there's not a medium in London whose future wouldn't be made by a real genuine star like that, say, twice a week.'

'But I wasn't run over in order that I might make the fortune of mediums,' said Mr. Tilly. 'I want to go: it's all rather degrading. And I want to see something of my new world. I don't know what it's like yet.'

'Oh, but, Mr. Tilly,' said she. 'You told us lovely things about it, how busy and happy you were.'

'No, I didn't. It was you who said that, at least it was you who put it into my head.'

Even as he wished, he found himself emerging from the dull waters of Mrs. Cumberbatch's mind.

'There's the whole new world waiting for me.' he said. 'I must go and see it. I'll come back and tell you, for it must be full of marvellous revelations . . .'

Suddenly he felt the hopelessness of it. There was that thick fluid of materiality to pierce, and, as it dripped off him again, he began to see that nothing of that fine rare quality of life which he had just begun to experience, could penetrate these opacities. That was why, perhaps, all that thus came across from the spirit-world, was so stupid, so banal. They, of whom he now was one, could tap on furniture, could light stars, could abound with commonplace, could read as in a book the mind of medium or sitters, but nothing more. They had to pass into the region of gross perceptions, in order to be seen of blind eyes and be heard of deaf ears.

Mrs. Cumberbatch stirred.

'The power is failing,' she said, in a deep voice, which Mr. Tilly felt was meant to imitate his own. 'I must leave you now, dear friends –'

He felt much exasperated.

'The power isn't failing,' he shouted. 'It wasn't I who said that.'

But he had emerged too far, and perceived that nobody except the medium heard him.

'Oh, don't be vexed, Mr. Tilly,' she said. 'That's only a formula. But you're leaving us very soon. Not time for just one materialisation? They are more convincing than anything to most inquirers.'

'Not one,' said he. 'You don't understand how stifling it is even to speak through you and make stars. But I'll come back as soon as I find there's anything new that I can get through to you. What's the use of my repeating all that stale stuff about being busy and happy? They've been told that often enough already. Besides, I have got to see if it's true. Good-bye: don't cheat any more.'

171

He dropped his card of admittance to the séance on the table and heard murmurs of excitement as he floated off.

The news of the wonderful star, and the presence of Mr. Tilly at the séance within half an hour of his death, which at the time was unknown to any of the sitters, spread swiftly through spiritualistic circles. The Psychical Research Society sent investigators to take independent evidence from all those present, but were inclined to attribute the occurrence to a subtle mixture of thought-transference and unconscious visual impression, when they heard that Miss Soulsby had, a few minutes previously, seen a news-board in the street outside recording the accident at Hyde Park Corner. This explanation was rather elaborate, for it postulated that Miss Soulsby, thinking of Mr. Tilly's non-arrival, had combined that with the accident at Hyde Park Corner, and had probably (though unconsciously) seen the name of the victim on another news-board and had transferred the whole by telepathy to the mind of the medium. As for the star on the ceiling, though they could not account for it, they certainly found remains of phosphorescent paint on the panels of the wall above the chimney-piece, and came to the conclusion that the star had been produced by some similar contrivance. So they rejected the whole thing, which was a pity, since, for once, the phenomena were absolutely genuine.

Miss Soulsby continued to be a constant attendant at Mrs. Cumberbatch's séances, but never experienced the presence of Mr. Tilly again. On that the reader may put any interpretation he pleases. It looks to me somewhat as if he had found something else to do.

Home, Sweet Home

It was pleasant to get out of the baked train into an atmosphere that tingled with the subtle vitality of the sea, and though nothing could be duller than the general prospect of flat fields and dusty hedgerows, and the long white road that lay straight as a ruled line between them, I surmised that when it had climbed that long upward slope there would be a new horizon altogether, grey and liquid. Eyethorpe Junction was the name of the station, and though that appeared a strange misnomer, for nothing seemed to join anything, I presently perceived a weedy, derelict branch-line, and a loquacious porter explained that the line to Eyethorpe had long been untraversed by railway traffic. There had once been high hopes that it would develop into a popular watering-place. But the public had preferred its established favourites.

The affairs that led to my disembarkation on this broiling August day at a jointless junction had been conducted in my sister Margery's most characterstic style. Her husband, Walter Mostyn, the eminent nerve specialist, had been threatened during July with a breakdown owing to overstrain in his work, and, in obedience to the ironical ordinance of, 'Physician, heal thyself', had prescribed for himself a complete rest. His idea of resting his mind was not, as is the usual practice of those on holiday, to overtire his body, but to get away to some place where there was no temptation to do anything of the kind. There must be no golf-links, or he would want to play golf, and he would prefer his retreat to be by the sea, because the very fact of being in a boat at all made him feel seasick, and he hated bathing. A rest-cure in a nursing-home would be horrible to him, and he thought that if Margery could find some deadly seaside resort, where there was nothing that could tempt him into activity of mind or body, that would do just as well. He wanted to be a beast of the field, and recover his nervous force by sheer vegetation.

Margery, with these instructions to guide her, had thereupon set off, and scoured the coasts of Kent and Sussex, discovering on the second day of her wild career this amazing and unique Eyethorpe. There was a house there to let, which she at once saw was just what she was looking for, and with that most unfeminine instinct of hers of knowing that she had got what she wanted, and not making any further search, she went straight to the house-agent at Hastings and took 'The Firs' for a month as from tomorrow. She drove back to London that evening, informed Walter what she had done, sent down her servants next morning, and took down her husband the same evening. A fortnight later she wrote to me that the cure was progressing splendidly, and that he, emerging from his languor, was getting rather cross and argumentative, which she took to be the sign of returning vitality. He was excessively bored with her, and wanted some man in the house, and had grudgingly said that I would 'do'. So would I come soon for a couple of weeks? In fact, I must, and she would expect me on Thursday. It was Thursday now, and, in consequence, I was driving up the straight, white road from Eyethorpe Junction.

We topped the rise, and there, as I had expected, was a new horizon. The sea sprang up to eye-level, the ground declined steeply over a stretch of open downland dotted with furze bushes to a line of low cliffs that fringed the shore. Along the edge of these was a huddle of red-roofed cottages, among which rose a conspicuous church-tower, and presently we jolted over the level-crossing of the line from Eyethorpe Junction, which the public had scorned. On the left was a small abandoned station with weed-grown platform, and a board, much defaced by the weather, bearing the inscription, 'Eyethorpe and Coltham.' The name Coltham stirred some remote vibration in my mind; I felt that I had heard the name before, but could not recall the reason for its faint familiarity. The road forked, the left-hand branch of it leading up the village street; the other, which we took, had a signpost with the information that Coltham was one mile distant. We traversed, I should have guessed, two or three furlongs, and there, close at hand, separated from the highway by a field, through which led a grass-grown drive, stood a big mellow-walled farmhouse. A clump of rather fine Scotch firs at one end of it was sufficient indication of its identity.

I was taken into and through a broad passage (you might call it a hall) which intersected the house, and from which a dignified staircase led to the upper storey. At its further end a glass-paned door opened into the garden. But there was no one here, and the servant supposed that they had gone strolling, perhaps down to the beach. The afternoon was still very hot, and, deciding to wait for them rather than vaguely pursue, I admired the luck that had attended Margery's search for a tranquil sanatorium. Not a house was visible; the clean emptiness of the downland was laid like a broad green riband east and west, and in front, through a V-shaped gap, gleamed the sea. A one-storeyed wing, evidently a later addition, sprouted from the west end of the house; this cast just now a very welcome shade over the square space, laid with old paving-stones, where long, low chairs and the tea-table stood. The added wing, it is scarcely necessary to mention, was of far more antique design than the house, and, looking in through its open door which gave on to this flagged space, I found a very big, pleasant room, with rafters in the ceiling, and small diamond-shaped panes in the mullioned windows. The oak floor was bare but for a few rugs, and at the far end, near an open fireplace, stood a grand piano. The lid was open, and I read there, to my great surprise, the world-famous name of Barenstein. That, too, was just like Margery, to take a remote farm-house and find a Barenstein grand waiting for her very gifted fingers, and this fine spacious room. How cool it was in here, too – more than cool, it was positively cold; and at that moment, hearing familiar voices outside, I stepped out again on to the paved space from which I had entered.

Certainly Walter did not look as if a fortnight ago he had been on the edge of nervous breakdown. His face was bronzed and ruddy, he strode along with a firm step, and was talking in that loud, confident voice that had so often brought comfort to sufferers.

'But I tell you, darling,' he was saying, 'that it isn't that our senses occasionally deceive us, they habitually deceive us. Ah, there he is. Welcome, my dear Ted. You have come to a place beyond the limits of the civilized world, and it has done me a world of good already. Distractions, things that interest us are what starves the nerves. Boredom, there's the panacea for nerves. I've never been so bored in my life, and I'm a new man.'

Margery laughed.

'I wonder how often you've told your patients exactly the opposite,' she said. (Ted, there's a magnificent Barenstein here; did you ever know such luck?) But isn't it so, Walter? You always say that there's hope even for people who take an interest in postage-stamps. Never mind. You hate being consistent, and I won't press it. What about the senses habitually deceiving us?'

'Obvious. Your eyes, for instance. If you see a house half a mile off your eyes tell you it is about a quarter of an inch in height. If another train passes you as yours is standing in a station, they will tell you that you are moving in the opposite direction. Smell and taste are the same; if you shut your eyes you have no idea whether your cigarette is alight. Your sense of warmth and cold too; if you put your hand on a piece of very cold metal, it gives you the sensation of burning. I'm just as bad as

176

you, perhaps worse, for my senses tell me that that room in there is bitterly cold today, but the thermometer says it is sixty-five degrees. I was suffering from some subjective disturbance, that was all, and my imbecile senses told me it was cold. There was the thermometer saying it was warm. The senses, as I tell you, are habitually deceptive. Liars!'

There was all his usual vehemence in this, and, so I thought, a little more. He was clearly upset at this divergence of view between his senses and the thermometer.

'But I'm on the side of your senses,' I said. 'I went in there just now, and I swear it was more than chilly.'

He threw a quick glance over to Margery before he answered.

'More liars, then!' he said. 'Another instance of the deceptiveness of the senses.'

He said this with the air of bringing the discussion to an end; our talk became desultory and trivial, and before long Margery closed it by saying that, whatever anybody else did, she intended to have a dip in the sea before dinner. Presently she appeared again, with sandals and a dressing-gown over her bathing-suit, for there was but this strip of empty downland between the garden and the steep short descent on the beach. She insisted on my accompanying her as far as that V-shaped gap, and her very casual manner made me sure that she had some communication to make. It came as soon as we were out of earshot.

'Walter's ever so much better, as you can see for yourself,' she said, 'and till today he has been lying fallow with the most excellent results. But now that awful activity of his mind has begun to work again, and twenty times since lunch he has alluded to that strange feeling of chill in the big room in the wing. He keeps on saying that it's subjective, but you and I know him, and that means he thinks there's something queer about it. And you felt it too, apparently.'

'I thought I did, but then I had just come into it from the broiling air outside. But hadn't he felt it before?'

'No, for the simple reason that he hadn't been into the room before,' said she. 'When we came here, and, indeed, till this morning, it was locked and shuttered. The gardener, who has been caretaker here, told me that the owner had stored things in it, and that it was to be left closed. Till this morning Walter did not seem to mind whether it was shut or open, but today he told the gardener that it was all nonsense to keep the biggest room in the house shut up, and demanded the key. Denton, that's his name, talked about disobeying his owner, but Walter insisted, and he produced the key. There was nothing stored there, and I drove over to the house-agent's at Hastings that morning to ask if there was any such order. None at all. What does it mean?'

'Nothing,' said I, 'except that Denton was a lazy brute, and didn't want the bother of airing and dusting the room before you came, and of putting it to rights again after you'd gone. Perhaps also the owner didn't want to prohibit your playing the great Barenstein, but hoped you wouldn't. Also this accounts for the fact that Walter and I found the room very chilly after it had been shut up for so long. When was the house last occupied, by the way?'

'I don't know. It had been unlet for some time, so the agent told me, and I didn't care in the least about its history provided I got it for Walter now.'

Her jolly brown eyes made a complete circuit round my head, instead of looking at me straight when she answered.

'Don't be so foolish, Margery,' I said, 'but look straight at me. You told me just now that Walter thought there was something queer about the room. What do you think?'

Her eyes rested on mine.

'I think there's something queer about the house,' she said. 'I find myself looking up suddenly from a book or a paper to see who is in the room. And I think Walter does the same. But he – he thinks he hears something, and then finds he hasn't, just as I think I see something, and

178

find I haven't. I cock an eye, he cocks an ear. But don't say a word to him. He hates the idea of anything you can't account for by the ordinary functions of the senses, which, he says, habitually deceive you. But since that room was opened he's been arguing with himself.'

'Oh, put the stopper in,' said I. 'Do you remember the gurgle of the hot-water pipes in the nursery thirty years ago, and how you knew it was the groan of a murdered woman? You frightened me out of my wits then, but I'm too old to be frightened now. You haven't seen anything, and he hasn't heard anything; eye hath not seen nor ear heard. Don't imagine things; half the trouble in the world comes from imagining. Have a nice bathe, and wash it all off.'

For a moment, as she looked at me, I saw somewhere behind her eyes a sense of uneasiness, but it vanished.

'I shan't wash off my gladness that you've joined us,' she said, and ran off down the steep little path to the beach.

I strolled back through the garden thinking how unlike Margery it was to be within the grip of vague apprehension like this, or to imagine that there was anything 'queer' about the house, for, in spite of the famous episode of the gurgling pipes, she was singularly free from imagined alarms. Even more unusual, if she was right about him, was it that Walter should be affected in the same sort of way. Margery certainly showed her good sense in demanding that her odd apprehensions should be kept apart from his, and not be given the meeting-ground of discussion. But she had noticed, or imagined, his, and I was soon to learn that he was not blind to hers.

Walter had gone up to his room when I got back, and I went into the lately opened sitting-room, where I found that my books and papers had been disposed on a big table, which was thus clearly consecrated to my use. I was engaged on a memoir which it interested me to write, though I had grave doubts about its interesting anybody else to read. The piano stood a little beyond my table, with the keyboard towards me; between it and me, on my left, was the open window looking on to the garden. The room still seemed chilly, but I speedily forgot that and, indeed, everything else but my delightful task.

How long I had been at work I had no idea, when suddenly – even as I turned a page to carry on the note I had begun – I became vividly aware of my surroundings again and knew with absolute conviction that I was not alone. I glanced up and saw that there was a man outside the window looking at the piano. For a second or two he gazed fixedly at it, and then, turning his head, perceived me at my table. He had not, I imagined, observed that there was anyone here, for he touched his hat, and would have gone away, but I called to him.

'Do you want anything?' I asked. 'Denton, is it?'

'Yes, sir. I – I was only just looking to see if the room was all right,' and immediately he withdrew. But, oddly enough, I felt that it was not Denton's presence at the window that gave me the sense that there was someone here; it had nothing to do with Denton. And why, I asked myself, as the man walked briskly off, why on earth should Denton look in to see if the room was all right? It was the piano that riveted him; did he want to be sure that all was well with the piano?

I tried to attach myself to my work again, but the connection would no longer hold. There was still that sense of some presence in the room, which came between me and my page. Time and again I held my mind down to its task, but it slipped away, and presently at its bidding my eyes left the paper and scrutinized the room. Certainly there was nothing behind me, nor at my side, but I found myself – was it Denton's example which had infected me? – looking at the piano as if what I sought was invisibly there. Its japanned case, darkly, like black glass, reflected my table, the white keys gleamed in their ebony setting. And then I saw that some of them were moving – a group, three or four at a time, and now a succession of single notes sank and recovered as if under the pressure of fingers.

I cannot hope to describe the curiosity and the dismay with which this filled my mind. I gazed fascinated at this inexplicable movement, but at the same time my mind cried out in horror at the invisible cause of it. Then, as suddenly as it had begun, this fantastic spectacle ceased, but the presence was still there. Then from outside there came the sound of steps. Walter entered.

'Margery here?' he asked. 'No? Was it you playing, then?'

'Deceptive senses,' I said. 'I haven't touched the piano.'

He looked at me a moment, puzzled.

'But I would swear I heard the piano,' he said.

Instantly I made up my mind not to tell Walter what I had seen, and already, so fantastic was it, I was beginning to doubt if I had seen anything. Yet deep in my mind remained that intense curiosity, and deeper yet some unreasoning terror.

The evening passed quite normally; Walter bewailed the hideous necessity of going in to Hastings next day to have his hair cut, and even the darker fate of having the vicar of Eyethorpe to dinner.

It was still early when we went up to bed and, conscious of an overwhelming somnolence, I instantly fell asleep. I woke, staring wide awake, with the answer to the question which had slightly worried me yesterday, as to why the name of the neighbouring Coltham was remotely familiar to me, clear in my mind. There had occurred there, about a year before, a very brutal murder, which still remained among the unsolved mysteries of criminal history. An elderly spinster lady, living with her spinster sister at some house there, had been found strangled on the floor of her sitting-room. It was supposed that robbery was the motive for the crime, but the murderer seemed to have heard some stir in the house, and left a cashbox containing thirty or forty pounds in the drawer he had just opened. I could remember no further details, but I thought I would stroll over to Coltham next morning and, with that appetite for the horrible which lurks in us all, find out which the house was.

The two went off to Hastings next morning and, in pursuance of my plan, I strolled up the road to Coltham. It was a melancholy little bunch of cottages perched on the edge of the downs, and I had just decided that a rather stricken-looking house, with a board up to say it was to let was a suitable site for the murder, when I saw Denton coming down the little street.

'Which was the house where that murder took place last year, Denton?' I asked him.

He stared at me a moment, and I saw his throat-apple jerk up and down. Then he pointed to the house I had picked out.

'That was the one, sir,' he said.

'And what was the name of the old lady?' I asked.

'Miss Ellershaw,' said he, and rather abruptly, much in the manner in which he had retreated from the window last night, he turned and left me. Rather pleased with myself for my perspicacity I strolled homewards again.

Margery and Walter, he shorn and self-respecting again, came back about one o'clock, and Margery announced her determination of writing overdue letters till the really intolerable heat of the day had declined.

'Hopeless arrears,' she said, 'bills and bills, and the rent of the house for the next fortnight, which ought to have been paid two days ago. But I'll send it straight to our landlord – or is it landlady? – instead of the agent; that will save a day.'

The clear burning of the sun had given place to an extreme sultriness; the sky was overcast with clouds which all afternoon thickened to a still density portending thunder. Margery retired to the piano-room to perform her overdues, Walter fell asleep and, leaving him on the paved space, I joined Margery for coolness. She jumped up as I entered.

'I was dying to be interrupted,' she said, 'because I long to see what's in that cupboard by the piano. I've

182

muddled up your papers, Ted, I'm afraid. Unmuddle them again while I have an interval.'

She had, indeed muddled my papers up. Half-finished letters, and addressed envelopes, and bills were mixed up with my notes. As I disentangled them, I came across a cheque she had drawn. It was made out to Miss Ellershaw. There was also a half-sheet on which Mrs. Mostyn 'much regretted not having sent cheque for a fortnight's rent sooner'.

. . . So Miss Ellershaw was owner of 'The Firs', and two Miss Ellershaws, one of whom had been murdered, lived together. Had they lived in that house at Coltham, where Denton had told me the murder was committed, or had they –

Margery interrupted these rather disquieting thoughts.

'What a disappointment!' she said. 'Empty cupboard, all but one leaf of a book of English songs, and that's "Home, Sweet Home"! You may laugh at it, but it's a wonderful melody. I must just play it, and then I shall get on with my jobs.'

The window close to which I sat commanded a view of the garden. Out of it, I could see Denton plucking sweet-peas. As the notes of the old-fashioned tune streamed out through the open window, I saw him drop his basket and stop his ears. Simultaneously I knew that there was some presence here in the room not Margery's nor mine.

She played two lines and stopped. She turned round and faced me.

'What is there here?' she said. 'And what –'

Walter whom I had left asleep, looked in at the door.

'Ah, it's you playing,' he said. 'That's all right.'

By strange interweavings of emotion, that common consciousness between us all of the presence of something that came not from among the humming wheels of life but from the grey mists that encompassed it, grew thicker in texture. There was some presence in the room – not mine, nor Margery's, nor Walter's – here now, though invisible, and somehow gathering strength

183

from our recognition of its existence. In our different ways we all contributed to it in that moment of absolute and appalling silence.

Some sort of babble broke it. I babbled of the disorder of my papers, Margery babbled apology and promised to put them straight, if she might be allowed to deal with them. Some sort of crisis passed. I can explain it no better than that.

As evening drew on the clouds gathered even more thickly. The sea was leaden, the air dead, and when, about half past ten that night, Mr. Bird, who had proved himself a charming guest, said good night, and I went with him to the door, we looked out on to a pit of impenetrable darkness. I saw the opportunity I wanted, and assuring him that I should really like a stroll to get such air as there was, insisted on fetching a lantern and lighting him back as far as the village. I then went straight to the point.

'There was a fearful tragedy in Coltham last year,' I said. 'Denton pointed me out the house where the murder was committed.'

Mr. Bird stopped dead.

'Denton pointed you out the house?' he asked.

'Yes, but perhaps he was wrong,' said I. 'In fact, Mr. Bird, I should be very much obliged to you if you would tell me whether I am not right in thinking that the scene of the tragedy was "The Firs". My sister and brother-in-law know nothing about it, and I hope they won't. But I learned accidentally today that she pays the rent to Miss Ellershaw, which I think is the name. And I hazard the guess that the precise scene was the room outside which we sat tonight.'

He did not reply for a moment.

'I can't deny what you suggest,' he said, 'and my mere refusal to reply would do no good. You are quite right. Denton's telling you, by the way, that the scene was in the village, itself, is quite intelligible, for Miss Ellershaw, who does not intend to live in the house again, wants to let it, and if it was known that the murder took place there it would be prejudicial; Denton knows that. And in turn I want to ask you something. Why do you guess that particular room?'

I hesitated as to whether I should tell him about the crop of strange impressions which were growing up round it, but decided not to.

'There are queer things,' I said. 'My sister was told, for instance, that there were orders that the room should not be used. Denton told her that.'

'I can understand that too,' he said. 'The room has terrible memories for those who were in the house at the time. Any more queer things?'

'None that I can think of at present,' I said. 'But I will wish you good night here, as the rest of your way is clear.'

I retraced my steps, and found that Walter and Margery had both gone upstairs. There was a lamp still burning on the paved space where we had sat after dinner, and I went out there, disinclined to go to bed, with my nerves all strung up by the stimulus of the approaching storm. All feeling of fear about what was creeping out into the light concerning this room, and what might, I felt, suddenly burst forth with some blaze of revelation, was gone, and I was conscious only of intense curiosity, as I summed up in my mind what I believed, owing to these strange hints and signals out of the mists, had actually taken place. I figured Miss Ellershaw as having been sitting at the piano when the strangling cord was slipped round her neck; I figured her as having been playing 'Home, Sweet Home'; I figured Denton as having heard her. Then there would have been silence, but for some few gasps, some quivering convulsions, like the shaking of leaves in a tree, and then the discovery, perhaps by Denton, of the crime which was still unexplained. Certainly that afternoon the fragment of the tune which Margery had played gave him a sudden shock of horror. . .

The night was absolutely still; neither from inside the house nor from outside came the slightest stir of life, and the silence rang in my ears. And then from the room close at hand I heard, faint but distinct, the tinkle of the piano. A couple of bars of the familiar tune were played, and some voice, thin and quavering, began to sing the air. Curiosity, violent and irresistible, drowned all other feeling in my mind, and taking up the lamp, I opened the door of the room and entered. It burned brightly, and by its light, which gleamed on the keys of the piano, I could see that the room was empty. But the tune went on, softly played and faintly sung, and looking more closely at the piano I saw that once more the keys were moving. At that the sense of fear which till then had lain coiled and quiet in my mind began to stir. But I felt absolutely powerless to go; fear, now in swift invasion of my mind, held me where I was.

Something began to form in the air by the piano, a mist, a greyness. Then in a second it solidified, and there sat with her back to me the figure of a little whitehaired woman. Then the singing stopped, her arms shot up with quivering, clutching fingers; she struggled, she turned, and I saw her face, swollen and purple, with gasping mouth and protruding eyes. Her head lolled and nodded; her body swayed backwards and forwards, and she slid off the music-stool to the ground. At that moment a blaze of light poured through the unsheltered windows, and I saw pressed against the pane, and seemingly quite unaware of my presence, Denton's white and staring countenance. His eyes were fixed on the piano. Simultaneously with the light came an appalling crack of thunder. The storm had burst.

For that moment Denton and I faced each other; the next he had gone, and I heard his feet running down the garden path. I had seen enough too, and with my mind submerged in terror I stumbled from the room. As I paused for a moment outside, another flash flooded the gross darkness, and I saw him scudding across the down to the white edge of the cliffs. Then down came the rain, solid and hissing; my lamp was extinguished, and by the flare of the lightning, standing still between the flashes, I groped my way up to bed.

186

All night the prodigious storm streamed and rattled, but about dawn, as I lay still sleepless, and quaking with the prodigy of horror I had looked upon, it passed away, and I dozed and then slept deeply, and woke to find the morning tranquil and fresh and sunny. All the intolerable depression of the day before, not physical alone, seemed to me to have vanished, the house was wholesome as the breeze from the sea, and so, too, when, not without making a strong call on my courage, I entered it, I found the room where last night I had witnessed that ghastly pageantry. In no way could I account for that inward conviction, even less could I question it; all I knew was that some tragic stain had passed from it.

I was down before either of the others, and strolling through the garden as I waited for them, I saw advancing along the paved walk the figure of the vicar.

'A very dreadful thing has happened,' he said. 'Denton's body was found half an hour ago by some fishermen at the foot of the cliff down there. His head was smashed in; he must have fallen sheer on to the rocks.'

Now the reader may put any interpretation he pleases on the events which I have here briefly recorded and on certain facts which may or may not seem to him to be connected with them, namely, that Miss Ellershaw, the elder of the two sisters who lived together at 'The Firs', was found strangled on the floor by the piano in the room which juts out into the garden; that her sister not many minutes before her body was found had heard her singing 'Home, Sweet Home' to her own accompaniment, and that the author of the murder had never been found. It is a fact also that late on the night of which I have been speaking I saw Denton looking in through the window of that room, and shortly afterwards running across the strip of downland towards the cliff, at the bottom of which next morning his body was found.

But beyond that point we deal not with material facts, but with impressions. Three separate people fancied that there was something strange about the room; one of them found herself expecting to see some unaccountable appearance; one of them thought there was a peculiar chill in the room, and also that he heard the piano being played when nobody had touched it; the third, as I have related, believed that he both saw and heard things in that room which he cannot explain. Whether Denton shared that experience we cannot tell, nor can we tell for certain whether it was a pure accident that he fell over the cliff, or whether he had seen and heard something which drove him to make an end of himself.

It remains only to add that Walter and Margery agreed that some strange sense, which they had both felt as of an unexplained presence in that room, had passed away from it during the night on which Denton met his death. Walter was inclined to attribute our original impressions to some purely subjective disturbance of the nerves caused by the approach of that great storm. Not then, but later, when, thoroughly restored, he had gone back to his work, I told him and Margery what I had seen that night and what, perhaps, Denton had seen.

The Sanctuary

Francis Elton was spending a fortnight's holiday one January in the Engadine, when he received the telegram announcing the death of his uncle, Horace Elton, and his own succession to a very agreeable property: the telegram added that the cremation of the remains was to take place that day, and it was therefore impossible for him to attend, and there was no reason for his hurrying home.

In the solicitor's letter that reached him two days later Mr. Angus gave fuller details: the estate consisted of sound securities to the value of about £80,000, and there was as well Mr. Elton's property just outside the small country town of Wedderburn in Hampshire. This consisted of a charming house and garden and a small acreage of building land. Everything had been left to Francis, but the estate was saddled with a charge of £500 a year in favour of the Reverend Owen Barton.

Francis knew very little of his uncle, who for a long time had been much of a recluse; indeed he had not seen him for nearly four years, when he had spent three days with him at this house at Wedderburn. He had vague but slightly uneasy memories of those days, and now on his journey home, as he lay in his berth in the rocking train, his brain, rummaging drowsily among its buried recollections, began to disinter these. There was nothing very definite about them: they consisted of suggestions and side-lights and oblique impressions, things observed, so to speak, out of the corner of his eye, and never examined in direct focus.

He had only been a boy at the time, having just left school, and it was in the summer holidays, hot sultry weather of August, he remembered, that he had paid him this visit, before he went to a crammer's in London to learn French and German.

There was his Uncle Horace, first of all, and of him he had vivid images. A grey-haired man of middle age, large and extremely stout with a cushion of jowl overlapping his collar, but in spite of this obesity, he was nimble and light in movement, and with a merry blue eye that was equally alert, and seemed constantly to be watching him. Then there were two women there, a mother and daughter, and, as he recalled them, their names occurred to him, too: they were Mrs. Isabel Ray and Judith. Judith, he supposed, was a year or two older than himself, and on the first evening had taken him for a stroll in the garden after dinner. She had treated him at once as if they were old friends, had walked with her arm round his neck, had asked him many questions about his school, and whether there was any girl he was keen on. All very friendly, but rather embarrassing. When they came in from the garden, certainly some questioning signal had passed between the mother and the girl, and Judith had shrugged her shoulders in reply.

Then the mother had taken him in hand; she made him sit with her in the window-seat, and talked to him about the crammer's he was going to: he would have much more liberty, she supposed, than he had at school, and he looked the sort of boy who would make good use of it. She tried him in French and found he could speak it very decently, and told him that she had a book which she had just finished, which she would lend him. It was by that exquisite stylist Huysman and was called *Là-Bas*. She would not tell him what it was about: he must find out for himself. All the time those narrow grey eyes were fixed on him, and when she went to bed, she took him up to her room to give him the book. Judith was there, too: she had read it, and laughed at the memory of it. 'Read it, darling Francis,' she said, 'and then go to sleep immediately,

190

and you will tell me tomorrow what you dreamed about, unless it would shock me.'

The vibrating rhythm of the train made Francis drowsy, but his mind went on disinterring these fragments. There had been another man there, his uncle's secretary, a young fellow, perhaps twenty-five years old, clean-shaven and slim and with just the same gaiety about him as the rest. Everyone treated him with an odd sort of deference, hard to define but easy to perceive. He sat next Francis at dinner that night, and kept filling his wine-glass for him whether he wanted it or not, and next morning he had come into his room in pyjamas, sat on his bed, looked at him with odd questioning eyes, had asked him how he got on with his book, and then taken him to bathe in the swimming-pool behind the belt of trees at the bottom of the garden... No bathing-costume, he said, was necessary, and they raced up and down the pool and lay basking in the sun afterwards. Then from the belt of trees emerged Judith and her mother, and Francis, much embarrassed, draped himself in a towel. How they all laughed at his delightful prudery... And what was the man's name? Why, of course, it was Owen Barton, the same who had been mentioned in Mr. Angus's letter as the Reverend Owen Barton. But why 'reverend,' Francis wondered. Perhaps he had taken orders afterwards.

All day they had flattered him for his good looks, and his swimming and his lawn-tennis: he had never been made so much of, and all their eyes were on him, inviting and beckoning. In the afternoon his uncle had claimed him: he must come upstairs with him and see some of his treasures. He took him into his bedroom, and opened a great wardrobe full of magnificent vestments. There were gold-embroidered copes, there were stoles and chasubles with panels of needle work enriched with pearls, and jewelled gloves, and the use of them was to make glorious the priests who offered prayer and praise to the Lord of all things visible and invisible. Then he brought out a scarlet cassock of thick shimmering silk,

191

and a cotta of finest muslin trimmed round the neck and the lower hem with Irish lace of the sixteenth century. These were for the vesting of the boy who served at the Mass, and Francis, at his uncle's bidding, stripped off his coat and arrayed himself, and took off his shoes and put on the noiseless scarlet slippers which were called sanctuary shoes. Then Owen Barton entered, and Francis heard him whisper to his uncle, 'God! What a server!' and then he put on one of those gorgeous copes and told him to kneel.

The boy had been utterly bewildered. What were they playing at, he wondered. Was it charades of some sort? There was Barton, his face solemn and eager, raising his left hand as if in blessing: more astonishing was his uncle, licking his lips and swallowing in his throat, as if his mouth watered. There was something below all this dressing-up, which meant nothing to him, but had some hidden significance for the two men. It was uncomfortable: It disquieted him, and he wouldn't kneel, but disrobed himself of the cotta and cassock. 'I don't know what it's about,' he said: and again, as between Judith and her mother, he saw question and answer pass between them. Somehow his lack of interest had disappointed them, but he felt no interest at all: just a vague repulsion.

The diversions of the day were renewed: there was more tennis and bathing, but they all seemed to have lost the edge of their keenness about him. That evening he was dressed rather earlier than the others, and was sitting in a deep window-seat of the drawing-room, reading the book Mrs. Ray had lent him. He was not getting on with it; it was puzzling, and the French was difficult: he thought he would return it to her, saying that it was beyond him. Just then she and his uncle entered: they were talking together, and did not perceive him.

'No, it's no use, Isabel,' said his uncle. 'He's got no curiosity, no leanings: it would only disgust him and put him off. That's not the way to win souls. Owen thinks so, too. And he's too innocent: why when I was his age . . .

Why, there's Francis. What's the boy reading? Ah, I see! What do you make of it?'

Francis closed the book.

'I give it up,' he said. 'I can't get on with it.'

Mrs. Ray laughed.

'I agree, too, Horace,' she said. 'But what a pity!'

Somehow Francis got the impression, he remembered, that they had been talking about him. But, if so, *what* was it for which he had no leanings?

He had gone to bed rather early that night, encouraged, he thought, to do so, leaving the rest at a game of Bridge. He soon slept, but awoke, thinking he heard the sound of chanting. Then came three strokes of a bell, and a pause and three more. He was too sleepy to care what it was about.

Such, as the train rushed through the night, was the sum of his impressions about his visit to the man whose substance he had now inherited, subject to the charge of £500 a year to the Reverend Owen Barton. He was astonished to find how vivid and how vaguely disquieting were these memories, which now for four years had been buried in his mind. As he sank into sounder sleep they faded again, and he thought little more of them in the morning.

He went to see Mr. Angus as soon as he got to London. Certain securities would have to be sold in order to pay death duties, but the administration of the estate was a simple matter. Francis wanted to know more about his benefactor, but Mr. Angus could tell him very little. Horace Elton had, for some years, lived an extremely sequestered life down at Wedderburn, and his only intimate associate was his secretary, this Mr. Owen Barton. Beyond him, there were two ladies who used often to stay with him for long periods. Their names? – and he paused, searching his memory.

'Mrs. Isabel Ray and her daughter Judith?' suggested Francis.

'Exactly. They were often there. And, not infrequently,

a number of people used to arrive rather late in the evening, eleven o'clock or even later, stay for an hour or two and then be off again. A little mysterious. Only a week or so before Mr. Elton died, there had been quite a congregation of them, fifteen or twenty, I believe.'

Francis was silent for a moment: it was as if pieces of jig-saw puzzle were calling for their due location. But their shapes were too fantastic. . .

'And about my uncle's illness and death,' he said. 'The cremation of his body was on the same day as that on which he died; at least so I understood from your telegram.'

'Yes: that was so,' said Mr. Angus.

'But why? I should instantly have come back to England in order to be present. Was it not unusual?'

'Yes, Mr. Elton, it was unusual. But there were reasons for it.'

'I should like to hear them,' he said. 'I was his heir, and it would have been only proper that I should have been there. Why?'

Angus hesitated a moment.

'That is a reasonable question,' he said, 'and I feel bound to answer it. I must begin a little way back. . . Your Uncle was in excellent physical health apparently, till about a week before his death. Very stout, but very alert and active. Then the trouble began. It took the form at first of some grievous mental and spiritual disturbance. He thought for some reason that he was going to die very soon, and the idea of death produced in him an abnormal panic terror. He telegraphed for me, for he wanted to make some alteration in his will. I was away and could not get down till the next day, and by the time I arrived he was too desperately ill to give any sort of coherent instructions. But his intention, I think, was to cut Mr. Owen Barton out of it.'

Again the lawyer paused.

'I found,' he said, 'that on the morning of the day I got down to Wedderburn, he had sent for the parson of his parish, and had made a confession to him. What that

194

was I have not, of course, the slightest idea. Till then he had been in this panic fear of death, but was physically himself. Immediately afterwards some very horrible disease invaded him. Just that: invasion. The doctors who were summoned from London and Bournemouth had no idea what it was. Some unknown microbe, they supposed, which made the most swift and frightful havoc of skin and tissue and bone. It was like some putrefying internal corruption. It was as if he was dead already. . . Really, I don't know what good it will do to tell you this.'

'I want to know,' said Francis.

'Well: this corruption. Living organisms came out as from a dead body. His nurses used to be sick. And the room was always swarming with flies; great fat flies, crawling over the walls and the bed. He was quite conscious, and there persisted this frantic terror of death, when you would have thought that a man's soul would have been only too thankful to be quit of such a habitation.'

'And was Mr. Owen Barton with him?' asked Francis.

'From the moment that Mr. Elton made his confession, he refused to see him. Once he came into the room, and there was a shocking scene. The dying man screamed and yelled with terror. Nor would he see the two ladies we have mentioned: why they continued to stop in the house I can't imagine. Then on the last morning of his life – he could not speak now – he traced a word or two on a piece of paper, and it seemed that he wanted to receive the Holy Communion. So the parson was sent for.'

The old lawyer paused again: Francis saw that his hand was shaking.

'Then very dreadful things happened,' he said. 'I was in the room, for he signed to me to be near him, and I saw them with my own eyes. The parson had poured the wine into the chalice, and had put the bread on the paten, and was about to consecrate the elements, when a cloud of those flies, of which I have told you, came about him.

195

They filled the chalice like a swarm of bees, they settled in their unclean thousands on the paten, and in a couple of minutes the chalice was dry and empty and they had devoured the bread. Then like drilled hosts, you may say, they swarmed on to your uncle's face, so that you could see nothing of it. He choked and he gasped: there was one writhing convulsion, and, thank God, it was all over.'

'And then?' asked Francis.

'There were no flies. Nothing. But it was necessary to have the body cremated at once and the bedding with it. Very shocking indeed! I would not have told you, if you had not pressed me.'

'And the ashes?' asked he.

'You will see that there is a clause in his will, directing that his remains should be buried at the foot of the Judas-tree beside the swimming pool in the garden at Wedderburn. That was done.'

Francis was a very unimaginative young man, free from superstitious twitterings and unprofitable speculations, and this story, suggestive though it was, of ghastly sub-currents, did not take hold of his mind at all or lead to the fashioning of uneasy fancies. It was all very horrible, but it was over. He went down to Wedderburn for Easter with a widowed sister of his and her small boy, aged eleven, and they all fairly fell in love with the place. It was soon settled that Sybil Marsham should let her house in London for the summer months, and establish herself here. Dickie, who was a delicate boy, rather queer and elfin, would thus have the benefit of country air, and Francis the benefit of having the place run by his sister and occupied and in commission whenever he was able to get away from his work.

The house was of brick and timber, with accommodation for half a dozen folk, and stood on high ground above the little town. Francis made a tour of it, as soon as he arrived, rather astonished to find how the sight of it rubbed up to clearness in the minutest details his memory of it. There was the sitting-room with its tall bookcases and its deep window-seats overlooking the garden, where he had sat unobserved when his uncle and Mrs. Ray came in talking together. Above was his uncle's panelled bedroom, which he proposed to occupy himself, with the big wardrobe containing vestments. He opened it: they were under their covering sheets of tissue paper, shimmering with scarlet and gold and finest lawn foamed with Irish lace: a faint smell of incense hung about them. Next that was his uncle's sitting-room, and beyond that the room which he had slept in before, and was now appropriated to Dickie. These rooms lay on the front of the house, looking westward over the garden and he went out to renew acquaintance with it. Flower-beds gay with spring blossoms ran below the windows: then came the lawn, and beyond the belt of trees that enclosed the swimming pool. He passed along the path that threaded it between tapestries of primrose and anemone, and came out into the clearing that surrounded the water. The bathing shed stood at the deep end of it by the sluice that splashed riotously into the channel below, for the stream that supplied the pool was running full with the rains of March. In front of the copse on the far side stood a Judas-tree decked gloriously with flowers, and the reflection of it was cast waveringly on the rippled surface of the water. Somewhere below those red-blossoming boughs, there was buried a casket of ashes. He strolled round the pool: it was quite sheltered here from the April breeze, and bees were busy in the red blossoms. Bees, and large fat flies, a quantity of them.

He and Sybil were sitting in the drawing-room with the deep window-seats as dusk began to fall. A servant came in to say that Mr. Owen Barton had called. Certainly they were at home, and he entered, and was introduced to Sybil.

'You will hardly remember me, Mr. Elton,' he said, 'but I was here when you paid a visit to your uncle: four years ago it must have been.'

'But I remember you perfectly,' he said. 'We bathed together, we played tennis: you were very kind to a shy boy. And are you living here still?'

'Yes: I took a house in Wedderburn after your uncle's death. I spent six very happy years with him as his secretary, and I got much attached to the country. My house stands just outside your garden palings opposite the latched gate leading into the wood round the pool.'

The door opened and Dickie came in. He caught sight of the stranger and stopped.

'Say "how do you do" to Mr. Barton, Dickie,' said his mother.

Dickie performed this duty with due politeness and stood regarding him. He was a shy boy usually; but, after this inspection, he advanced close to him, and laid his hands on his knees.

'I like you,' he said confidently, and leant up against him.

'Don't bother Mr. Barton, Dickie,' she said rather sharply.

'But indeed he's doing nothing of the kind,' said Barton, and he drew the boy towards him so that he stood clipped between his knees.

Sybil got up.

'Come, Dick,' she said. 'We'll have a walk round the garden before it gets dark.'

'Is he coming, too?' asked the boy.

'No: he's going to stop and talk to Uncle Francis.'

When the two men were alone Barton said a word or two about Horace Elton, who had always been so generous a friend to him. The end, mercifully short, had been terrible, and terrible to him personally had been the dying man's refusal to see him during the last two days of his life.

'His mind, I think, must have been affected,' he said, 'by his awful sufferings. It happens like that sometimes: people turn against those with whom they have been most intimate. I have often mourned over that, and deeply regretted it... And I owe you a certain word of explanation, Mr. Elton. No doubt you were puzzled to find in your uncle's will that I was entitled "the Reverend." It is quite true, though I do not call myself so. Certain spiritual doubts and difficulties caused me to give up my orders, but your uncle always held that if a man is once a priest he is always a priest. He was very strong about that, and no doubt he was right.'

'I didn't know my uncle took any interest in ecclesiastical affairs,' said Francis. 'Ah, I had forgotten about his vestments. Perhaps that was only an artistic taste.'

'By no means. He regarded them as sacred things, consecrated to holy uses... And may I ask you what happened to his remains? I remember he once expressed a wish to be buried by the swimming pool.'

'His body was cremated,' said Francis, 'and the ashes were buried there.'

Barton stayed but little longer, and Sybil on her return was frankly relieved to find he had gone. Simply, she didn't like him. There was something queer, something sinister about him. Francis laughed at her: quite a good fellow, he thought.

Dreams, of course, are a mere hash-up of recent mental images and associations, and a very vivid dream that came to Francis that night could easily have arisen from such topics. He thought he was swimming in the bathing pool with Owen Barton, and that his uncle, stout and florid, was standing underneath the Judas-tree watching them. That seemed quite natural, as is the way of dreams: merely he was not dead at all. When they came out of the water, he looked for his clothes, but found that there was laid out for him a scarlet cassock and a white lace-trimmed cotta. This again was quite natural; so, too, was the fact that Barton put on a gold cope.

His uncle, very merry and licking his lips, joined them, and each of them took an arm of his and they walked back to the house together singing a hymn. As they went the daylight died, and by the time they crossed the lawn it was black night, and the windows of the house were lit. They walked upstairs, still singing, into his uncle's bedroom which was now his own. There was an open door, which he had never noticed before opposite his bed, and there came a very bright light from it. Then the sense of nightmare began, for his two companions, gripping him tightly, pulled him along towards it, and he struggled with them knowing there was something terrible within. But step by step they dragged him, violently resisting, and now out of the door there came a swarm of large fat flies that buzzed and settled on him. Thicker and thicker they streamed out, covering his face, and crawling into his eyes, and entering his mouth as he panted for breath. The horror grew to breaking-point, and he woke sweating with a hammering heart. He switched on the light, and there was the quiet room and the dawn beginning to be luminous outside, and the birds, just tuning up.

Francis's few days of holiday passed quickly. He went down to the village to see Barton's house, and found it a most pleasant little dwelling, and its owner an exceedingly pleasant fellow. Barton dined with them one evening, and Sybil went so far as to admit that her first judgement of him was hasty. He was charming with Dickie, too, and that disposed her in his favour, and the boy adored him. Soon it was necessary to find some tutor for him, and Barton readily agreed to undertake his education, and every morning Dickie trotted across the garden and through the wood where the swimming pool lay to Barton's house. His ill-health had made him rather backward in his studies, but he was now eager to learn and to please his instructor, and he got on quickly.

II

It was now that I first met Francis, and during the next few months in London we became close friends. He told me that he had lately inherited this place at Wedderburn from his uncle, but for the present I knew no more than that of the previous history which I have just recorded. Sometime during July he told me he was

200

intending to spend the month of August there. His sister, who kept house for him, and her small boy would be away for the first week or two, for she had taken him off to the seaside. Would I then come and share his solitude, and get on there, uninterrupted, with some work I had on hand. That seemed a very attractive plan, and we motored down together one very hot afternoon early in August, that promised thunder. Owen Barton, he told me, who had been his uncle's secretary was coming to dine with us that night.

It wanted an hour or so yet to dinner-time when we arrived, and Francis directed me, if I cared for a dip, to the bathing pool among the trees beyond the lawn. He had various household businesses to look into himself, so I went off alone. It was an enchanting place, the water still and very clear, mirroring the sky and the full-foliaged trees, and I stripped and plunged in. I lay and floated in the cool water, I swam and dived again, and then I saw, walking close to the far bank of the pool, a man of something more than middle-age, and extremely stout. He was in dress-clothes, dinner-jacket and black tie, and instantly it struck me that this must be Mr. Barton coming up from the village to dine with us. It must therefore be later than I thought, and I swam back to the shed where my clothes were. As I climbed out of the water, I glanced round. There was no one there.

It was a slight shock, but very slight. It was odd that he should have come so unexpectedly out of the wood and disappeared again so suddenly, but it did not concern me much. I hurried home, changed quickly and came down, expecting to find Francis and his guest in the drawing-room. But I need not have been in such haste for now my watch told me that there was still a quarter of an hour before dinner-time. As for the others, I supposed that Mr. Barton was upstairs with Francis in his sitting-room. So I picked up a chance book to beguile the time, and read for a while, but the room grew rather dark, and, rising to switch on the electric light, I saw standing outside the French window into the garden the

201

figure of a man, outlined against the last of a stormy sunset, looking into the room.

There was no doubt whatever in my mind that he was the same person as I had seen when I was bathing, and the switching on of the light made this clear, for it shone full on his face. No doubt then Mr. Barton finding he was too early was strolling about the garden till the dinner-hour. But now I did not look forward at all to this evening: I had had a good look at him and there was something horrible about him. Was he human, was he earthly at all? Then he quietly moved away, and immediately afterwards there came a knock at the front door just outside the room, and I heard Francis coming downstairs. He went to the door himself: there was a word of greeting, and he came into the room accompanied by a tall, slim fellow whom he introduced to me.

We had a very pleasant evening: Barton talked fluently and agreeably, and more than once he spoke of his friend and pupil Dickie. About eleven he rose to go, and Francis suggested to him that he should walk back across the garden which gave him a short cut to his house. The threatening storm still held off, but it was very dark overhead, as we stood together outside the French window. Barton was soon swallowed up in the blackness. Then there came a bright flash of lightning, and in that moment of illumination I saw that there was standing in the middle of the lawn, as if waiting for him, the figure I had seen twice already. 'Who is that?' was on the tip of my tongue, but instantly I perceived that Francis had seen nothing of it, and so I was silent, for I knew now what I had already half-guessed that this was no living man of flesh and blood whom I had seen. A few heavy drops of rain plopped on the flagged walk, and, as we moved indoors, Francis called out 'Good night, Barton!' and the cheery voice answered.

Before long we went up to bed, and he took me into his room as we passed, a big panelled chamber with a great wardrobe by the bed. Close to it hung an oil-portrait of kit-cat size.

202

'I'll show you what's in that wardrobe tomorrow,' he said. 'Rather wonderful things. . . That's a picture of my uncle.'

I had seen that face before this evening.

For the next two or three days I had no further glimpse of that dreadful visitant, but never for a moment was I at ease, for I was aware that he was about. What instinct or what sense perceived that, I have no idea: perhaps it was merely the dread I had of seeing him again that gave rise to the conviction. I thought of telling Francis that I must get back to London; what prevented me from so doing was the desire to know more, and that made me fight this cold fear. Then very soon I perceived that Francis was no more at ease than I was. Sometimes as we sat together in the evening he was oddly alert: he would pause in the middle of a sentence as if some sound had attracted his attention, or he would look up from our game of bezique and focus his eyes for a second on some corner of the room or, more often, on the dark oblong of the open French window. Had he, I wondered, been seeing something invisible to me, and, like myself, feared to speak of it?

These impressions were momentary and infrequent, but they kept alive in me the feeling that there was something astir, and that something, coming out of the dark and the unknown, was growing in force. It had come into the house, and was present everywhere. . . And then one awoke again to a morning of heavenly brightness and sunshine, and surely one was disquieting oneself in vain.

I had been there about a week when something occurred which precipitated what followed. I slept in the room which Dickie usually occupied, and awoke one night feeling uncomfortably hot. I tugged at a blanket to remove it, but it was tucked very tightly in between the mattresses on the side of the bed next to the wall. Eventually I got it free, and as I did so I heard something drop with a flutter on to the floor. In the morning I remembered that, and found underneath the bed a little paper note-book. I opened it idly enough, and within were a dozen pages written over in a round childish handwriting, and these words struck my eye:

'Thursday, July 11th. I saw great-uncle Horace again this morning in the wood. He told me something about myself which I didn't understand, but he said I should like it when I got older. I mustn't tell anybody that he's here, nor what he told me, except Mr. Barton.'

I did not care one jot whether I was reading a boy's private diary. That was no longer a consideration worth thinking about. I turned over the page and found another entry.

'Sunday, July 21st. I saw Uncle Horace again. I said I had told Mr. Barton what he had told me, and Mr. Barton had told me some more things, and that he was pleased, and said I was getting on and that he would take me to prayers some day soon.'

I cannot describe the thrill of horror that these entries woke in me. They made the apparition which I had seen infinitely more real and more sinister. It was a spirit corrupt and malign and intent on corruption that haunted the place. But what was I to do? How could I, without any lead from Francis, tell him that the spirit of his uncle – of whom at present I knew nothing – had been seen not by me only, but by his nephew, and that he was at work on the boy's mind? Then there was the mention of Barton. Certainly that could not be left as it was. He was collaborating in that damnable task. A cult of corruption (or was I being too fantastic?) began to outline itself. Then what did that sentence about taking to prayers mean? But Dickie was away, thank goodness, for the present, and there was time to think it over. As for that pitiful little notebook, I put it into a locked despatch case.

The day, as far as outward and visible signs were concerned, passed pleasantly. For me there was a morning's work, and for both of us an afternoon on the golf-links. But below there was something heavy; my knowledge of that diary kept intervening with mental telephone-calls asking 'What are you going to *do?*' Francis, on his side, was troubled; there were sub-currents, and I did not know what they were. Silences fell, not the natural unobserved silences between those who are intimate, which are only a symbol of their inti-macy, but the silences between those who have some-thing on their minds of which they fear to speak. These had got more stringent all day: there was a growing tenseness: all common topics were banal, for they only cloaked a certain topic.

We sat out on the lawn before dinner on that sultry evening, and breaking one of these silent intervals, he pointed at the front of the house.

'There's an odd thing,' he said. 'Look! There are three rooms aren't there on the ground floor: dining-room, drawing-room, and the little study where you write. Now look above. There are three rooms there: your bedroom, my bedroom, and my sitting-room. I've measured them. There are twelve feet missing. Looks as if there was a sealed-up room somewhere.'

Here at any rate, was something to talk about.

'Exciting,' I said. 'Mayn't we explore?'

'We will. We'll explore as soon as we've dined. Then there's another thing: quite off the point. You remember those vestments I showed you the other day? I opened the wardrobe, where they are kept, an hour ago, and a lot of big fat flies came buzzing out. A row like a dozen aero-planes overhead. Remote but loud, if you know what I mean. And then there weren't any.'

Somehow I felt that what we had been silent about was coming out into the open. It might be ill to look upon. . .

He jumped from his chair.

'Let's have done with these silences,' he cried. 'He's here, my uncle, I mean. I haven't told you yet, but he died in a swarm of flies. He asked for the Sacrament, but before the wine was consecrated the chalice was choked with them. And I know he's here. It sounds damned rot, but he is.'

205

'I know that, too,' I said. 'I've seen him.'

'Why didn't you tell me?'

'Because I thought you would laugh at me.'

'I should have a few days ago,' said he. 'But I don't now. Go on.'

'The first evening I was here I saw him at the bathing pool. That same night, when we were seeing Owen Barton off, a flash of lightning came, and he was there again standing on the lawn. '

'But how did you know it was he?' asked Francis.

'I knew it when you showed me the portrait of him in your bedroom that same night. Have you seen him?'

'No; but he's here. Anything more?'

This was the opportunity not only natural but inevitable.

'Yes, much more,' I said. 'Dickie has seen him too.'

'That child? Impossible.'

The door out of the drawing-room opened, and Francis's parlour-maid came out with the sherry on a tray. She put the decanter and glasses down on the wicker table between us, and I asked her to bring out the despatch case from my room. I took the paper notebook out of it.

'This slipped out from between my mattresses last night. It's Dickie's diary. Listen:' and I read him the first extract.

Francis gave one of those swift disconcerting glances over his shoulder.

'But we're dreaming,' he said. 'It's a nightmare. God, there's something awful here! And what about Dickie not telling anybody except Barton what he told him? Anything more?'

'Yes. "Sunday, July 21st. I saw Uncle Horace again. I said I had told Mr. Barton what he told me, and Mr. Barton told me some more things, and that he was pleased and said I was getting on, and that he would take me to prayers some day soon. I don't know what that means." '

Francis sprang out of his chair.

'What?' he cried. 'Take him to prayers? Wait a minute. Let me remember about my first visit here. I was a boy of nineteen, and frightfully, absurdly innocent for my age. A woman staying here gave me a book to read called *Là-Bas*. I didn't get far in it then, but I know what it's about now.'

'Black Mass,' said I. 'Satan worshippers.'

'Yes. Then one day my uncle dressed me up in a scarlet cassock, and Barton came in and put on a cope and said something about my being a server. He used to be a priest, did you know that? And one night I awoke and heard the sound of chanting and a bell rang. By the way, Barton's coming to dine tomorrow. . .'

'What are you going to do?'

'About him? I can't tell yet. But we've got something to do tonight. Horrors have happened here in this house. There must be some room where they held their Mass, a chapel. Why, there's that missing space I spoke of just now.'

After dinner we set to work. Somewhere on the first floor on the garden front of the house there was this space unaccounted for by the dimensions of the rooms there. We turned on the electric light in all of them, and then going out into the garden we saw that the windows in Francis's bedroom and in his sitting-room next door were far more widely spaced than they should have been. Somewhere, then, between them lay the area to which there was no apparent access and we went upstairs. The wall of his sitting-room seemed solid, it was of brick and timber, and large beams ran through it at narrow intervals. But the wall of his bedroom was panelled, and when we tapped on it, no sound came through into the other room beyond.

We began to examine it.

The servants had gone to bed, and the house was silent, but as we moved about from garden to house and from one room to another there was some presence watching and following us. We had shut the door into his bedroom from the passage, but now as we passed and felt about the panelling, the door swung open and closed again, and something entered, brushing my shoulder as it passed.

'What's that?' I said. 'Someone came in.'

'Never mind that,' he said. 'Look what I've found.'

In the border of one of the panels was a black stud like an ebony bell-push. He pressed it and pulled, and a section of the panelling slid sideways, disclosing a red curtain cloaking a doorway. He drew it aside with a clash of metal rings. It was dark within, and out of the darkness came a smell of stale incense. I felt with my hand along the frame of the doorway and found a switch, and the blackness was flooded with a dazzling light.

Within was a chapel. There was no window, and at the West end of it (not the East) there stood an altar. Above it was a picture, evidently of some early Italian school. It was on the lines of the Fra Angelico picture of the Annunciation. The Virgin sat in an open loggia, and on the flowery space outside the angel made his salutation. His spreading wings were the wings of a bat, and his black head and neck were those of a raven. He had his left hand, not his right, raised in blessing. The Virgin's robe of thinnest red muslin was trimmed with revolting symbols, and her face was that of a panting dog with tongue protruding.

There were two niches at the East end, in which were marble statues of naked men, with the inscriptions 'St. Judas' and 'St. Gilles de Raies.' One was picking up pieces of silver that lay at his feet, the other looked down leering and laughing at the prone figure of a mutilated boy. The place was lit by a chandelier from the ceiling: this was of the shape of a crown of thorns and electric bulbs nestled among the woven silver twigs. A bell hung from the roof, close beside the altar.

For the moment, as I looked on these obscene blasphemies, I felt that they were merely grotesque and no more to be regarded seriously than the dirty inscriptions written upon empty wall-spaces in the street. That indifference swiftly passed, and a horrified consciousness of

208

the devotion of those who had fashioned and assembled these decorations took its place. Skilled painters and artificers had wrought them and they were here for the service of all that is evil; that spirit of adoration lived in them dynamic and active. And the place was throbbing with the exultant joy of those who had worshipped here.

'And look here!' called Francis. He pointed to a little table standing against the wall just outside the altar-rails.

There were photographs on it, one of a boy standing on the header-board at the bathing pool about to plunge.

'That's me,' he said. 'Barton took it. And what's written underneath it? "Ora pro Francisco Elton." And that's Mrs. Ray, and that's my uncle, and that's Barton in a cope. Pray for him, too, please. But it's childish!'

He suddenly burst into a shout of laughter. The roof of the chapel was vaulted and the echo that came from it was loud and surprising, the place rang with it. His laughter ceased, but not so the echo. There was some-one else laughing. But where? Who? Except for us the chapel was empty of all visible presences.

On and on the laughter went, and we stared at each other with panic stirring. The brilliant light from the chandelier began to fade, dusk gathered, and in the dark there was brewing some hellish and deadly force. And through the dimness I saw, hanging in the air, and oscil-lating slightly as if in a draught the laughing face of Horace Elton. Francis saw it too.

'Fight it! Withstand it!' he cried as he pointed to it. 'Desecrate all that it holds sanctified! God, do you smell the incense and the corruption?'

We tore the photographs, and we smashed the table on which they stood. We plucked the frontal from the altar and spat on the accursed table: we tugged at it and it toppled over and the marble slab split in half. We hauled from the niches the two statues that stood there, and crash they went on to the paved floor. Then appalled at the riot of our iconoclasm we paused. The laughter had ceased and no oscillating face dangled in the dimness. Then we left the chapel and pulled across the doorway the panel that closed it.

Francis came to sleep in my room, and we talked long, laying our plans for next day. We had forgotten the picture over the altar in our destruction, but now it worked in with what we proposed to do. Then we slept, and the night passed without disturbance. At the least we had broken up the apparatus that was hallowed to unhallowed uses, and that was something. But there was grim work ahead yet, and the issue was unconjecturable.

Barton came to dine that next evening, and there hung on the wall opposite his place the picture from the chapel upstairs. He did not notice it at first, for the room was rather dark, but not dark enough yet to need artificial light. He was gay and lively as usual, spoke amusingly and wittily, and asked when his friend Dickie was to return. Towards the end of dinner the lights were switched on, and then he saw the picture. I was watching him, and the sweat started out on his face that had grown clay-coloured in a moment. Then he pulled himself together.

'That's a strange picture,' he said. 'Was it here before? Surely not.'

'No: it was in a room upstairs,' said Francis. 'About Dickie? I don't know for certain when he'll come back. We have found his diary, and presently we must speak about that.'

'Dickie's diary? Indeed!' said Barton, and he moistened his lips with his tongue.

I think he guessed then that there was something desperate ahead, and I pictured a man condemned to be hanged waiting in his cell with his warders for the imminent hour, as Barton waited then. He sat with an elbow on the table and his hand propping his forehand. Immediately almost the servant brought in our coffee and left us.

'Dickie's diary,' said Francis quietly. 'Your name figures in it. Also my uncle's. Dickie saw him more than once. But, of course, you know that.'

Barton drank off his glass of brandy.

'Are you telling me a ghost story?' he said. 'Pray go on.'

'Yes, it's partly a ghost story, but not entirely. My uncle – his ghost if you like – told him certain stories and said he must keep them secret except from you. And you told him more. And you said he should come to prayers with you some day soon. Where was that to be? In the room just above us?'

The brandy had given the condemned man a momentary courage.

'A pack of lies, Mr. Elton,' he said. 'That boy has got a corrupt mind. He told me things that no boy of his age should know: he giggled and laughed at them. Perhaps I ought to have told his mother.'

'It's too late to think of that now,' said Francis. 'The diary I spoke of will be in the hands of the police at ten o'clock tomorrow morning. They will also inspect the room upstairs where you have been in the habit of celebrating the Black Mass.'

Barton leant forward towards him.

'No, no,' he cried 'Don't do that! I beg and implore you! I will confess the truth to you. I will conceal nothing. My life has been a blasphemy. But I'm sorry: I repent. I abjure all those abominations from henceforth: I renounce them all in the name of Almighty God.'

'Too late,' said Francis.

And then the horror that haunts me still began to manifest itself. The wretched man threw himself back in his chair, and there dropped from his forehead on to his white shirt-front a long grey worm that lay and wriggled there. At that moment there came from overhead the sound of a bell, and he sprang to his feet.

'No!' he cried again. 'I retract all I said, I abjure nothing. And my Lord is waiting for me in the sanctuary. I must be quick and make my humble confession to him.'

With the movement of a slinking animal he slid from the room, and we heard his steps going swiftly upstairs.

'Did you see?' I whispered. 'And what's to be done? Is the man sane?'

'It's beyond us now,' said Francis.

There was a thump on the ceiling overhead as if some-one had fallen, and without a word we ran upstairs into Francis's bedroom. The door of the wardrobe where the vestments were kept was open, some lay on the floor. The panel was open, too, but within it was dark. In terror at what might meet our eyes, I felt for the switch and turned the light on.

The bell which had sounded a few minutes ago was still swinging gently, though speaking no more. Barton, clad in the gold-embroidered cope, lay in front of the overturned altar, with his face twitching. Then that ceased, the rattle of death creaked in his throat, and his mouth fell open. Great flies, swarms of them, coming from nowhere, settled on it.

Pirates

For many years this project of sometime buying back the house had simmered in Peter Graham's mind, but whenever he actually went into the idea with practical intention, stubborn reasons had presented themselves to deter him. In the first place it was very far off from his work, down in the heart of Cornwall, and it would be impossible to think of going there just for week-ends, and if he established himself there for longer periods what on earth would he do with himself in that soft remote Lotus-land? He was a busy man who, when at work, liked the diversion of his club and of the theatres in the evening, but he allowed himself few holidays away from the City, and those were spent on salmon river or golf-links with some small party of solid and like-minded friends. Looked at in these lights, the project bristled with objections.

Yet through all these years, forty of them now, which had ticked away so imperceptibly, the desire to be at home again at Lescop had always persisted, and from time to time it gave him shrewd little unexpected tugs, when his conscious mind was in no way concerned with it. This desire, he was well aware, was of a sentimental quality, and often he wondered at himself that he, who was so well-armoured in the general jostle of the world against that type of emotion, should have just this one joint in his harness. Not since he was sixteen had he set eyes on the place, but the memory of it was more vivid than that of any other scene of subsequent experience. He had married since then, he had lost his wife, and

213

though for many months after that he had felt horribly
lonely, the ache of that loneliness had ceased, and now,
if he had ever asked himself the direct question, he
would have confessed that bachelor existence was more
suited to him than married life had ever been. It had not
been a conspicuous success, and he never felt the least
temptation to repeat the experiment.

But there was another loneliness which neither
married life nor his keen interest in his business had
ever extinguished, and this was directly connected with
his desire for that house on the green slope of the hills
above Truro. For only seven years had he lived there,
the youngest but one of a family of five children, and
now out of all that gay company he alone was left. One
by one they had dropped off the stem of life, but as each
in turn went into this silence, Peter had not missed them
very much: his own life was too occupied to give him time
really to miss anybody, and he was too vitally constituted to do otherwise than look forwards.

None of that brood of children except himself, and he
childless, had married, and now when he was left without intimate tie of blood to any living being, a loneliness
had gathered thickly round him. It was not in any sense a
tragic or desperate loneliness: he had no wish to follow
them on the unverified and unlikely chance of finding
them all again. Also, he had no use for any disembodied
existence: life meant to him flesh and blood and material
interests and activities, and he could form no conception
of life apart from such. But sometimes he ached with this
dull gnawing ache of loneliness, which is worse than all
others, when he thought of the stillness that lay con-
gealed like clear ice over these young and joyful years
when Lescop had been so noisy and alert and full of
laughter, with its garden resounding with games, and
the house with charades and hide-and-seek and multi-
tudinous plans. Of course there had been rows and
quarrels and disgraces, hot enough at the time, but now
there was no one to quarrel with. 'You can't really quarrel with people whom you don't love,' thought Peter,

214

'because they don't matter.' . . . Yet it was ridiculous to feel lonely; it was even more than ridiculous, it was weak, and Peter had the kindly contempt of a successful and healthy and unemotional man for weaknesses of that kind. There were so many amusing and interesting things in the world, he had so many irons in the fire to be beaten, so to speak, into gold when he was working, and so many palatable diversions when he was not (for he still brought a boyish enthusiasm to work and play alike), that there was no excuse for indulging in senti-mental sterilities. So, for months together, hardly a stray thought would drift towards the remote years lived in the house on the hill-side above Truro.

He had lately become chairman of the board of that new and highly promising company, the British Tin Syn-dicate. Their property included certain Cornish mines which had been previously abandoned as non-paying propositions, but a clever mineralogical chemist had recently invented a process by which the metal could be extracted far more cheaply than had hitherto been pos-sible. The British Tin Syndicate had bought the patent, and having acquired these derelict Cornish mines was getting very good results from ore that had not been worth treating. Peter had very strong opinions as to the duty of a chariman to make himself familiar with the practical side of his concerns, and was now travelling down to Cornwall to make a personal inspection of the mines where this process was at work. He had with him certain technical reports which he had received to read during the uninterrupted hours of his journey, and it was not till his train had left Exeter behind that he finished his perusal of them, and, putting them back in his despatch-case, turned his eye at the swiftly passing panorama of travel. It was many years since he had been to the West Country, and now with the thrill of vivid recognition he found the red cliffs round Dawlish, interspersed between stretches of sunny sea-beach, startlingly familiar. Surely he must have seen them quite lately, he thought to himself, and then, ransacking his

215

memory, he found it was forty years since he had looked at them, travelling back to Eton from his last holidays at Lescop. The intense sharp-cut impressions of youth!

His destination tonight was Penzance, and now, with a strangely keen sense of expectation, he remembered that just before reaching Truro station the house on the hill was visible from the train, for often on these journeys to and from school he had been all eyes to catch the first sight of it and the last. Trees perhaps would have grown up and intervened, but as they ran past the station before Truro he shifted across to the other side of the carriage, and once more looked out for that glimpse. . . There it was, a mile away across the valley, with its grey stone front and the big beech-tree screening one end of it, and his heart leaped as he saw it. Yet what use was the house to him now? It was not the stones and the bricks of it, nor the tall hay-fields below it, nor the tangled garden behind that he wanted, but the days when he had lived in it. Yet he leaned from the window till a cutting extinguished the view of it, feeling that he was looking at a photograph that recalled some living presence. All those who had made Lescop dear and still vivid had gone, but this record remained, like the image on the plate. . . And then he smiled at himself with a touch of contempt for his sentimentality.

The next three days were a whirl of enjoyable occupation: tin-mines in the concrete were new to Peter, and he absorbed himself in these, as in some new game or ingenious puzzle. He went down the shafts of mines which had been opened again, he inspected the new chemical process, seeing it at work and checking the results, he looked into running expenses, comparing them with the value of the metal recovered. Then, too, there was substantial traces of silver in some of these ores, and he went eagerly into the question as to whether it would pay to extract it. Certainly even the mines which had previously been closed down ought to yield a decent dividend with this process, while those where the lode was richer would vastly increase their profits. But economy, economy. . . Surely it would save in the end, though at a considerable capital expenditure now, to lay a light railway from the works to the railhead instead of employing these motor-lorries. There was a piece of steep gradient, it was true, but a small detour, with a trestle-bridge over the stream, would avoid that.

He walked over the proposed route with the engineer and scrambled about the stream-bank to find a good take-off for his trestle-bridge. And all the time at the back of his head, in some almost subconscious region of thought, were passing endless pictures of the house and the hill, its rooms and passages, its fields and garden, and with them, like some accompanying tune, ran that ache of loneliness. He felt that he must prowl again about the place: the owner, no doubt, if he presented himself, would let him just stroll about alone for half an hour. Thus he would see it all altered and overscored by the life of strangers living there, and the photograph would fade into a mere blur and then blankness. Much better that it should.

It was in this intention that, having explored every avenue for dividends on behalf of his company, he left Penzance by an early morning train in order to spend a few hours in Truro and go up to London later in the day. Hardly had he emerged from the station when a crowd of memories, forty years old, but more vivid than any of those of the last day or two, flocked round him with welcome for his return. There was the level-crossing and the road leading down to the stream where his sister Sybil and he had caught a stickleback for their aquarium, and across the bridge over it was the lane sunk deep between high crumbling banks that led to a footpath across the fields to Lescop. He knew exactly where was that pool with long ribands of water-weed trailing and waving in it, which had yielded them that remarkable fish: he knew how campions red and white would be in flower on the lane-side, and in the fields the meadow-orchis. But it was more convenient to go first into the town, get his lunch at the hotel, and to make enquiries from a house-agent as to the present owner of Lescop; perhaps he would walk back to the station for his afternoon train by that short cut.

Thick now as flowers on the steppe when spring comes, memories bright and fragrant shot up round him. There was the shop where he had taken his canary to be stuffed (beautiful it looked!): and there was the shop of the 'undertaker and cabinet-maker,' still with the same name over the door, where on a memorable birthday, on which his amiable family had given him, by request, the tokens of their good-will in cash, he had ordered a cabinet with five drawers and two trays, varnished and smelling of newly cut wood, for his collection of shells. . . There was a small boy in jersey and flannel trousers looking in at the window now, and Peter suddenly said to himself, 'Good Lord, how like I used to be to that boy: same kit, too.' Strikingly like indeed he was, and Peter, curiously interested, started to cross the street to get a nearer look at him. But it was market-day, a drove of sheep delayed him, and when he got across the small boy had vanished among the passengers. Farther along was a dignified house-front with a flight of broad steps leading up to it, once the dreaded abode of Mr. Tuck, dentist. There was a tall girl standing outside it now, and again Peter involuntarily said to himself, 'Why, that girl's wonderfully like Sybil!' But before he could get more than a glimpse of her, the door was opened and she passed in, and Peter was rather vexed to find that there was no longer a plate on the door indicating that Mr. Tuck was still at his wheel. . . At the end of the street was the bridge over the Fal just below which they used so often to take a boat for a picnic on the river. There was a jolly family party setting off just now from the quay, three boys, he noticed, and a couple of girls, and a woman of young middle-age. Quickly they dropped downstream and went forth, and with half a sigh he said to himself, 'Just our number with Mamma.'

He went to the Red Lion for his lunch: that was new ground and uninteresting, for he could not recall having set foot in that hostelry before. But as he munched his cold beef there was some great fantastic business going on deep down in his brain: it was trying to join up (and it believed it could) that boy outside the cabinet-maker's, that girl on the threshold of the house once Mr. Tuck's, and that family party starting for their picnic on the river. It was in vain that he told himself that neither the boy nor the girl nor the picnic-party could possibly have anything to do with him: as soon as his attention relaxed that burrowing underground chase, as of a ferret in a rabbit-hole, began again... And then Peter gave a gasp of sheer amazement, for he remembered with clear-cut distinctness how on the morning of that memorable birthday, he and Sybil started earlier than the rest from Lescop, he on the adorable errand of ordering his cabinet, she for a dolorous visit to Mr. Tuck. The others followed half an hour later for a picnic on the Fal to celebrate the great fact that his age now required two figures (though one was a nought) for expression. 'It'll be ninety years, darling,' his mother had said, 'before you want a third one, so be careful of yourself.'

Peter was almost as excited when this momentous memory burst on him as he had been on the day itself. Not that it meant anything, he said to himself, as there's nothing for it to mean. But I call it odd. It's as if something from those days hung about here still...

He finished his lunch quickly after that, and went to the house-agent's to make his enquiries. Nothing could be easier than that he should prowl about Lescop, for the house had been untenanted for the last two years. No card 'to view' was necessary, but here were the keys; there was no caretaker there.

'But the house will be going to rack and ruins,' said Peter indignantly. 'Such a jolly house, too. False economy not to put a caretaker in. But of course it's no business of mine. You shall have the keys back during the afternoon: I'll walk up there now.'

'Better take a taxi, sir,' said the man. 'A hot day, and a mile and a half up a steep hill.'

'Oh, nonsense,' said Peter. 'Barely a mile. Why, my brother and I used often to do it in ten minutes.'

It occurred to him that these athletic feats of forty years ago would probably not interest the modern world. . .

Pyder Street was as populous with small children as ever, and perhaps a little longer and steeper than it used to be. Then turning off to the right among strange new-built suburban villas he passed into the well-known lane, and in five minutes more had come to the gate leading into the short drive up to the house. It drooped on its hinges, he must lift it off the latch, sidle through and prop it in place again. Overgrown with grass and weeds was the drive, and with another spurt of indignation he saw that the stile to the pathway across the field was broken down and had dragged the wires of the fence with it. And then he came to the house itself, and the creepers trailed over the windows, and, unlocking the door, he stood in the hall with its discoloured ceiling and patches of mildew growing on the damp walls. Shabby and ashamed it looked, the paint perished from the window-sashes, the panes dirty, and in the air the sour smell of chambers long unventilated. And yet the spirit of the house was there still, though melancholy and reproachful, and it followed him wearily from room to room – 'You are Peter, aren't you?' it seemed to say. 'You've just come to look at me, I see and not to stop. But I remember the jolly days just as well as you.' . . . From room to room he went, dining-room, drawing-room, his mother's sitting-room, his father's study: then upstairs to what had been the school-room in the days of governesses, and had then been turned over to the children for a play-room. Along the passage was the old nursery and the night-nursery, and above that attic-rooms, to one of which, as his own exclusive bedroom, he had been promoted when he went to school. The roof of it had leaked, there was a brown-edged stain on the sagging ceiling just above where his bed had been. 'A nice state to let my room get into,' muttered Peter. 'How am I to sleep underneath that drip from the roof? Too bad!'

The vividness of his own indignation rather startled him. He had really felt himself to be not a dual personality, but the same Peter Graham at different periods of his existence. One of them, the chairman of the British Tin Syndicate, had protested against young Peter Graham being put to sleep in so damp and dripping a room, and the other (oh, the ecstatic momentary glimpse of him!) was indeed young Peter back in his lovely attic again, just home from school and now looking round with eager eyes to convince himself of that blissful reality, before bouncing downstairs again to have tea in the children's room. What a lot of things to ask about! How were his rabbits, and how were Sybil's guinea-pigs, and had Violet learned that song 'Oh 'tis nothing but a shower,' and were the wood-pigeons building again in the lime-tree? All these topics were of the first importance. . .

Peter Graham the elder sat down on the window-seat. It overlooked the lawn, and just opposite was the lime-tree, a drooping lime making a green cave inside the skirt of its lower branches, but with those above growing straight, and he heard the chuckling coo of the wood-pigeons coming from it. They were building there again then: that question of young Peter's was answered.

'Very odd that I should just be thinking of that,' he said to himself: somehow there was no gap of years between him and young Peter, for his attic bridged over the decades which in the clumsy material reckoning of time intervened between them. Then Peter the elder seemed to take charge again.

The house was a sad affair, he thought: it gave him a stab of loneliness to see how decayed was the theatre of their joyful years, and no evidence of newer life, of the children of strangers and even of their children's children growing up here could have overscored the old sense of it so effectually. He went out of young Peter's room and paused on the landing: the stairs led down in two short flights to the storey below, and now for the moment he was young Peter again, reaching down with his hand along the banisters, and preparing to take the first flight in one leap. But then old Peter saw it was an impossible feat for his less supple joints.

Well, there was the garden to explore, and then he would go back to the agent's and return the keys. He no longer wanted to take that short cut down the steep hill to the station, passing the pool where Sybil and he had caught the stickleback, for his whole notion, sometimes so urgent, of coming back here, had wilted and withered. But he would just walk about the garden for ten minutes, and as he went with sedate step downstairs, memories of the garden, and of what they all did there began to invade him. There were trees to be climbed, and shrubberies – one thicket of syringa particularly where goldfinches built – to be searched for nests and moths, but above all there was that game they played there, far more exciting than lawn-tennis or cricket in the bumpy field (though that was exciting enough) called Pirates... There was a summer-house, tiled and roofed and of solid walls at the top of the garden, and that was 'home' or 'Plymouth Sound,' and from there ships (children that is) set forth at the order of the Admiral to pick a trophy without being caught by the Pirates. There were two Pirates who hid anywhere in the garden and jumped out, and (counting the Admiral who, after giving his orders, became the flagship) three ships, which had to cruise to orchard or flower-bed or field and bring safely home a trophy culled from the ordained spot. Once, Peter remembered, he was flying up the winding path to the summer-house with a pirate close on his heels, when he fell flat down, and the humane pirate leaped over him for fear of treading on him, and fell down too. So Peter got home, because Dick had fallen on his face and his nose was bleeding...

'Good Lord, it might have happened yesterday,' thought Peter. 'And Harry called him a bloody pirate, and Papa heard and thought he was using shocking language till it was explained to him.

The garden was even worse than the house, neglected utterly and rankly overgrown, and to find the winding path at all, Peter had to push through briar and thicket. But he persevered and came out into the rose-garden at the top, and there was Plymouth Sound with roof collapsed and walls bulging, and moss growing thick between the tiles of the floor.

'But it must be repaired at once,' said Peter aloud. . . 'What's that?' He whisked round towards the bushes through which he had pushed his way, for he had heard a voice, faint and far off coming from there, and the voice was familiar to him, though for thirty years it had been dumb. For it was Violet's voice which had spoken and she had said, 'Oh, Peter: here you are!'

He knew it was her voice, and he knew the utter impossibility of it. But it frightened him, and yet how absurd it was to be frightened, for it was only his imagination, kindled by old sights and memories, that had played him a trick. Indeed, how jolly even to have imagined that he had heard Violet's voice again.

'Vi!' he called aloud, but of course no one answered. The wood-pigeons were cooing in the lime, there was a hum of bees and a whisper of wind in the trees, and all round the soft enchanted Cornish air, laden with dream-stuff.

He sat down on the step of the summer-house, and demanded the presence of his own common sense. It had been an uncomfortable afternoon, he was vexed at this ruin of neglect into which the place had fallen, and he did not want to imagine these voices calling to him out of the past, or to see these odd glimpses which belonged to his boyhood. He did not belong any more to that epoch over which grasses waved and headstones presided, and he must be quit of all that evoked it, for, more than anything else, he was director of prosperous companies with big interests dependent on him. So he sat there for a calming five minutes, defying Violet, so to speak, to call to him again. And then, so unstable was his mood today, that presently he was listening for her. But Violet was always quick to see when she was not wanted, and she must have gone, to join the others. . . .

He retraced his way, fixing his mind on material environments. The golden maple at the head of the walk, a sapling like himself when last he saw it, had become a stout-trunked tree, the shrub of bay a tall column of fragrant leaf, and just as he passed the syringa, a goldfinch dropped out of it with dipping flight. Then he was back at the house again where the climbing fuchsia trailed its sprays across the window of his mother's room and hot thick scent (how well-remembered!) spilled from the chalices of the great magnolia.

'A mad notion of mine to come and see the house again,' he said to himself. 'I won't think about it any more: it's finished. But it was wicked not to look after it.'

He went back into the town to return the keys to the house-agent.

'Much obliged to you,' he said. 'A pleasant house, when I knew it years ago. Why was it allowed to go to ruin like that?'

'Can't say, sir,' said the man. 'It has been let once or twice in the last ten years, but the tenants have never stopped long. The owner would be very pleased to sell it.'

An idea, fanciful, absurd, suddenly struck Peter.

'But why doesn't he live there?' he asked. 'Or why don't the tenants stop long? Was there something they didn't like about it? Haunted: anything of that sort? I'm not going to take it or purchase it: so that won't put me off.'

The man hesitated a moment.

'Well, there were stories,' he said, 'if I may speak confidentially. But all nonsense, of course.'

'Quite so,' said Peter. 'You and I don't believe in such rubbish. I wonder now: was it said that children's voices were heard calling in the garden?'

The discretion of a house-agent reasserted itself.

'I can't say, sir, I'm sure,' he said. 'All I know is that the house is to be had very cheap. Perhaps you would take our card.'

Peter arrived back in London late that night. There was a tray of sandwiches and drinks waiting for him, and having refreshed himself, he sat smoking awhile thinking of his three days' work in Cornwall at the mines: there must be a directors' meeting as soon as possible to consider his suggestions. . . Then he found himself staring at the round rosewood table where his tray stood. It had been in his mother's sitting-room at Lescop, and the chair in which he sat, a fine Stuart piece, had been his father's chair at the dinner-table, and that book-case had stood in the hall, and his Chippendale card-table . . . he could not remember exactly where that had been. That set of Browning's poems had been Sybil's: it was from the shelves in the children's room. But it was time to go to bed, and he was glad he was not to sleep in young Peter's attic.

It is doubtful whether, if once an idea has really thrown out roots in a man's mind, he can ever extirpate it. He can cut off its sprouting suckers, he can nip off the buds it bears, or, if they come to maturity, destroy the seed, but the roots defy him. If he tugs at them something breaks, leaving a vital part still embedded, and it is not long before some fresh evidence of its vitality pushes up above the ground where he least expected it. It was so with Peter now: in the middle of some business-meeting, the face of one of his co-directors reminded him of that of the coach-man at Lescop; if he went for a week-end of golf to the Dormy House at Rye, the bow-window of the billiard-room was in shape and size that of the drawing-room there, and the bank of gorse by the tenth green was no other than the clump below the tennis-court: almost he expected to find a tennis ball there when he had need to search it. Whatever he did, wherever he went, something called him from Lescop, and in the evening when he returned home, there was the furniture, more of it than he had realized, asking to be restored there: rugs and pictures and books, the silver on his table all joined in the mute appeal. But Peter stopped his ears to it: it was a senseless sentimentality, and a purely materialistic one to imagine that he could recapture the life over which so many years had flowed, and in which none of the actors but himself remained, by restoring to the house its old amenities and living there again. He would only emphasize his own loneliness by the visible contrast of the scene, once so alert and populous, with its present emptiness. And this 'butting-in' (so he expressed it) of materialistic sentimentality only confirmed his resolve to have done with Lescop. It had been a bitter sight but tonic, and now he would forget it.

Yet even as he sealed his resolution, there would come to him, blown as a careless breeze from the west, the memory of that boy and girl he had seen in the town, of the gay family starting for their river-picnic, of the faint welcoming call to him from the bushes in the garden, and, most of all, of the suspicion that the place was supposed to be haunted. It was just because it was haunted that he longed for it, and the more savagely and sensibly he assured himself of the folly of possessing it, the more he yearned after it, and constantly now it coloured his dreams. They were happy dreams; he was back there with the others, as in old days, children again in holiday time, and like himself they loved being at home there again, and they made much of Peter because it was he who had arranged it all. Often in these dreams he said to himself 'I have dreamed this before, and then I woke and found myself elderly and lonely again, but this time it is real!'

The weeks passed on, busy and prosperous, growing into months, and one day in the autumn, on coming home from a day's golf, Peter fainted. He had not felt very well for some time, he had been languid and easily fatigued, but with his robust habit of mind he had labelled such symptoms as mere laziness, and had driven himself with the whip. But now it might be as well to get a medical overhauling just for the satisfaction of being told there was nothing the matter with him. The pronouncement was not quite that. . .

'But I simply can't,' he said. 'Bed for a month and a winter of loafing on the Riviera! Why, I've got my time filled up till close on Christmas, and then I've arranged to go with some friends for a short holiday. Besides, the Riviera's a pestilent hole. It can't be done. Supposing I go on just as usual: what will happen?'

Dr. Dufflin made a mental summary of his wilful patient.

'You'll die, Mr. Graham,' he said cheerfully. 'Your heart is not what it should be, and if you want it to do its work, which it will for many years yet, if you're sensible, you must give it rest. Of course, I don't insist on the Riviera: that was only a suggestion for I thought you would probably have friends there, who would help to pass the time for you. But I do insist on some mild climate, where you can loaf out of doors. London with its frosts and fogs would never do.'

Peter was silent for a moment.

'How about Cornwall?' he asked.

'Yes, if you like. Not the north coast of course.'

'I'll think it over,' said Peter. 'There's a month yet.'

Peter knew that there was no need for thinking it over. Events were conspiring irresistibly to drive him to that which he longed to do, but against which he had been struggling, so fantastic was it, so irrational. But now it was made easy for him to yield and his obstinate colours came down with a run. A few telegraphic exchanges with the house-agent made Lescop his, another gave him the address of a reliable builder and decorator, and with the plans of the house, though indeed there was little need of them, spread out on his counterpane, Peter issued urgent orders. All structural repairs, leaking roofs and dripping ceilings, rotted woodwork and crumbling plaster must be tackled at once, and when that was done, painting and papering followed. The drawing-room used to have a Morris-paper; there were

227

spring flowers on it, blackthorn, violets, and fritillaries, a hateful wriggling paper, so he thought it, but none other would serve. The hall was painted duck-egg green, and his mother's room was pink, 'a beastly pink, tell them,' said Peter to his secretary, 'with a bit of blue in it: they must send me sample by return of post, big pieces, not snippets' . . . Then there was furniture: all the furniture in the house here which had once been at Lescop must go back there. For the rest, he would send down some stuff from London, bedroom appurtenances, and linen and kitchen utensils: he would see to carpets when he got there. Spare bedrooms could wait; just four servants' rooms must be furnished, and also the attic which he had marked on the plan, and which he intended to occupy himself. But no one must touch the garden till he came: he would superintend that himself, but by the middle of next month there must be a couple of gardeners ready for him.

'And that's all,' said Peter, 'just for the present.' 'All?' he thought, as, rather bored with the direction of matters that usually ran themselves, he folded up his plans. 'Why, it's just the beginning: just underwriting.'

The months' rest-cure was pronounced a success, and with strict orders not to exert mind or body, but to lie fallow, out of doors whenever possible, with quiet strolls and copious restings, Peter was allowed to go to Lescop, and on a December evening he saw the door opened to him and the light of welcome stream out on to his entry. The moment he set foot inside he knew, as by some interior sense, that he had done right, for it was not only the warmth and the ordered comfort restored to the deserted house that greeted him, but the firm knowledge that they whose loss made his loneliness were greeting him. . . That came in a flash, fantastic and yet soberly convincing; it was fundamental, everything was based on it. The house had been restored to its old aspect, and though he had ventured to turn the small attic next door to young Peter's bedroom into a bathroom, 'after all,' he

228

thought, 'it's my house, and I must make myself comfortable. They don't want bathrooms, but I do, and there it is.' There indeed it was, and there was electric light installed, and he dined, sitting in his father's chair, and then pottered from room to room, drinking in the old friendly atmosphere, which was round him wherever he went, for They were pleased. But neither voice nor vision manifested that, and perhaps it was only his own pleasure at being back that he attributed to them. But he would have loved a glimpse or a whisper, and from time to time, as he sat looking over some memoranda about the British Tin Syndicate, he peered into corners of the room, thinking that something moved there, and when a trail of creeper tapped against the window he got up and looked out. But nothing met his scrutiny but the dim starlight falling like dew on the neglected lawn. 'They're here, though,' he said to himself, as he let the curtain fall back.

The gardeners were ready for him next morning, and under his directions began the taming of the jungly wildness. And here was a pleasant thing, for one of them was the son of the cowman, Calloway, who had been here forty years ago, and he had childish memories still of the garden where with his father he used to come from the milking-shed to the house with the full pails. And he remembered that Sybil used to keep her guinea-pigs on the drying-ground at the back of the house. Now that he said that Peter remembered it too, and so the drying-ground all overgrown with brambles and rank herbage must be cleared.

'Iss, sure, nasty little vermin I thought them,' said Calloway the younger, 'but 'twas here Miss Sybil had their hutches and a wired run for 'em. And a rare fuss there was when my father's terrier got in and killed half of 'em, and the young lady crying over the corpses.'

That massacre of the innocents was dim to Peter; it must have happened in term-time when he was at school, and by the next holidays, to be sure, the prolific habits of her pets had gladdened Sybil's mourning.

229

So the drying-ground was cleared and the winding path up the shrubbery to the summer-house which had been home to the distressed vessels pursued by pirates. This was being rebuilt now, the roof timbered up, the walls rectified and whitewashed, and the steps leading to it and its tiled floor cleaned of the encroaching moss. It was soon finished, and Peter often sat there to rest and read the papers after a morning of prowling and supervising in the garden, for an hour or two on his feet oddly tired him, and he would doze in the sunny shelter. But now he never dreamed about coming back to Lescop or of the welcoming presences. 'Perhaps that's because I've come,' he thought, 'and those dreams were only meant to drive me. But I think they might show that they're pleased: I'm doing all I can.'

Yet he knew they were pleased, for as the work in the garden progressed, the sense of them and their delight hung about the cleared paths as surely as the smell of the damp earth and the uprooted bracken which had made such trespass. Every evening Calloway collected the gleanings of the day, piling them on the bonfire in the orchard. The bracken flared, and the damp hazel stems fizzed and broke into flame, and the scent of the wood smoke drifted across to the house. And after some three weeks' work all was done, and that afternoon Peter took no siesta in the summer-house, for he could not cease from walking through flower-garden and kitchen-garden and orchard now perfectly restored to their old order. A shower fell, and he sheltered under the lime where the pigeons built, and then the sun came out again, and in that gleam at the close of the winter day he took a final stroll to the bottom of the drive, where the gate now hung firm on even hinges. It used to take a long time in closing, if, as a boy, you let it swing, penduluming backwards and forwards with the latch of it clicking as it passed the hasp: and now he pulled it wide, and let go of it, and to and fro it went in lessening movement till at last it clicked and stayed. Somehow that pleased him immensely: he liked accuracy in details.

But there was no doubt he was very tired: he had an unpleasant sensation, too, as of a wire stretched tight across his heart, and of some thrumming going on against it. The wire dully ached, and this thrumming produced little stabs of sharp pain. All day he had been conscious of something of the sort, but he was too much taken up with the joy of the finished garden to heed little physical beckonings. A good long night would make him fit again, or, if not, he could stop in bed tomorrow. He went upstairs early, not the least anxious about himself, and instantly went to sleep. The soft night air pushed in at his open window, and the last sound that he heard was the tapping of the blind-tassel against the sash.

He woke very suddenly and completely, knowing that somebody had called him. The room was curiously bright, but not with the quality of moonlight; it was like a valley lying in shadow, while somewhere, a little way about it, shone some strong splendour of noon. And then he heard again his name called, and knew that the sound of the voice came in through the window. There was no doubt that Violet was calling him: she and the others were out in the garden.

'Yes, I'm coming,' he cried, and he jumped out of bed. He seemed – it was not odd – to be already dressed: he had on a jersey and flannel trousers, but his feet were bare and he slipped on a pair of shoes, and ran downstairs, taking the first short flight in one leap, like young Peter. The door of his mother's room was open, and he looked in, and there she was, of course, sitting at the table and writing letters.

'Oh, Peter, how lovely to have you home again,' she said. 'They're all out in the garden, and they've been calling you, darling. But come and see me soon, and have a talk.'

Out he ran along the walk below the windows, and up the winding path through the shrubbery to the summer-house, for he knew they were going to play Pirates. He must hurry, or the pirates would be abroad before he got there, and as he ran, he called out:

'Oh, do wait a second: I'm coming.'

He scudded past the golden maple and the bay tree, and

there they all were in the summer-house which was home. And he took a flying leap up the steps and was among them.

It was there that Calloway found him next morning. He must indeed have run up the winding path like a boy, for the new-laid gravel was spurned at long intervals by the toe-prints of his shoes.

THE END

Lucia in Wartime
Tom Holt

"WE WILL PAY ANYTHING FOR LUCIA BOOKS"
NOEL COWARD: GERTRUDE LAWRENCE: NANCY MITWORD:
W.H. AUDEN

1939: On the continent of Europe a battle rages, but on the Tilling side of the Channel the conflict is deadlier by far. For here, re-inforced by patriotism, armed with Union Jacks and gas-masks, are those two arch-friends, Lucia and Elizabeth Mapp-Flint.

Each must make sacrifices: Italians and *Mozartino* are out, Polish and Elgar are in. Elizabeth nobly surrenders Major Benjy to the Home Guard, while Georgie – for a while – outshines Lucia as a man who can do anything with cornbeef and parsnips.

All is glorious, glorious enmity, until that last magnificent moment when Lucia triumphs in what must be recognised as her Finest Hour.

"Michael MacLiammoir tells us that at the time of E.F. Benson's death he had a dream. It was a summer morning in Tilling, the characters gathered in the High Street to hear the awful news,
'Not Mr Benson?' Lucia murmured . . .
'Oh, Georgie! Oh, Elizabeth! What is going to *happen* to all of us?'

Tom Holt has provided the answer in this first novel, which will be most welcome to old members of the society of Luciaphiles and new ones recruited by the TV series"
MOLLIE HARDWICK, BOOKS AND BOOKMEN

"It's a successful and funny imitation."
BRITISH BOOK NEWS

0 552 99202 X   £3.95

BLACK SWAN

A SELECTED LIST OF OTHER BLACK SWAN TITLES

The prices shown below were correct at the time of going to press. However Transworld Publishers reserve the right to show new retail prices on covers which may differ from those previously advertised in the text or elsewhere.

☐	99198 8	THE HOUSE OF THE SPIRITS	Isabel Allende	£3.95
☐	99201 1	THE GOVERNESS	Patricia Angadi	£3.95
☐	99185 6	THE DESPERADOES	Stan Barstow	£3.95
☐	99193 7	A RAGING CALM	Stan Barstow	£4.95
☐	99186 4	A KIND OF LOVING	Stan Barstow	£3.95
☐	99189 9	WATCHERS ON THE SHORE	Stan Barstow	£3.95
☐	99187 2	THE RIGHT TRUE END	Stan Barstow	£3.95
☐	99159 7	THE GLAD EYE AND OTHER STORIES	Stan Barstow	£3.50
☐	99176 7	JOBY	Stan Barstow	£2.50
☐	99075 2	QUEEN LUCIA	E.F. Benson	£2.95
☐	99076 0	LUCIA IN LONDON	E.F. Benson	£3.50
☐	99083 3	MISS MAPP	E.F. Benson	£2.95
☐	99084 1	MAPP AND LUCIA	E.F. Benson	£3.95
☐	99087 6	LUCIA'S PROGRESS	E.F. Benson	£2.95
☐	99088 4	TROUBLE FOR LUCIA	E.F. Benson	£2.95
☐	99202 X	LUCIA IN WARTIME	Tom Holt	£3.50
☐	99163 5	BEAUTIFUL	Rachel Billington	£3.95
☐	99166 X	COCK ROBIN	Rachel Billington	£3.95
☐	99164 3	ALL THINGS NICE	Rachel Billington	£3.50
☐	99165 1	THE BIG DIPPER	Rachel Billington	£2.95
☐	99191 0	LADY ADDLE REMEMBERS	Mary Dunn	£2.50
☐	99192 9	THE MEMOIRS OF MIPSIE (Lady Addle Part 2)	Mary Dunn	£2.50
☐	99130 9	NOAH'S ARK	Barbara Trapido	£3.95
☐	99056 6	BROTHER OF THE MORE FAMOUS JACK	Barbara Trapido	£3.50
☐	99117 1	MRS POOTER'S DIARY	Keith Waterhouse	£3.95
☐	99074 4	IN THE MOOD	Keith Waterhouse	£2.95
☐	99210 0	HARNESSING PEACOCKS	Mary Wesley	£3.95
☐	99126 0	THE CAMOMILE LAWN	Mary Wesley	£3.95
☐	99082 5	JUMPING THE QUEUE	Mary Wesley	£1.95

ORDER FORM

All these books are available at your book shop or newsagent, or can be ordered direct from the publisher. Just tick the titles you want and fill in the form below.

Transworld Publishers, Cash Sales Department,
61-63 Uxbridge Road, Ealing, London, W5 5SA

Please send cheque or postal order, not cash. All cheques and postal orders must be in £ sterling and made payable to Transworld Publishers Ltd.

Please allow cost of book(s) plus the following for postage and packing:

U.K./Republic of Ireland Customers:
Orders in excess of £5; no charge
Orders under £5 add 50p

Overseas Customers:
All orders; add £1.50

NAME (Block Letters) ....

ADDRESS ....

....